"Can you risk a kiss?" The dimple shone in the corner of Ragn's mouth. "Or are you too busy with your feast preparations?"

"Is it the only way to seal our agreement to marry?" Gunnar asked.

"The most pleasurable way."

He dipped his head and brushed his lips against hers, no more than the touch of a butterfly but also all fire and heat. Her legs became weak, and she clutched his tunic.

A little moan escaped her throat, and his arms came around her, molding her against him.

Someone dropped a pan and Ragn realized what she was doing. She jumped backward. He allowed her to go.

Her mouth felt pangs of disappointment at the kiss's briefness. She kept her eyes on the rushes, but his ragged breathing echoed in her ears.

"I believe the experiment was a success."

Author Note

This story came about because I visited the fabulous Scottish island of Jura where George Orwell wrote *Nineteen Eighty-Four* and the purple Paps loom. Something timeless hangs in the island's air and I considered it the perfect setting for a Viking romance. Because it is very close to Colonsay and Islay, I seized the opportunity to briefly check in with characters from *The Warrior's Viking Bride*. Also, I loved being able to explore how the Vikings celebrated their winter festival.

I do hope you will enjoy Ragn and Gunnar's story as much as I enjoyed writing it.

I love getting comments from readers and can be reached at michelle@michellestyles.co.uk, through my publisher, on Facebook or on Twitter, @michellelstyles.

MICHELLE STYLES

SENT AS THE VIKING'S BRIDE

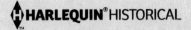

Recycling programs
for this product may
not exist in your area.

ISBN-13: 978-1-335-63488-7

Sent as the Viking's Bride

Copyright © 2018 by Michelle Styles

Printed in U.S.A.

Born and raised near San Francisco, California, **Michelle Styles** currently lives near Hadrian's Wall with her husband and a menagerie of pets in an Edwardian bungalow with a large and somewhat overgrown garden. An avid reader, she became hooked on historical romances after discovering Georgette Heyer, Anya Seton and Victoria Holt. Her website is www.michellestyles.co.uk and she's on Twitter and Facebook.

Books by Michelle Styles

Harlequin Historical

His Unsuitable Viscountess
Hattie Wilkinson Meets Her Match
An Ideal Husband?
Paying the Viking's Price
Return of the Viking Warrior
Saved by the Viking Warrior
Taming His Viking Woman
Summer of the Viking
Sold to the Viking Warrior
The Warrior's Viking Bride
Sent as the Viking's Bride

Harlequin Historical *Undone!* ebook

The Perfect Concubine

Visit the Author Profile page
at Harlequin.com for more titles.

To Tim and Kathy de la Fosse because he asked so nicely when we visited and you gave us the most memorable rooster aka Hugo Buff-Orpington to protect the hens from foxes.

Prologue

January AD 877—Colbhasa, modern-day Colonsay

Gunnar Olafson had spent a lifetime dreaming of his own land, but after he learned of his excellent fortune, all he could do was sit in stunned silence. Others would be shouting the news to the rafters, calling for more ale for everyone, but he wanted to savour it and hug it close.

He closed his hand about the tiny carved stone man his mother had given him the last time he'd seen her and recited the vow he'd made on her grave. It had seen him through two shipwrecks, five severe injuries and countless minor skirmishes.

His mind skittered away from the memory of the day he'd made that vow, the day when he knew the soothsayer's dying words had power to harm those he loved. The curse still clung to his soul, but he wanted to believe that maybe one day, if he made his new lands prosperous, he'd show the gods that he was worthy and those words—*all the women he loved would crumble to dust*—would cease to have any power.

'Are you going to tell me why Kolbeinn wanted to

speak with you alone? What have you done wrong this Jul? Your oath of loyalty was as loud as any man's.' Eylir Rokrson banged his fists together as he settled on the bench next to Gunnar. 'I won't have it. We're still treated poorly because we once followed his ex-wife and then his daughter.'

Gunnar slipped the stone man back into his pouch for safekeeping and regarded his best friend and drinking companion. They had fought long and hard together. He had hugged his good fortune to his chest for long enough. 'Against all expectation, he has offered me land...on Jura. I had thought he was about to send me to Ireland on another impossible mission. Just to test my loyalty again.'

'You thrive on such things.'

Gunnar examined the dregs of his Jul ale. 'He hasn't been able to kill me yet despite his best efforts. He thinks to put my back to better use and have me till soil even if the island is windswept and nearly unin-habited. We will only truly last long in this land if we put down roots.'

'Yours is the better fate.' His friend nodded. 'Many of our former comrades were put to death.'

'They betrayed Dagmar.' Gunnar ignored the clench-ing of his stomach. 'In the end I proved my loyalty and that I'd been tricked into giving her that cup of ale.'

'Which was switched and made you ill.'

Gunnar winced, remembering how he'd inadver-tently contributed to his former leader's abduction. He had rejoiced at her restoration, but his punishment had been to serve her father, Kolbeinn. 'For the last two seasons, I've served Kolbeinn well.'

'What made him agree to honour the promise of land?'

'I saved Lord Ketil's life last season during that storm and, as Kolbeinn's overlord, he demanded Kolbeinn reward me with land.' Gunnar regarded the bottom of his goblet. Even now it was hard for him to believe that the man who had come from nothing and who had lost everything had the chance of making his dreams come true. His land. No more fighting in the stinking mud for someone else. No more offering his sword and oath to the highest bidder. He was going to build a hall which all would envy. His success should taste better than it did.

'Far too modest.' Eylir clapped him on the shoulder. 'What next? Acquiring that northern wife you have always talked of? The one with the come-hither smile and plump bosom?'

Gunnar shook his head. 'First the land tamed, then the marriage. One wild thing at a time.'

'Send word for her now.' Eylir made an expansive gesture with his hands. 'Wanted: one sweet-tempered, buxom blonde who knows northern customs. Someone who doesn't have inconvenient relatives, but does have accommodating thighs. One who listens, but forgets to open her mouth, except for your tongue.'

Gunnar laughed along with his friend, while privately wondering how much the other warrior had had to drink. 'It sounds like a description for the woman of your dreams.'

Eylir shook his head. 'Not I. I want a woman I can share my life with. But I've watched you long enough to know what you want—the type of woman who warms your bed when you can be bothered, but who plays no other part in your life.'

Gunnar twisted the goblet between his fingers. It was true he preferred blondes who asked for no more than he was prepared to give. 'Do you indeed? When I go looking, I will remember your counsel. But I shall require a wife, not a concubine. We can discuss it further the first time you visit me in Jura.'

'I'm required in the north. It is why I have come to find you.' Eylir leant towards him, blasting him with alcohol fumes. 'My younger brother sent word. My sword arm must return north or the family faces destruction. The usual exaggeration, I'm sure.'

Eylir launched into his familiar tirade against familial obligations. Gunnar swirled his ale and listened with greedy ears while he tried not to think about the three snow-covered corpses of his mother and two young sisters before a darkened hut. Families were wasted on those who had them.

'Family. You'd never forgive yourself if something happened to them,' Gunnar said when Eylir reached the end of his recital.

'Aye, you spoke true there.' Eylir gestured with his hand, sloshing ale everywhere. 'It is why I will provide you with a wife, the perfect wife for your new venture, one you can get sons on.'

Gunnar stood. 'Your drunken prattling puts our friendship in peril.'

'Serious.' Eylir grabbed Gunnar's arm. 'You require a northern bride, but you have land to till, a hall to build. You admirably hold fast to the vow you gave to your mother before you departed, the one about only marrying a worthy northern woman. Wasn't that the excuse you gave that Irish warlord who commanded you to marry his daughter last season? The redhead who gave you hungry glances and had no eyes for anyone else?'

Gunnar tightened his grasp on the goblet. 'You should know better than to believe what I say in drink!'

'Same excuse you gave that pretty widow from Bernicia with her many acres of lands. Or one of the dozen other women who have buzzed around you like bees searching for a honeypot. You've acquired your land. What excuse are you going to give for failing to travel northwards and find this elusive bride of yours?'

Gunnar instinctively fingered his mother's stone man. 'You exaggerate as usual.'

'Nevertheless, I will send you a Jul present to remember if you win the wrestling competition.'

'How much Jul ale have you consumed?'

A self-satisfied smile crossed Eylir's face. 'I watched you in practice this morning. Peak physical condition. A man would have to be a fool to bet against you.'

'Then there are plenty of fools. Maurr is the favourite.'

'Nobody ever called me a fool.'

The wrestling was a high point on the Jul celebration. During the last two seasons, he had made it to the quarter-final and the semi, never to the final. He'd be out in one of the first rounds this year by his best guess.

'Your gold to waste.'

His first and second opponents were inebriated and then the next warrior was someone Gunnar personally disliked. And so it continued until he was proclaimed champion.

When he looked over his shoulder as all around him shouted his name, Eylir was there, gesturing with the sack of gold he'd won. 'Look for your northern bride before next Jul.'

Gunnar allowed the shouts to wash over him. The last thing he needed to worry about was a drunken friend's idle promise—he had a hall to construct.

Chapter One

November AD 877—Jura, Viking-controlled Alba, modern-day Jura, Scotland

The newly built longhouse shone like a beacon of hope in the thin grey light and behind rose the great purple mountains or *paps* which dominated the island. The ship had come the long way around, avoiding the great whirlpool. According to the captain, on a day like today, the whirlpool would writhe like a great cauldron and suck the life out of any ship which ventured close.

Ragnhild Thorendottar gripped the side of the boat with her hands and willed it onward towards the shore. Nearly there. Nearly safe. A new life for her and her younger sister, a safe life away from her brother-in-law and his murderous greed beckoned. Some day she would get her revenge and regain her lands, but for now she required safety.

Hard work on a desolate island failed to frighten her. She feared other things such as berserkers in the night, burning houses and, most importantly, her brother-in-law's fury if he knew that she and Svana had escaped.

If he ever discovered they had not perished in the fire, he would send his berserkers after them again. For who would go against one of the King's closest advisors? Who would take the risk? Who would believe her? Even now, with her burns nearly healed, Ragn scarce credited how completely her safe world had been destroyed.

She tucked Svana's hand into hers and squeezed. Her sister gave a tremulous smile. Her right eye turned in more than ever, but there was no rolling back of the eyes or the fearful twitching which had begun the night of the attack, after Svana took the blow to her head, a blow meant for Ragn when her back had been turned and which would have certainly ended her life.

Ragn heaved a sigh of relief. Maybe Svana's affliction would vanish. Maybe her actions had not damaged her sister for ever. Maybe this island would truly be a fresh start, one where the shadows of the past failed to flicker. She pushed the thought to one side and concentrated on the tangible. Dreams had tumbled her into this mess and she refused to indulge in that luxury ever again.

'Our new home,' she said, pointing to the gabled hall which shone in the gathering gloom. 'Soon you will be running in the pastures, helping me to brew the Jul ale and a thousand other things. We will make it a Jul to remember, something to make this year good.'

Unlike last Jul, which had been one to forget, she silently added.

Her sister's face lit up. 'Jul is my favourite time of year. I love everything about it—the flaming wheel, the Jul log burning bright during the days of darkness when the Sun Maiden is in the belly of the wolf and most of all the feasting and celebrating when she returns.'

A pucker appeared between Svana's brows. 'Will this Gunnar Olafson understand everything which needs to be done? And in the proper fashion?'

'Jul will happen, sweetling. I promise.' Ragn tightened her grip and willed Svana to keep her thoughts silent—Ragn had ruined so many things recently, could she be trusted not to ruin this as well?

'Are you certain he will welcome me as well as you?'

'Smile,' she said, putting an arm about Svana. 'See the great purple mountains? Gunnar Olafson's farm is at the base of the middle one. It has a good bay and there are good forests with straight trees for building ships. It is as his friend told me. A true home, Svana. Think about that.'

Svana gave her a brave but uncertain nod. Ragn's heart contracted. 'A true home. I'd like that. We haven't had one since…'

'It is going to happen, love,' Ragn said before Svana attempted again to blame herself for the tragedy. Svana had been the innocent one. Ragn had been the one to arrange the witch woman's visit attempting to end the quarrel between her husband and his brother over the inheritance. She'd never anticipated the old crone would prophesy that Svana would bring about her brother-in-law's death or that her husband would take Svana's part, refusing his brother's demand for her immediate death and instead bodily removed him from the hall.

'Do you think I will be able to meet the farm's *nisser*? To make sure he knows that I intend to look after him properly with porridge and everything. That way he will know to favour this farm,' Svana said, interrupting Ragn's thoughts.

Ragn stared at the rapidly approaching spit of land,

trying to decide if her sister asking about the mischievous elf who was supposed to guard homes but often played tricks on the inhabitants was a good thing. Such creatures in Ragn's experience did not exist or, if they did, they were not inclined to assist her.

'Tending to your chores will do more to ensure the farm prospers than putting out porridge. Believe me. This farm will prosper with me in charge.'

'And this will be my home for ever? You won't make me marry unless I want to?' Svana gestured towards her inward-turning eye. 'No true man will want me like this. I have heard the whispers. What the men on board this ship said about me, what they wanted to do.'

'Stop doubting my schemes. I might start to think you have lost faith,' Ragn said lightly.

Svana squeezed her hand. 'I trust you, Ragn. I just can't help overhearing what other people are saying.'

Ragn clucked her under the chin. 'Would you believe them if they said the sky was green? So why believe them about that? We will be fine.'

We have to be, I have no other plan to save her life, she added under her breath.

The boat made a scraping noise as it hit the shore. Ragn was jolted forward and her stomach hit the railing. The ill-favoured crew leaped out and dragged the boat further up the shingle.

Ragn's legs wobbled slightly when she first set foot on the rough shingle. She forced them to stagger a few steps. 'Svana, firm ground. Good ground. Safe ground.'

'It wobbles.'

'Only because we have been on the sea. It will pass quickly.' Ragn prayed to any god that her words were correct.

She glanced about the barren windswept beach. Their approach had to have been noted. They had come in peacefully with the shields down. And it was obvious from the smoke lazily curling in the sky that someone was at home.

To hide her discomfort, she directed the long-nosed captain to put her trunks on the shore above the tide-line. The man shrugged his shoulders, muttering about the tide turning and having to leave quickly.

When she was about to give in to despair, a large man came out of the hall. A shaft of winter sunshine illuminated him, turning his skin and hair golden. His shoulders were broad and powerful, a man used to fighting and hard work, rather than a courtier like her late husband, a man a woman could count on to fight for her and her family and win. Her next thought was why in the name of Freya did a man who looked like that need to send to the north for a wife? Women would be buzzing about him like bees around a honeycomb.

'He isn't very friendly and wants us gone. He should have tankards of ale to offer strangers, but his hands are empty.' A worried frown puckered Svana's forehead. 'Something is very wrong, Ragn, isn't it?'

Ragn forced a laugh. 'They do things differently here, I suspect. We will soon have their manners.'

Svana glanced over her shoulder and lowered her voice. 'On the ship, they said I brought that storm. I didn't. I promise. I am not bad luck and shouldn't be thrown overboard.'

'As if I'd allow that to happen to you!'

'You are wearing your serious face, like you did when you spied Vargr and his berserkers riding towards our old home.'

Ragn forced her lungs to fill with air. Vargr believed them dead in the fire he and his men had set. He did not know they had escaped just as the roof caved in. He would not come looking for them, particularly not with the North Sea between them. Vargr had feared the North Sea ever since his father perished on it.

'Nothing is wrong, sweetling. Wives are for civilising. Warriors are for defending their land. It is why he has sent for a wife—to learn how to be civil. I can do that.'

'Who goes there?' her soon-to-be husband asked, placing a hand on the large sword he wore. 'We are a simple farm, not a market. I've little wish to waste your time or mine. Best be gone before the tide turns.'

Despite its roughness, his deep voice was easy on the ear. Ragn placed her hand on her stomach and bid the butterflies to be gone. It was possible the captain had made a mistake and this golden mountain of a man wasn't her intended. Her husband was probably old, missing a limb and confined to bed. This warrior would lead her to him.

'Ragnhild Thorendottar, the contracted wife of Gunnar Olafson, come from Viken as requested.' She made the sort of low curtsy she'd make to the King or Queen.

The only sound was the cawing of the seagulls. The man's stance turned more foreboding. He drew his brows together.

'Contracted wife?' he said after what appeared to be a lifetime. 'Of whom did you say? Gunnar Olafson?'

'Are you Gunnar Olafson, also known as Gunnar the Strong Arm, of Kolbeinn's *felag*? Or his steward?' she asked, tilting her head to one side. Her voice sounded thin on the breeze. She swallowed hard and tried again. 'Or must I seek him elsewhere?'

Ragn watched the man from under her lashes now that she clearly saw him. His features were regular, his hair was a dark blond which had begun to go to brown and had been shaved at the sides but allowed to grow long on top. He sported two golden rings in his beard. Everything about him proclaimed vitality and virility.

She pressed her hands together to stop them from trembling. His gaze raked her form, making her immediately aware of her many failings from her lack of curves to her above-average height and overbearing manner which made men's manhood shrivel to nothingness. Her late husband's taunts, the ones he said when he drank far too much ale, echoed in her mind. She tried to list the good things she brought to a marriage—her willingness to work hard, her knowledge of making ale, and…her mind went blank. She no longer possessed any land or riches of any kind, nothing to tempt a successful warrior like this one.

'I seek Gunnar Olafson.'

'I am he,' the man confirmed with a puzzled expression. 'But I've made no contract for a wife. Ever. I have no wish or desire for one at the present. Who plots against me?'

Ragn's stomach swooped and knotted. There had to be some mistake. She refused to risk Svana on the sea again with that crew. The captain of the boat had driven a hard bargain to bring her and Svana out here—a one-way passage only, no return or onward. Eylir the Black had paid for her passage as the morning gift for the marriage, but the captain had demanded double for Svana. She had relinquished both her grandmother's gold brooches to pay for it. After sacrificing her gold necklace to calm the waves during the storm, all she had left was her mother's silver necklace, but that would not pay for the return passage or safeguard Svana from being tossed overboard if the ship encountered another storm.

'Eylir Rokrson, whom some call Eylir the Black, made the contract,' she said, banging her fists together and bidding the doubts to be gone. 'Are you saying that he played me false? Or are you not the Gunnar Olafson who grew up on the fjord near Kaupang? The Gunnar who served with Dagmar Kolbeinndottar and now serves her father?'

The man's mouth became a thin white line, but without the slightest sign of a welcome. 'I am that Gunnar Olafson, but I've never asked for a wife to be sent from anywhere. You came on the whisper of a false promise. Go back to where you came from.'

He turned his back and marched towards the hall. The rudeness of it nearly took her breath away. She had travelled here on more than a whisper or a promise.

Behind her, the long-nosed captain rubbed his hands together with glee at the thought of her paying more gold, gold which she didn't have.

'Eylir paid for the passage as the morning gift,' she called out. 'Why would he pay that much gold if the promise was untrue? Is he always that reckless with his gold?'

The man halted. His eyes narrowed. 'Why in the name of all the gods would Eylir send a woman like you?'

His words hammered like physical blows, proof if she needed it that men always failed to look beyond the physical unless there was a possibility of material gain. Her sister's fingers had grown ice-cold. The air chilled and the first spots of hard rain began to fall. Ragn wanted the earth to swallow her up. Her day of hope and triumph was fast turning into one of despair.

'He informed me you were occupied in building your new hall, but required a wife from your home fjord as soon as possible. Have I been lied to?' Ragn tightened her hold of Svana and resisted the temptation to hide her face. Her troubles were supposed to be behind her in this foreign land—instead, everything had become far worse. 'Have I travelled here for nothing?'

'Have you? Only Eylir can answer.' Gunnar Olafson scratched his neck. 'All I know is that your arrival is news to me. I never requested a wife from anyone, least of all from Eylir. I've no intention of taking one simply because some woman turns up on my beach, making outlandish claims. Now I bid you good day. May the gods guide your journey to wherever you need to go. I'm sure you will make some poor man a very able wife.'

Ragn squared her shoulders. This man, the person who was supposed to be her saviour, was not going to get away that easily. She would make him see reason. She marched up to him and caught his arms, halting his progress. His look was dark and furious. She released his arm and backed up two steps.

'We have travelled a long way.' She kept her head up and ignored the rain dripping off her nose. 'Why would I have travelled this far on a whisper? Why would I leave my home and friends at this time of year? Will you listen to my tale? Please?'

The man brought his upper lip over his teeth. 'If I

listen, will I be rid of you quicker? Many matters require my attention.'

'Please, my sister shivers from the cold. We have travelled across the winter sea because of your friend's promise.'

He tugged at his beard. 'You have until the tide turns.'

Gunnar Olafson ground his teeth as he stared at the slim dark-haired woman standing in front of him declaring with a toss of her head that she was his contracted wife and demanding to be heard. A wife! He'd never asked for such a thing and most certainly he didn't require one. Until the curse was lifted, how could he risk any woman's life?

The idea was laughable that Eylir would send this woman. Her face was far too angular, her mouth oversized and all teeth, her curves non-existent and her hair from what he saw peeping out from under the kerchief was dark as a raven's wing. His tastes ran towards buxom blondes with easy smiles, few expectations and little taste for conversation, rather than sharp-tongued raven-haired women who had desire to order everything.

Eylir and his blasted bag of gold at Jul.

'The tide will be turning soon.'

'You gave me until it actually turned. My sister needs to get out of the damp.' She paused as if she expected him to invite her to the hall.

A silver-haired girl of no more than ten ran to the woman and grasped the woman's hand so tightly that her knuckles shone white. There was a resemblance, but there was no way they were mother and daughter as the age gap was not enough. She, too, watched him with big eyes, inward-turning eyes which reminded him of his youngest sister, stirring unwanted memories. He turned towards the longboat. The crew were an ill-favoured lot.

'Where is Eylir? Precisely.' He half-expected to see his so-called friend rising up from the boat, his eyes creasing with laughter. Eylir's jokes had finally transgressed beyond acceptable. He would have to teach the man a lesson about interfering in other people's lives, but that was a task for another time.

Her eyes flashed with a hidden fire, but her voice was steady. 'I've no idea where Eylir is. We parted company on Kaupang's quayside.'

'I swear he is trickier than Loki. Come out, Eylir, you have had your fun. Now let's see what you are truly on about.'

The sailors stopped moving the trunks and regarded him as if he had lost his mind, but his friend failed to appear.

Gunnar swallowed hard and tried again. 'Is this the wife you have been threatening to acquire? She has your same sense of humour. This prank has gone on long enough, Eylir.'

The seagulls mocked his call, but otherwise the only sound was that of the waves. The woman watched him with perfectly arched brows and a faint supercilious smile on her overly large mouth.

'He remained in the north. He had business to attend to, but will arrive in the new year.' The woman adopted a tone more suited towards talking to a young child than a grown man.

'What business?'

'His second cousin died. He needed to get the estate in order before sailing again to the west.' Her hand trembled, betraying her nerves. 'We agreed that it was best for all concerned if I undertook the journey immediately. There was nothing to keep me in the north.'

Her voice trembled on the last word. Fear? Fear of what? Why had she braved the sea at this time of year? What drove her to risk her life and that of her sister's?

Gunnar frowned. Becoming interested in this woman's problems was the last thing he needed. Better to get rid of her and be done with it. It was a slippery slope to caring and, if he cared, women died.

The soothsayer's dying prediction resounded in his ears. His friends had warned him the old man had supernatural power, but he'd refused to allow the man to slaughter those young girls. He'd lost his temper and killed him. The necessary sacrifice to the gods instead of the girls who reminded him of his sisters, he'd proclaimed with a laugh. He'd stopped laughing when he'd discovered the bodies of his mother and sisters. By his reckoning, they had died about the same time as the soothsayer. And then it happened again with Dyrfinna's betrayal and death. He forced his mind away from the past and back to the present.

The woman was connected to Eylir. How? He narrowed his gaze. Family matters had forced Eylir across the North Sea. Eylir had no sister. She had to be the family-forced bride as she was not the sort Eylir would take as a concubine.

'Indeed.' He forced a short laugh. 'I suspect he wished to avoid being torn limb from limb once I got my hands on him. Your husband is notorious for his pranks, my lady.'

'Eylir is most definitely not my husband.' The

woman made an imperious gesture towards where the longboat was pulled up on shore. 'Ask the captain if you doubt me.'

'He did tell Ragn to come!' the girl called out. 'He is soon to be married to our cousin, Trana Ragnardottar.'

'How did you know that, Svana?' Ragnhild asked, drawing her brows together.

'I overheard them speaking as we left. He was kissing her.' The girl smacked her lips. 'They will have to get married after that as they will have lots of babies.'

'You are being ridiculous, Svana. Trana's father requires a different husband for his only daughter. Not a penniless sell-sword like Eylir.'

Gunnar kept his face impassive. Eylir had hidden his wealth from them.

'After what he did for us, Trana will defy her father.' The girl lifted her chin. 'I just know it. And I made a wish about it as we left.'

Ragnhild gave an exasperated sigh. 'You and your pronouncements. Would that the world was ordered the way you wish. One must be practical, child.'

'Trana thinks he has fine legs and a good backside,' Svana confided from behind her hand. Gunnar struggled to keep a straight face.

Ragnhild pinched the bridge of her nose, making her skin appear even more sallow. 'That is more than anyone, let alone Gunnar Olafson, needs to know. Curb your tongue.'

Svana hung her head. 'I'm sorry, Sister.'

'Next time remember some things remain private, but you are young, Svana, and I forgive you.'

Young. The girl was indeed too young to have made this journey in the winter. The fact knifed through him.

While Eylir might enlist the aid of a woman, he would not stoop so low as to send a child on a perilous autumn journey.

'Why did Eylir send vulnerable women alone on the sea?'

The woman gave a small cough. 'We agreed that I'd travel alone as the circumstances dictated.'

Circumstances—whose? Eylir's or this woman's? Something had driven her across the seas, but she wanted to keep it a secret. 'Truly?'

'Would that he was here! You would greet your friend properly and we would not be forced to stand in the mizzle.' A convulsive shiver racked her slender frame, but she kept her head proudly erect and her hands at her sides.

Gunnar winced at the accusation of less-than-proper hospitality. Worse, her words rang true. His mother would have been appalled. He'd allowed a lady, any lady let alone a lady of breeding, to stand outside while the rain pelted down. Despite the years since her death and against his instinct, divorcing himself from his mother's teachings was impossible. 'Into the hall with you. Get dry.'

Her eyes gleamed triumph. 'Thank you.'

She motioned for her trunks. Gunnar gritted his teeth. Ragnhild would learn that he might have given on one point, but he would not give in on the other. She was most definitely not the wife for him.

'No, they stay outside. It should not take long to clear this mess up.'

With its piles of filthy rushes, half-finished benches and the nearly cold hearth, the best thing Ragn thought about the hall was that it was out of the icy rain. But she was inside and that was a start. She would make this warrior understand that they needed to stay for the night, that returning on the boat to Kaupang was not an option. She'd worry about the future after that. Little steps, rather than focusing on the mountain looming in front of her.

'Has there been a mistake, Ragn?' Svana whispered. 'He is going to allow us to stay, isn't he? He won't behave like... Vargr?'

Ragn glanced towards where Gunnar was busily filling tankards.

'The future is in front of us.' Ragn bent down so that her face was level with Svana's. 'Keep the past behind you. Never mention Vargr again. He is dead to us.'

Svana gave a little nod. Her sister was too young to understand that if Gunnar knew her brother-in-law's identity, or the danger they faced in Viken, that he'd close his doors to them as many of her so-called friends had done. Survival depended on keeping their troubled past hidden.

'Promise me you will remember that.'

Svana worried her bottom lip. 'I'll try.'

Ragn withdrew the rune stick, which she had insisted Eylir write, from her pouch. It should be sufficient to make Gunnar Olafson see reason now that he was being hospitable.

Once he had finished ensuring the captain and his men had drinks, Gunnar returned to where they stood. His face had settled into even harsher lines. Svana shrank back against her.

'You are out of the wet. Explain.'

No please. No courtesy of any kind. Perhaps he had

taken one look at her and decided, no, that she wasn't attractive enough. Ragn stiffened her spine. This marriage wasn't supposed to be about attraction, but mutual assistance. 'We need to discuss our contracted marriage.'

Gunnar allowed his breath through clenched teeth. 'I know my friend better than that. Tell me the truth. Where is Eylir?'

Two bright spots appeared on the woman's pale cheeks, flooding her face with colour. A strong wind would blow her over. He knew her type. He had encountered enough of them back in the old country when he was growing up. She'd know about court gossip or the ways to recite a saga or how to fix a sweetmeat, but he doubted if she understood the hard back-breaking work life on this rugged western isle required. He was doing her a favour by sending her back.

'I was given to understand that you required a wife and that I satisfied those requirements. It seemed like the perfect alternative to my life in Kaupang. My husband recently died and we had no other male protectors.' Her mouth turned down. 'Someone may have been playing a joke, Gunnar Olafson, but the joke was on me and my sister, not you. I accepted the offer under false pretences. I have left my home and everything I held dear to travel here for a new life. I cannot return with these men. Know that much.'

Her voice was clear and steady and not unpleasant to the ear. Her gaze direct, rather than downcast. The tilt of her chin reminded him of how his mother acted when the world was against her and the silver fire shone again in her eyes.

A tiny voice inside Gunnar questioned why he was

watching this woman so closely if he was going to send her on her way. He ignored it. No man or woman dictated what he should do or whom he should marry. He'd earned the right to make his own choice. And this woman wasn't his choice.

'My friend acted without thinking things through properly.' Gunnar roughly shoved the remaining tankard of ale in her general direction and waited for her to refuse it. Fine ladies should be served mead or wine as they turned their noses up at ale, according to his mother's dictates.

Her fingers brushed his and he was aware of her—the sweep of her neck, the length of her fingers and how her dress hinted at her slender curves, rather than revealing them. He wanted to reveal those curves and explore them more in depth.

Gunnar buried the unexpected feeling down deep. It was merely because he had been busy with the estate, rather than seeking female companionship. Jul was coming and with it, his annual oath-taking at Kolbeinn's hall. There he was certain to find an instantly forgettable buxom blonde who would attend to his physical needs.

She regarded him from under her lashes with those silver-flecked eyes. 'What are we to do about this non-authorised promise? Forget that it ever happened?'

Gunnar ran a hand through his hair. Better she went now before he started to hope for the curse's end. Before he was responsible for another woman's death.

'Eylir overstepped. That much is clear. When I spoke of acquiring a bride last Jul, I expected to travel northwards once the hall and the farm were prosperous. Ketil would have understood the necessity of waiting.'

He pronounced the name of the overlord of the Western Isles and Manx with enough lack of reverence for Ragnhild to understand his status.

Ragnhild held out a rune stick. '*King* Harald has issued new decree about men needing to be married in order to hang on to the gifted lands. Eylir acted in your best interests.'

Her tone implied he would be an idiot for acting otherwise. Gunnar clenched his jaw. Harald Fine-Hair had once been a close comrade-in-arms when they'd served in the Byzantine Emperor's personal guard. He doubted if the King intended to enforce the decree on everyone. The King would use it as he used other decrees, to chivvy those he disagreed with and reward his cronies.

'Exceptions can be made. They have been in the past. Harald uses such decrees to further his own ends, enforcing where he chooses. Kolbeinn will keep his own counsel about this. I never considered Eylir for being an old woman worrier.'

'As your friend is in Kaupang, he is better placed than you to judge the mood of the King and his court.'

'How did your husband die?'

'A boring story which has little relevance to me standing here in front of you.'

'We differ on that view. Had he lived, you would not be here. Had he left you with lands, you would have remained on them.'

'Neither of us can rewrite history.'

Gunnar frowned. 'You must think me naïve to take everything on trust. How do I even know Eylir sent you?'

She shoved the rune stick towards him again with an overly bright smile. 'Read the runes. I can tell you what any of the unfamiliar marks means, if you like.'

Gunnar gritted his teeth. What secrets had Eylir confided? The last thing he wanted was to be laughed at by this woman because of his trouble with reading runes, because he was more skilled at the sword and axe than at learning and frippery. 'They are clear enough.'

'Your eyes remain sceptical. Do you require more proof? Captain, come here and inform this man who paid my passage and why.' She gestured towards the captain who hurried up and confirmed the woman's story. Eylir the Black had paid for the passage for this woman. One way for the bride of Gunnar Olafson, extra because of the time of year. The woman had paid for her sister, but it had been barely enough because everyone knew women with eyes like that offended the sea gods.

Gunnar caught his top lip between his teeth. The fool should trust his skill, rather than seeking to sacrifice the innocent when the first squall blew up.

The boatman gave a shout about the shifting tide and the need to be away from the rocks sharpish. He wanted to know where he should put the trunk. Ragnhild shouted to hold on, that the tide would wait a while longer.

'Your friend said that you were a fair man. I have travelled far and staked a great deal on this marriage which now turns out to be a false promise.' She took a step forward and her eyes blazed a deep silver, making her pale face come alive.

He screwed his eyes tightly shut. A fair man. He pictured Eylir saying that with one of his careless laughs, the sort that made the unwary relax.

'Where will you go? Will you return to your family in Viken?'

'For a price, I am sure the captain will take me somewhere.' She glared at him with her silver-blue eyes and he fancied fear underneath the bravado.

'For a great price.' The captain smacked his lips. Behind him, the crew sniggered. In his gut, Gunnar knew neither woman would reach another shore.

'Wait.' Gunnar put a hand on her trembling arm. Something stirred deep inside of him. He was aware of her, the way her chest rose and fell and how the ends of her flyaway tendrils curled about her forehead. All Ragnhild Thorendottar had done was behave like his mother might have done after his father's death, if the option had been open to her.

'Why wait? The tide shifts.' She gave his hand a pointed look and he slowly released her. 'You've already decided. I regret troubling you or in any way causing you embarrassment. I must accept my fate.'

'Eylir sent you to me. I have an obligation to ensure your safety, but I will choose my own bride. You remain here.'

Her eyes widened. 'Why are you willing to do this?' she whispered. 'My sister and I are strangers.'

'I would hate for your shades to haunt me. That boat appears barely seaworthy,' he said, opting for a half-truth.

Her bitter laugh rang out. 'My shade would be haunting others first.'

'The least I can do after you have travelled all this way.' Gunnar took a deep breath. He was providing shelter, not allowing this woman and girl into his life.

She held out her hand. 'I accept as a guest, not a bride.'

Chapter Two

A hard, soaking rain lashed down and the pale light from the sky made the looming mountain turn a deep brooding purple, but Ragn knew her feet were on firm ground. Being here with a reluctant host was a thousand times better than being on that ship where, when this storm hit, she and Svana would have been tossed overboard. Best of they'd escaped Vargr's reach. Small gifts from the gods. She had the most precious of commodities—time.

'Where are the women of the household?' Ragn asked as it became increasingly clear Gunnar's men had deserted his cold hall for their own homes rather than bedding down there.

'I manage well enough on my own. I can even brew ale and boil meat. My men's wives turn their hand to the spindle and loom as well as any and I enjoy the silence.'

He gave a superior sort of smile, but one which made his features become breath-taking. One smile and the women in his life must melt and do his bidding. She silently resolved that she would not join the legion of panting followers.

'Indeed.'

'Years of warring. In time, when I marry, there will be women, but for now it is just me and my dogs.'

'Surely you have servants or...' Ragn hesitated. How to explain that Svana was terrified of the dogs? Any explanation would have to include Vargr. Then there would be awkward questions about the estate, why no man would fight for her rights and why they were on their own. Later, she promised that little voice in her head, once they were warm and dry, once she had formulated a new plan now that there would be no marriage.

His brow lowered. 'I see no point in acquiring women as then I'd have to endure their prattling and twittering company.'

Endure their company.

Ragn's heart sank. Eylir had kept quiet about his friend's views on women and their usefulness. 'Eylir failed to mention that you disliked women.'

A dimple shone in his cheek. 'I love women at the right time and in the right place. Other than in my bed, most women flutter about like birds, chirp up all the time about nonsense until my back teeth ache and leave messes to be cleaned up.'

Ragn took three deep breaths of air. 'The reasons why your friend despaired of you ever marrying become ever clearer.'

'A few more days and I would have departed for Colbhasa and the start of the Jul celebrations,' he said, pointedly changing the subject. 'Not the comfort you must be used to, but it will serve until for the short time you will be here. You depart and my solitude can return. Have I mentioned that I enjoy the quiet?'

Ragn ignored the words about going. Her head pounded enough as it was. She had to concentrate on the positives, starting with not being in the boat.

'When did you plan to go to the north? To find a bride?' She deliberately paused, racking her brain for what Eylir had said about his story. The truth was that she hadn't paid much attention. She'd been that grateful for a way out of the shadows and hiding, half-expecting every knock on the door to bring Vargr and his berserker assassins. 'Or would you have found a reason why you need to be somewhere else rather than bride-hunting?'

'Eylir has been telling his usual far-fetched tales.' The planes on his face hardened to chiselled stone. 'I have lands to tame. What good is having a bride if she shivers without a proper house to keep her? What good children if they starve because you failed to have enough stores because you lack the proper buildings? Once I know for certain they can survive, I will find my bride.'

'And the King's decree that owners of gifted lands must be married?'

'There is a great deal of water between me and the King's shining new hall, the one which shimmers like gold on a summer evening and many other unmarried *jaarls* who are closer.'

Her heart felt a little easier. It wasn't her, it was the entire concept of marriage he objected to. Maybe in time… She rejected the thought before it started. She was not going to start weaving wishes again. If she had looked like Trana with spun gold for hair, pouting lips and a bosom for a man to bury his face in, they would be married. Instead she knew what she looked like—all teeth and no figure with her one beauty, her long hair, burnt away in the fire, along with her dowry.

'Returning to Viken is not an option. Let me—'

'I choose my own bride, not Eylir. I will travel to the north to find her, like I vowed on my mother's grave.' His blue-eyed gaze raked her form. 'The sort of bride I have in mind will be entirely different from what you keep offering.'

The words cut far deeper than they should. She should be used to it after Hamthur's barbs, but that small part of her which hoped her late husband had been wrong had never been entirely extinguished. Somewhere in this world there had to be a man who would appreciate what she brought to a marriage and treat her with respect. Right now, she'd settle for safety for Svana and that meant finding somewhere far from Vargr's influence.

'Thank you for the clarity,' she said in a tight voice.

All the amusement fled from his face. 'Pardon for any offence. I merely meant my bride will not have to travel on her own. Those men would have killed you or your sister if you'd travelled with them further.'

'I see.' Ragn inclined her head and allowed the untruth.

He ran a hand through his unruly hair, making it stand upright. 'I'm more used to the company of warriors than ladies. It is something I must work on before I travel north to woo.'

'Ladies do expect a certain amount of honey-coated words when they are wooed.'

He gave a rich laugh which warmed her to her toes. 'You possess a tart tongue and are unafraid to mince words. Perhaps you should learn honey-coating as well.'

'Curbing my tongue has always been a problem.

Allow me to try again.' She made a curtsy. 'I'm pleased you have taken pity on me and my sister and have allowed us to stay. I will trust your assessment of the captain who brought me. No good would have come of our returning to the north.'

'Your family would not welcome your return.'

She examined the dirty rushes. His words were far too close to the truth. She need to seize control of the conversation and steer it away from tricky subjects like why her family would not assist her. 'Perhaps one day I will thank you for choosing not to marry me. I know I certainly have no wish for an unwilling husband. However, *I* believe in looking forward, not harping on past mistakes.'

'I'm sure you will.' His laugh rang out. 'My temper is far too short. I've a certain disregard for the niceties of polite conversation and little care for life's luxuries. Past women have detailed my defects.'

'Then we should be friends as we've both avoided something that was destined to make us unhappy.'

He examined her from hooded eyes. 'Can men and women ever be friends?'

'I like to think they can be.' Ragn hoped she was telling the truth. Her parents had had a deep friendship until her mother's death. She'd listened to her father's despairing sobs after every feast until his death. 'I consider you one for giving me and my sister a place to stay instead of forcing us back on that ship. You saved our lives.'

He bowed his head. 'I'll take you to Ile in the morning. The commander, Sigurd Sigmundson, is a friend. He can find you passage on a ship northwards when the ships begin to move in the spring.'

Ragn firmed her mouth. She had heard of Ile. Vargr had had something to do with it a few years before, but she believed the commander of the fort had changed. 'The captain and his crew feared Svana's eyes. I sacrificed a gold necklace to calm the sea. If such a thing happened on the return journey, I doubt I could prevent it.'

'Fools.' Gunnar shook his head. 'As if how a passenger looks matters more than the skill of the navigator or the pilot. They should remember Odin only has one eye, but still manages to navigate his ship. Your sister has two good eyes, even if one turns inward.'

A dog's howl made him stop and cock his head to one side.

'Is there something amiss?' Ragn asked as Svana froze at the sound. In another breath Svana would throw herself on the ground and reveal precisely why the sailors feared her.

'I shut my dogs in the barn when I spied the ship. They dislike strangers.'

'Do they come into the hall?' she asked, trying to calculate how she had to prepare Svana.

'You and your sister remain here out of the cold and damp. Wait here until I return.'

Ragn grasped Svana's hand. 'All will be well, sweetling. We are safe.'

Svana gave the barest hint of a nod. 'Safe is good.'

Ragn watched Gunnar stride away into the murky gloom. She had until morning to convince him to change his mind and allow them to stay.

When the final embers of the meagre fire vanished, a steady and insistent cold crept around Ragn. Despite

Gunnar's request for her to wait, she knew she had to act. Her breath made great plumes in the air and keeping her hands busy made it easier for her to think.

In the silence, Svana sniffled and rubbed her eyes. 'Are we truly going to have to leave here tomorrow? Will the dogs come in to eat me up?'

'I protected you once from dogs, I can do so again.'

'Is it my eyes the man fears? Is that why he wanted to send us away? The witch woman said my eyes would only bring sorrow.'

Ragn's heart clenched. Typical Svana thinking, blaming herself when Ragn knew the truth—it was her he didn't want. 'The witch woman was Vargr's creature, even though she pretended otherwise. How many times do I have to tell you that?'

'Ragn, my stomach hurts. Will we starve?'

'Not if I can help it.' Ragn hunkered down so her face was about level with Svana's. 'Trust me—I will see us safe.'

Svana's eyes widened. 'How are you going to do that?'

'First, I am going to make us a hot meal. A solid one. Hard to think straight when your belly rumbles. Remember I brought dried herbs and mushrooms in our trunks. I spied the kitchen building when he had the trunks dragged up here. No need to stay in this ice palace.'

Svana wrinkled her nose, but her face lost its terrified expression. 'How will that help us stay?'

'His friend said that he longed for the old country, perhaps once he has a taste of it…he will be in a better mood. And as a general rule, dogs stay out of kitchens so you will be safe there.'

The tightness of Svana's face eased. 'Truly?'

Ragn made her voice sound positive and hoped her words rang true about the dogs. If her scheme failed, they would at least have a decent meal in their bellies, something they hadn't had since before they left the north.

Svana clapped her hands. 'You will succeed. I know you will. You're a good cook and you make the best ale. You can show this man that he needs to have you here. I can't face the sea again and the waves.'

'You won't have to,' Ragn whispered as she started searching through her trunks. 'I will find a way. I promised and you know I try hard to keep my promises.'

'Most of the time.'

Ragn banged the pots about with vigour.

Gunnar struggled to control his temper as he strode towards the barn. The biting autumn rain helped to cool him off. This woman, this Ragnhild, had no idea about him or the way he might behave. She agreed with Eylir's assessment that his solid reasons for not marrying were excuses. The gods save him from meddlesome women. His mother had been like that, but she had done it from a good heart. He had no idea what sort of heart this woman had. She simply had worn that proud look as if she expected everyone to bow down before her.

He imagined the rules she'd impose if her feet were under his table. What Eylir had been thinking when he sent her, he had no idea. There was something more to her story, some reason for her journey.

When he undid the barn door, his two wolfhounds leapt out to greet him. His mood always improved when he encountered them. Kolka, the older, gave a sharp bark as if to ask what took him so long to get rid of the boat.

'We've visitors,' he said to the pair who cocked their heads to one side and gave the impression of understanding him. 'Behave until I get rid of them.'

Kefla, the brindle one of the pair, whimpered, reminding him various chores needed to be done before night fell such as feeding the cattle and making sure the pigs were properly slopped out, things he'd been doing when the ship had appeared. He could order one of his men to do the night-time chores, but he enjoyed the simple tasks which were a world away from the stink and filth of battle.

He concentrated on the mundane tasks, while promising himself that in the morning he'd send the women somewhere safer where they'd be properly looked after.

When the animals were settled, he realised that he'd not eaten since yesterday. Kolka and Kefla were hungry as well. He swore under his breath. And the visitors would be expecting food.

He knew Ragnhild's type. Such women rarely lifted a finger. It was why she asked about the servants. She wanted someone to order about. But he'd manage something. The girl had appeared half-starved.

'Hard bread and cheese is better than nothing.'

The dogs looked at him with tilted heads and trotted off towards the hall.

He followed them towards the hall, but stopped as a delicious scent filled the yard. It instantly transported him back to his childhood. He shook his head to get rid of the memory. He had to be hungrier than he considered. He was imagining his mother's stew.

He went into the kitchen. A fire had been lit in the

hearth. Meat bubbled away, but rather than smelling and looking like shoe leather as it always did for him, it appeared appetising. The woman was bent over the pot and he saw the curve of her backside and the way her waist nipped in. There was far more to her than he'd first considered.

His stomach growled, announcing his presence. She jumped slightly, dropping a long-handled spoon with a clatter.

'We were hungry and you have timed it perfectly,' she said with a smile as she retrieved the spoon. 'I hope you don't mind. I thought it best to make a meal. A simple stew from the leftovers I discovered. There should be plenty. It has been such a long time since Svana had hot food…'

'You made stew?'

'After a fashion.' She gave a casual shrug. 'The meat is less tender than I would like, but a growing girl needs to eat. Waiting is next to impossible when you are Svana's age.'

He had forgotten the last time he'd eaten a proper stew. Lately he'd been too busy to do more than boil a bit of meat for the dogs and eat hard cheese and bread.

'The smell takes me back to my childhood,' he admitted as his stomach rumbled again.

'Funny how scents can do that. Freshly mown hay always has me thinking of my grandfather and the way he used to lift me up into the hay barn.' She tucked a tendril of hair behind her ear. He noticed that her skin was now a far healthier pink and white as opposed to the green-yellow tinge it had had when she'd first arrived on the shore. While not conventionally beautiful, Ragnhild was striking. More Skaldi, the giant's daughter who won her place amongst the gods, rather than the golden loveliness of Sif. 'I brought the herbs with me and it seemed a shame to not use them on a day like today.'

'It certainly smells delicious.'

'I put some dried cloudberries into the porridge for the morning. I always find it best to have it sitting overnight in the embers. Saves time in the morning.' Her cheeks coloured. 'I like my hands to be busy.'

'My mother used to do that. Cloudberries when she had them for a special treat, but making it the day before. She'd have to chase me out of the kitchen to keep me from sneaking them.' After he found his family's bodies, he could not bear anything which reminded him of those times, but now a sharp longing to taste cloudberries' tart tang filled him. 'Something I'd forgotten.'

'Then we are agreed—cloudberries for the morning.'

'Earlier...' he said as she put out several bowls, ones he'd not seen before.

'Shall we leave it in the past?' She deftly scooped out a bowl of stew and placed it in front of him before serving up two more bowls. 'Behind us both. A new beginning.'

He took a taste and the stew was every bit as good as it smelled. 'It might be best. Hunger always makes me irritable, or so my mother used to claim. She'd ensure I had a bowl of stew when I came home.'

'Hunger does that to many people.'

Gunnar took another bite. He had been far too hasty in dismissing Ragnhild as someone who was content to be decorative. To his surprise, the bowl seemed to have emptied without his realising it. Kolka and Kefla advanced and sat before Ragnhild, wagging their tails and making little whimpering noises.

'Your dogs are hungry?'

'They have a soft spot for stew.'

Ragnhild ladled several spoons into wooden bowls and put them in front of the dogs before she put another steaming bowl in front of him. The traitors lapped it very quickly.

'You should eat,' he said, dipping his spoon into the broth. He'd forgotten how good food tasted, rather the burnt mess he always seemed to create. His stomach growled in appreciation.

'In good time. Svana, come here and get your food. It is going cold.'

Gunnar glanced over towards the girl sat rigid on the bench, her eyes wide.

'You promised, Ragn! No dogs. Not in here! Not in a kitchen! Please, no!'

'Svana, come here!' She held out her hand. 'The dogs are busy eating their supper.'

The girl got up and made a big circuit about the dogs. The dogs, seeing her, gave sharp welcoming barks, but each time she heard the noise, she visibly shuddered. Her silver eyes grew wider. When she reached Ragnhild, she threw her arms about her and made little whimpering noises. Gunnar frowned. It was unnatural that a child would be that afraid of dogs.

'Svana, what will our host think of you?' Ragnhild said, picking the child up and carrying her to where her stew sat. 'His dogs are very well behaved. They will not hurt you. They simply wanted their supper. Time you ate and stopped this nonsense. A full belly makes everything better. Gunnar agrees with me.'

The girl stopped making sniffing noise and peeped out from behind a curtain of hair. 'I didn't mean to be bad. I never mean to be.'

'Eat. Leave the poor dogs in peace to enjoy their supper. Once they have finished, I am sure they will have better things to do than bother one girl who is busy with her supper.'

Ragn put a few more ladles of stew in the dogs' bowls before adding another to his.

The child dropped her spoon and instantly Kefla headed towards it to investigate. The child's face became white and pinched.

'Your sister's hands shake,' he said, frowning as he recalled long-buried memories about Asa his youngest sister, her affliction and how the other villagers had shunned the family because of it.

'The sea voyage has unsettled her.'

Svana gave another cry of sheer terror and drew her feet up. Kefla stopped, tilting her head in confusion.

'Could they go out?' Ragnhild asked. 'Maybe just for the night.'

'My dogs like the fire on a cold and wet night.'

Ragnhild pointedly cleared her throat. 'Svana, we need to find you a place to sleep. You are clearly overtired. Remember we are here on sufferance. Gunnar Olafson has been kind. You hated the storm-tossed sea. After you are rested, the world won't be as scary as it seems now.'

The girl screwed up her nose. 'Will the dogs eat me if I sleep? They are awfully large. If I don't give my stew to them, they will eat me.'

Ragnhild pressed her hands on the table as she gave him a nervous glance. 'Svana. Please.'

'They look like the sort which Mor-Mor told me about—the sort who snap up little girls when they are naughty,' the girl whispered in a voice which he had to strain to hear as she clapped her hands in imitation of a dog gnashing its jaws.

Another memory of Asa slammed into him, rising from that forbidden place where he kept all the memories of his family. It was the sort of thing she'd have said and then she'd have given one of her piercing screams to prove her point. She, too, had loved the terrifying stories their grandmother or *mor-mor* had told on long winter nights.

The last thing he required right now was a piercing wail which set the dogs off. The entire situation would career out of control, worse than a long ship which had lost its steering oar.

He knelt down so his face was closer to her level. She did not shrink away from him, but stared with a solemn gaze.

'Kolka and Kefla are my wolfhounds,' he said in as soft a tone as he could manage. 'They listen to me. You are safe here.'

Svana put her hands over her mouth. 'I once saw some dogs in a battle. Spittle dripped from their great fangs.'

'Hush, Svana. That is in the past.' Her sister put an arm about the girl. 'Things in the past can't hurt you. Only things in the present. We discussed this.'

'I know, Ragn. Forgive me?'

'Always. Now breathe slowly and finish the stew.'

The room went quiet as the dogs put their heads on their paws and the child ate a few more mouthfuls.

'Does he know about putting out porridge for the

nisser?' the girl asked in a loud whisper when she'd
finished.

The innocent words sent a knife through his heart.
Nissers… He'd nearly forgotten about them. His sisters
had believed in them as well, declaring the *nisser* would
only stay if he put out porridge and said goodbye to him.
He'd scoffed that last time. By the time he returned in
the dead of winter, the farm had failed and his family
had starved to death. He abruptly stood.

Sensing the change in atmosphere, Kefla gave a
small whine and the girl cringed again.

'Hush, Svana. You have too many notions in your
head. Gunnar Olafson has enough to think about. *Nissers* indeed.'

'But you put the barley on to seep, that works,' the
child persisted, sounding just like Asa and Brita had.

'No porridge,' he said, his head erupting with tre-
mendous pain.

The girl winced and Ragnhild's mouth pressed to a
thin white line. He frowned. The words had come out
far harsher than he'd intended. 'My dogs tend to gobble
porridge up given half a chance. *Nissers* respect hard
work. When one realises how hard I've worked, then
he will come.'

'It is quite a new hall,' Ragnhild added. 'Anyone can
see how hard Gunnar worked. The stout walls keep out
the wind and rain. Remember the ruined hut we sheltered in, Svana?'

'Oh. I hadn't thought about that.' Svana stifled a
small yawn and her eyelids fluttered. 'I know a *nisser*
will be here soon. This place is safe and *nissers* require
such things.'

Safety. A lump came into Gunnar's throat. And for

the umpteenth time, he wished he could have made the old farm safe for Brita, Asa and his mother.

Ragn put an arm around her sister. 'My sister needs a place to sleep. She is exhausted.'

'There is a small chamber you two can use. I made up a bed in case Eylir visited. It will suffice for the night.' He clenched his jaw. The woman might infuriate him, but she had regard for her sister. None of his business. They were leaving in the morning but he would find them somewhere safe, just somewhere away from his farm. 'I know how women value their privacy. It is unfinished and probably not up to the standard you are used to, but it will serve for now.'

'You have little idea what we are used to. A pig sty would be a luxury after that ship.'

Swift anger at the implied criticism went through him and he took refuge in it. 'I believe my hall extends to more comfort than a pig sty.'

Her cheeks went pink. 'I didn't mean…' she said. 'My tongue sometimes runs away. I merely didn't want you to go to any more trouble. You've been too kind already.'

Kind was the last word he expected her to use. Remorse tugged at him. He held up his hand. 'My friend sent you on a fool's errand. Nothing more. Nothing less. But abandoning women to the wilds… I was raised better.'

'There are not many who would have taken us in. I am pleased that we won't have to go back on the boat.' She bit her bottom lip, turning it the colour of summer berries. 'I worry that Svana would not have survived the return journey.'

'I have the chores to finish. This farm doesn't run

on its own. The dogs always assist me. I would suggest you and your sister are in bed before I return to avoid misunderstandings.'

The corners of her mouth curved upwards. 'You mean your *nisser* fails to live up to expectation? What a surprise!'

His smile answered hers. '*Nissers* only assist those who are prepared to put the hard work in. If you had trouble in the past, perhaps you failed to work hard enough.'

'My problems stem from something other than hard work.'

'Would you care to tell me about them?' The words tumbled out before he stopped them.

'My problems, not yours.' She quickly busied herself, collecting up the bowls.

Rather than answering, he made a clicking noise at the back of his throat and the dogs followed him out of the hall. One night, then his life returned to its predictable pace. He liked the solitude. He ignored the little voice which called him a liar.

Chapter Three

'The dogs obeyed him. Instantly. Hamthur's dogs rarely obeyed him,' Svana declared, stifling another large yawn. 'Are you certain we will have to leave tomorrow? I thought you were married to Gunnar.' Her brow furrowed with concentration. 'A proxy marriage.'

'I gambled everything on a few vague promises. I should have seen Gunnar's friend only wanted to impress Trana.'

Ragn forced the bitter bile back down and kept her hands moving, reshaping the straw in the mattress into a serviceable bed instead of a heap. The straw had seen better days, but it was clean and smelt of summer meadows.

Cleaning the kitchen had gone far more quickly than she'd anticipated, with Svana, having recovered from her earlier fright, eagerly drying the dishes, carefully sweeping the floor while humming a little song about how the *nissers* always help the helpers.

Hearing Svana's lisping tones had lifted her spirits and made her long for easier days, when she, too, had believed in such things.

Rather than give her a lecture about making friends with the dogs, Ragn banked the fire in preparation for Gunnar's return and marched Svana into the tiny cupboard of a room.

'You must be able to do something.' Svana's hand clutched hers. 'A reason to keep us here. Our luck is changing, Ragn. I can feel it. My hands are all tingly. See.'

Ragn's breath caught in her throat. Another of Svana's attacks? They were there on sufferance already. She pushed Svana's hair from her forehead. Her skin wasn't clammy, a good sign. Gunnar might not mind the inward-turning eye, but if he discovered Svana flailing about and foaming at the mouth? What would his great dogs do then? Might they not be better off just leaving? Ragn worried her bottom lip. They had a roof over their heads here and she had no idea of what the conditions were like on Ile.

'Hopefully I can convince him that he requires a housekeeper, instead of relying on a magical sprite. He certainly needs help.' Ragn's breath caught. She knew how to make a household prosper despite Hamthur's extravagances. However, she'd utterly failed in the marriage bed. She'd been young and eager to please at the start of the marriage, but nothing she did seemed to please him. Hamthur had rapidly grown disenchanted with her efforts and mostly sought other women's beds.

When she'd first heard he'd been waylaid and murdered, she had felt relief. It was only later she'd learnt that Vargr had ordered the murder as retribution for Hamthur's continued refusal to kill Svana. If she had known that he cared or even had done it out of selfish interests to protect his own skin, knowing his brother would find another excuse to attack or because he was in no mood to yield to his brother's demands, she might have behaved differently, might have insisted that he take armed guards, instead of accepting his easy assurance he was a grown man. She accepted that she could never know for certain why he'd protected Svana, but he had and that was enough to make her feel sorry that she hadn't tried harder to protect him. She should have guessed that Vargr would have behaved in that fashion.

'You're the best at managing,' Svana said with a sleepy smile. 'Far used to say that you magicked grain from any barrel, and ale from the lake—the sort of wife any man would be proud of.'

'My lack of womanly charms is an established fact.'

'Hamthur was jealous because everyone looked to you.' Svana gave a big yawn. 'Gunnar should marry you like he was supposed to. Once I catch that *nisser*'s shirt tail, you will see only good things for my sister, the best sister in all the world.'

The best sister. Ragn hated how her throat tightened. Did good sisters cause their sisters to get hurt? Did sisters ruin their younger sisters' lives by inviting witch women to give predictions? Bitterness filled her mouth. Her great plan for restarting their lives in Jura had come to nothing.

'*Nissers* don't exist.' She smoothed a lump out in the straw and discovered a small stone figurine, the sort her grandmother used to wear on a string around her neck. She carefully pocketed it before Svana proclaimed it a gift from the *nisser*.

'You are his Jul present from his best friend. One should not give presents like that away.'

'Presents of that sort are best not given as a surprise.'

Ragn swallowed hard. How much of her story Eylir had guessed or been told she hadn't asked and he hadn't volunteered. His offer had enabled them to escape Vargr's murderous clutches.

Had she known the truth would she have accepted Eylir's offer? Ragn sighed. Undoing the past was futile. She could only make the future better. For the thousandth time, she whispered her new resolution—past behind her and forgotten, the future was the only thing which mattered.

'Gunnar never asked his friend for a bride,' she said. 'I will not hold him to the words Eylir said. Some day we will laugh about it and be glad that he refused me. We have a better future coming, sweetling.'

'But he allowed us to stay the night and his eyes twinkled, particularly after he ate the stew. That means he likes you.' Svana gave a smug smile.

'It is character which matters. I learned that particular lesson the hard way. And Gunnar Olafson is grumpy.'

'He is a hard worker. He built this all on his own.'

'He has no interest in me.'

'His eyes followed you. I saw them. Even if you didn't. You always believed Hamthur about your looks and never me. Why?'

Ragn's cheeks burned. She well imagined the sort of woman a man like Gunnar would like and it wasn't a flat-chested, dried-up stick like her. 'That is beside the point.'

'It isn't.'

'You are over-tired and emotional. We will be leaving here in the morning for Ile, a great big island with lots of people. I will find a husband there.'

'But…' Svana's bottom lip stuck out.

'We won't have to stay in Ile if we don't like it,' Ragn continued before the tears started. 'We can go to another island, or possibly even the Isle of Colbhasa where Kolbeinn rules. He was our father's friend and will find a place for us at his court. Then, there is Lord Ketil whose word holds sway over the Western reaches of King Harald's domain. Our father had dealings with him as well. We haven't travelled all this way simply to starve or give up.'

The hard knot in her stomach eased. The *jaarls* Kolbeinn and Ketil probably wouldn't even remember their father, but it was a plan of sorts. From the stories her father told about his former comrade-in-arms, she doubted if Kolbeinn bent his knee to anyone, let alone someone like Vargr who thrived on the intrigues at court, rather than on the battlefield.

'You give up too easily, Ragn.' Svana looped her arms about her knees. '*Nissers* are happier where there is a family. Mor-Mor told me that. He will want us to stay so he can have a really real family to look after.'

Ragn was very glad she had not mentioned the little carved man she'd found. There would have been no stopping Svana's pronouncements and then there would have been a full-blown fit when she realised that they would have to leave despite her predictions. 'The self-proclaimed expert on *nissers* must get her sleep. To-morrow will be another long day. Sleep.'

Svana started to get up. 'If I sit beside the porridge, I can catch him by his shirt tail and force him to make Gunnar fall for you. Mor-Mor said *nissers* must grant wishes if you catch their shirt tail.'

'You talk an awful lot of nonsense.' She placed a kiss

on her sister's forehead. 'May your dreams be pleasant ones. Your eyes are closing.'

Svana stifled a yawn. 'In the morning then, I'll go looking. He is probably hiding from those pesky dogs.'

'Only if you do the tasks I set first. We must show Gunnar that we are grateful for his kindness. And that means working hard while we remain on this island.'

'When I catch the *nisser*, you will have to admit you were wrong.'

Ragn sighed. Admitting that she was wrong was something she spent far too much time doing lately. This journey had seemed like the right thing to do back in Kaupang, but had she dragged Svana halfway around the world for nothing? Another mistake to beg forgiveness for?

'It is not our home.'

Svana snuggled down into the bedding. 'This time, Sister, I am right.'

In the morning she'd find a reason to distract Svana and hopefully her brain would work better. There was no point in believing in things you couldn't see as you set yourself up for disappointment. She'd learned that lesson the first year of her ill-fated marriage.

Hard work and a pragmatic attitude were what was required. She had managed to get them this far. No one, particularly not Gunnar Olafson and his arrogant attitude, was going to force her to give up. She simply needed to find a plan which would work.

A faint noise made Ragn glance up from where she lay next to the softly slumbering Svana. She knew she should sleep, but every time she closed her eyes, she saw

the flames which had nearly engulfed her and Svana.
She'd vowed then to keep Svana safe and she would.

The bumping noise sounded again. As if something
heavy was being dragged across the floor. Svana, however, seemed utterly oblivious to the noise and gave a
soft snore.

'Is something wrong?' she called out and reached
for her shawl. 'Was I wrong to leave the fire banked?'

Gunnar stood looking at her from the doorway. The
light from the hearth silhouetted him and the bundle
he carried.

'I've brought furs. It can be cold and damp at this
time of year.'

Ragn scrambled to her feet, aware that all she wore
was her under-gown. She contemplated reaching for
her proper gown, but decided it was silly. The darkness
obscured her form, not that there was much to see. She
winced, recalling Hamthur's jibes. 'You brought furs?
Whatever for?'

'I can't risk you or the girl getting sick. You will
have to stay longer if you do.' He dropped the furs on
the ground beside the door. 'Do what you like with
them, but don't go blaming me if you are uncomfortable or cold.'

'Thank you for them. My sister will be appreciative.'

He stared at her a long time. 'Thank you for the meal
earlier. It has been a long time since anyone laid things
out for me. The dogs appreciated it.'

Saying that, he turned on his heel and strode out of
the room before she said anything further.

Ragn rushed over to the bundle and withdrew several
thick pelts. And there were so many that they could easily cover both Svana and herself. Gunnar made a show

of being harsh, but underneath he had a kind heart. She needed to reach the man behind the rude mask, the one whose eyes had deepened to summer-sea-blue when he spoke of cloudberries. She shook her head—mooning over Gunnar's eyes and the width of his shoulders would not solve her immediate problem.

She held the little figurine in her hand. There had to be a way of making him want to keep them there, just until she figured out somewhere safe for Svana, somewhere where Vargr and his followers would never think to look. Her actions had taken away so many things in that girl's life, starting with their mother's life and ending with Svana's health.

She gave a half-smile as she recalled one of her grandmother's sayings. *Faint hearts never won anything except a cold.* Acting now while she had her courage was better than regretting the missed opportunity in the morning.

Gunnar stirred the embers of the kitchen's fire as the faint snuffling noises from the pair made sleep impossible. Not that sleep was ever easy. He worked himself to exhaustion to avoid the dreams.

In the morning, once the current was right, he'd take Ragnhild and her sister to Ile and when he returned, he'd be back to his peace. It was what he wanted. He cursed Eylir for his rashness in sending them and hated that he kept trying to guess why his friend sent Ragnhild and her sister when he recollected Eylir teasing him about buxom blondes. He should have no interest in unpicking her mysteries. He shouldn't have enjoyed the aroma of her stew, clashing wits with her earlier, or even watching her mouth relax into a smile. But he had.

A rustle made him glance towards the door. Ragnhild hovered on the step. Her hair was unbound, but far shorter than he had previously thought. A woman of her quality should have long hair. He narrowed his eyes. In the firelight, the vivid scars on her feet and ankles were visible. They were at most a few weeks' old. The woman had been through a fire and possibly a raid. That fire and the girl's fear of dogs were related.

Rather than trying to get rid of her to pursue the cousin, had Eylir sent her to the one place where she'd be safe? Where he trusted his friend would look after her?

Gunnar ground his teeth. Speculation did no one any good. Keeping someone safe and marrying them were two separate things entirely. He intended to get Ragnhild and her sister to safety—away from here and out of his life.

'Yes? Do you require more furs?'

'I found this in the bedding. I assume it belongs to you and is not a gift from any stray *nisser*.' She held out a small carved man with a smile.

Time and his breath stopped. Her lips softly parted as she leant towards him with it. Their fingers brushed, sending a warm pulse jolting through him. She jumped backwards, dropping the stone.

Even as he caught it in mid-air, he knew it would be his good-luck charm, the one he'd misplaced weeks ago and had spent days searching for. His temper had become so foul that even his dogs had avoided him. He'd finally given up all hope and had become resigned to its loss.

His fingers curled around the amulet, warm from her palm. The anguished part of his soul eased. His last tangible connection to his family had been regained.

'You found it in the bedding?' he asked, trying to puzzle out where it had fallen. 'You mean in the furs that I brought in?'

'In the straw. If Svana had found it, there would've been no stopping her. Her belief in *nissers* inhabiting this place would have been proved true. She'd have clung to the doorframe to stay and see one.' Her slight frown indicated that was the last thing she required.

His eyes widened. 'And you know what it is?'

'My father's mother had a stone-man amulet like that. She used to swear it kept her safe. Perhaps it worked—she lived a long and prosperous life. It went missing after her death.' She ducked her head and he saw how the fire had left her fringe long but burned the back of her neck. Her sister showed no such signs of injury.

Gunnar frowned. She and her sister would be safe... in Ile where she would be able to choose a better man than he as a husband. An unexpected twinge of jealousy at the unknown man stabbed him.

He pushed it away. It was for the best. His fate had been sealed the instant he spotted the soothsayer abusing those girls. An older warrior would have turned a blind eye, but he had acted to save those girls. Unfortunately, they had been too injured and died later. Now he lived with the consequences of the dying soothsayer's prophecy.

She drew her brows together. 'Is everything all right? Did you intend to lose the amulet? Is it bad luck?'

'It belonged to my mother. All I have left of her.' There was little point in telling Ragnhild that his mother had wanted to ensure he returned safely home for the start of Jul.

He turned the stone man over and over, feeling its familiar carvings. He almost heard his mother's laugh as she told him that it would help him find the right partner in life.

He remembered Dyrfinna's scorn about the crudely carved man when she discovered it. She'd pulled it from around his throat, saying it frowned at her. He'd intended on proposing marriage to her that evening, but her reaction made him question their relationship and possibly even saved his life. Rather than adoring him as she had pretended, Dyrfinna owed a debt to the soothsayer Gunnar had slain and had been determined to avenge his death. However, thanks to the stone man, they'd been arguing instead of being wrapped in the throes of passion when the assassins entered her house. The attackers were no match for his sword that day. But Dyrfinna had perished in the ensuing fight. Her last words had been that he'd been a gullible fool to love someone like her. Gunnar had hunted down the men until none remained.

Why did this woman have to find it? His mother would have approved of her—she was a good cook, came from the north and had a fine manner about her. And she was in trouble. His mother had raised him never to turn his back on women who sought his help. To be fair, it was the coming from the north part which his mother would have approved of most.

The walls pressed in on him. Ragnhild was standing a mere breath away. Her mouth was softly parted and her eyes large. Her lips would taste of summer strawberries or possibly cloudberries. They were ripe for the nibbling. All he had to do was to take her in his arms and declare he'd changed his mind, that he wanted her for his bride after all.

What would he look like then? *'A gullible fool'*—the words resounded in his brain, dripping with Dyrfinna's precise intonations.

He shook his head to clear it and walked over to the hearth, putting the man next to his silver horn with a bang. 'I will choose my own bride.'

The dogs and Ragnhild looked at him strangely. He rubbed the back of his neck. He hadn't meant to say it out loud.

'The King's decree about marriage you spoke of earlier,' Gunnar said quickly before she started asking awkward questions and he confessed about his mother's prediction. 'I must go north for a wife in the spring. The Lords Ketil and Kolbeinn will hold off enforcing the decree on me until then.'

She gave a half-shrug which revealed the swanlike beauty of her throat. 'If you think you have until then.'

'I do.' He drew a breath and regained control of his wayward thoughts. 'Kolbeinn will give me time to choose a bride, rather than forcing me to accept the first one who crosses my path, once he learns of the decree.'

'Bringing you that stone man was an act of kindness, not an expectation of a marriage offer.' Her laugh sounded hollow as she started for the door.

'Stay. Keep me company.'

She halted so quickly the material flattened against her, revealing the shapeliness of her legs. 'Is there something more we can say to each other? Returning the amulet was the only reason I bothered you.'

He knew she lied. The deep hollows into which

her eyes had sunk betrayed her. Ragnhild disliked her dreams every bit as much as he disliked his own dreams.

'Your sister is far too thin,' he said in desperation to change the subject. Ragnhild was not the sort of lady who would agree to the only thing he was prepared to offer a woman—one night of pleasure to keep the bad dreams away. 'You can see her collarbones.'

'I know. Once she ate like a horse, but the sea voyage failed to agree with her. She was often sick. Her appetite will return in time.'

'The dogs like her, even if she doesn't like them.' He leant down and fondled the tan dog Kolka's ears. 'I trust their judgement. They are rarely wrong about people.'

Ragn watched him with wary eyes. She longed to ask what the dogs thought of her. Gunnar had clearly not meant to say the earlier words about choosing his own bride aloud. Once she'd taken it for a positive sign, but that was the problem with believing in such things, one ignored reality.

Right now, the marriage was unimportant, the staying here was. And his remark about going north in the spring had given her an idea. 'There are not many who have been kind to Svana lately.'

Gunnar motioned to her to come closer. Both dogs looked up briefly and then settled their heads on their paws. They seemed to accept her. The stew had worked with them, if not with him. 'And you? How did the men react to you?'

She carefully shrugged a shoulder. The men had kept their distance. 'They were less than kind and I no longer expect kindness.'

'But it is welcomed when you receive it.'

'I've no wish to seem ungrateful or forward. I fear

I might have been. I find it hard to be idle. I see a task which needs to be accomplished and I start. But worse than that my tongue runs away with itself when I have ideas for improvement.'

'My mother was one like you.'

She gave a careful laugh, aware that one wrong word and the chance would slip through her fingers. 'I hope that is a good thing. Finding your charm seemed to alarm you more than anything.'

He took a stick and stirred the fire so that bright sparks leapt in the air. 'Night-time is the right time to sleep. We can speak in the morning as we cross the channel to Ile.'

'My mind races far too much to sleep,' Ragn admitted, pressing her hands together to keep them from trembling. Gunnar's mood had improved from earlier and there was an intimacy about the night which would vanish with the sunrise.

'It is good that you will be going north in the spring. You have worked too hard on this hall to risk losing it for the want of a little thing like a bride.'

His eyes flickered to the stone man. 'The bride I choose, not one which is foisted on me by well-intentioned friends.'

'Did I say differently?' She swallowed hard and tried to ignore the tightening of the knots in her stomach. 'When you go north, you will leave this place empty. You need someone you trust to look after it. A caretaker to ensure it remains in good order.'

'Eylir remains in the north.'

'I meant me. I know how to run an estate. My husband used to leave me in charge when he went…when he went away.' Ragn watched the glowing embers.

'When your husband was off warring.'

'That and other things. He served the King and was required at court.'

'At court without you?'

'Someone had to ensure the smooth running of the estate.' She forced a placating smile. She needed to keep this conversation away from her past for both their sakes. 'If you give my sister and me a place to stay, we will have every reason to be loyal.'

'When I return, will I find my hall standing? The scarring on your limbs makes me believe your last hall burned to the ground.'

Ragn kept her chin up. 'We were the only ones to escape the inferno. My servants…the loyal ones… perished.'

'You carried her, shielded her.'

She fingered the indentations on her neck. The burns no longer hurt as they had done when they'd sheltered in that barn, but they still sometimes pained her. 'How did you guess?'

'Simple enough.' He moved closer and his breath brushed her cheek. 'Your hair is short while Svana's remains long. You have scars. She doesn't. Her right foot twists inward. She moves quickly enough so I'm guessing she was born with it, but outrunning flames would be beyond her.'

Ragn bowed her head. 'The fire took hold quickly. A few more breaths and we would have died.'

He nodded. 'How far did you carry her?'

'A tale for another day. I ensured she survived. That is all you need to know.'

'Quarrels with your husband? You must tell me the truth if you wish to stay here. Trust me.'

Ragn drew a shuddering breath. Where to begin and what to leave out. 'My late husband quarrelled with his brother over his inheritance. My brother-in-law became determined to win at all costs. When his petition to the assembly was refused, he had my husband murdered and sought to take the lands. When I defied him and refused to leave the hall which had been my childhood home, he had it burned, leaving us for dead.'

'Does he still consider you dead?' Gunnar asked quietly.

That question had circled around her brain for days. 'I must believe so. No one searched for us after the first night. Once I'd healed enough to walk, we made our way to Kaupang. Trana was the first person I encountered there and she offered a way out. It was better for everyone that we go.'

He tapped his fingers together. 'Don't you care about regaining your lands?'

'I learned that day that the people you love are more important than any land. He is welcome to all of it—the part that was his father's and the greater part which belonged to my family.' She leant towards him. 'I can keep this hall safe, better than safe. I can make this hall a place your bride will run towards instead of running from. Give me a chance to prove it.'

His eyes narrowed and for a horrible heartbeat she worried she'd overstepped. 'Why here? What is special about this hall?'

'I trust my sister's instincts much as you trust your dogs'. She is convinced she will see a *nisser*. It will give her a chance to regain her strength and put meat on her bones.'

He nodded. 'Fair enough.'

The breath whooshed out of her. He had not questioned her more about Svana and why she'd been incapable of running beyond her foot. Maybe he would never need know about the affliction she'd caused Svana. Maybe he would not need to know about Vargr and the power he now enjoyed as one of the King's closest advisors. All those things happened a world away. It was the present which was important, not the past.

'Then we may stay? Beyond tomorrow morning?'

'I expect you to work hard.'

'Hard work was never my problem.'

His eyes skittered to where the stone man perched. It appeared as if the man was grinning broadly. The firelight flickered and the expression disappeared.

'You may stay until I bring my chosen bride home. I won't have her displaced.'

She held out her hand. 'Done.'

'Done.' His fingers curled about hers, strong and safe. The warm liquefying of her insides that she'd had when she returned the amulet increased. Her breath left her with a gasp. She stumbled forward. His mouth loomed large over hers and his arms came about her.

She rapidly pushed against him before her bones completely melted into him, before she begged him to kiss her and make her feel desirable. Before she made a fool of herself. 'We agreed—marriage between us will not happen.'

Her voice was far too breathless for her liking.

His arms fell to his side and the cool air rushed between them. 'Is there harm in sharing a kiss? I have shared many pleasurable kisses and remain unmarried.'

Ragn schooled her features. Hamthur's taunts about her passion-killing abilities reverberated in her brain.

'I know where such things can lead, particularly in the night. I refuse to jeopardise our agreement by adding coupling into it.'

'Is it Eylir? Are you waiting for him?' He stroked his chin. 'Aye, I can understand that. Commendable even, but Eylir is a flighty man, constantly falling in and out of love.'

The lie trembled on her lips. Eylir was pleasant looking, but he was not the sort of man who made her blood run hot.

'Eylir?' She rapidly shook her head. 'No, it is not him.'

His eyes were hooded. 'Then what is it? A kiss to seal our bargain will not lead anywhere…unless you want it to.'

Ragn tightened her shawl about her shoulders and kept her chin up. 'I refuse to become a warm body in the night where there is no marriage in the offing. I refuse to play some sort of seduction game with you where I can only lose.'

'And marriage is the only situation in which you will consider a man in your bed?' His voice purred, making her knees go weak. 'You are resolved to make a stand?'

Ragn hastily backed up and her cheeks became hot. In her mind she repeated the reasons why starting anything with this man would be a mistake. 'I have my principles to keep me warm.'

He made a bow. 'I will abide by your *principles*… until you change your mind.'

'Do women often change their mind about inhabiting your bed?'

'I've never notice a shortage in past.' He gave a husky laugh. 'Eylir claimed bed-sport is the only use I have for women.'

Ragn lifted her chin and met his dancing eyes, eyes she happily drowned in. 'I look forward to demonstrating to you that women have a use beyond the bedchamber.'

Gunnar raised her hand to his lips. The hot pulse which travelled up her arm gave a lie to her words of not being attracted to him. 'I always enjoy discovering new ideas.'

Chapter Four

The sound of the cockerel's crow dragged Ragn from her fitful dreams. She rapidly dressed, placing the *couvrechief* over her shorn hair. She froze. Last night's offer to allow them to stay instead of removing them to Ile could not be some terrible dream. She rushed to the kitchen, saw the little man sitting on the mantel and breathed again.

When she returned to the bedchamber, Svana had snuggled into the warm place Ragn had vacated, her face smooth instead of scrunched up. Best of all, her limbs remained relaxed, not the restless twitching Ragn had witnessed every morning since the fire.

'A good night's sleep can cure much,' she whispered. 'Mor-Mor was right.'

Ragn blinked to clear the prickling tears. Perhaps she should have said something to Gunnar last night about the blow Svana had taken when he asked about why she'd carried Svana. She would do after she had demonstrated how much use they both could be.

'Ragn?' There was no mistaking the panicked note in Svana's voice. 'Are you there? I dreamt you disappeared. Have you?'

'Time to get up, Sleepy Bones.' She made her voice bright to keep from worrying Svana. 'Much to do today.'

'You mean travel again. No, thanks.' Svana burrowed deeper in the furs. Ragn smoothed Svana's hair from her forehead. After one night's rest, her eyes seemed straighter and her skin less like parchment. Ragn struggled to remember when Svana had last looked this well.

Ragn put her hand on Svana's shoulder. 'We stay here if we work hard. Gunnar Olafson agreed to my proposition.'

'When? What proposition?'

'We remain here as housekeepers until Gunnar returns with his bride from the north. No uncertain future in Ile. You can heal here.'

Svana scrubbed her eyes with the back of her hand. 'Gunnar is going to marry you after all? I knew once he had a proper look at you, he'd see how truly lovely you are with your black hair like a raven's wing and the way your eyes shine, not to mention your excellent figure, sleek and elegant. Not at all lumpy like...like...'

'Stop spinning idle tales,' Ragn said before Svana mentioned Hamthur's final mistress, the one whose body had been found next to his. 'My hair burnt to very nearly my scalp. My one beauty, as Mor-Mor used to say, is gone. It is prickly and more than a bit itchy, not at all like it was.'

'You are beautiful to me. You always have been.' Svana caught Ragn's fingers. 'You saved my life. You carried me out of the hall and then for ages and ages with the dogs howling all around.'

'A life which will not be worth living if we don't prove how industrious we are.'

'But you remain beautiful. Your skin glows this morning. Something else happened.'

Ragn quickly shook her head. Last night's near-kiss with Gunnar was because of the time of night rather than because of any physical attraction he felt for her. Hamthur had been like that after she'd lost the baby, using her when he couldn't find one of his mistresses. She'd kept very still and thought about the housekeeping. It had been easier than resisting, because then Hamthur used his fists.

'He liked my stew, something you only picked at.'

Svana scrunched up her face. 'If not as his bride, what are you?'

'The potential caretaker of his estate.' Ragn held out Svana's over-gown for her to slip into. 'I will stay here and run his house until he has time to fetch a bride back from the north next spring. He wants to choose his own. But first he needs to know I can look after this estate and run it well.'

'No bride could be better than you. You'll see. He will return empty-handed, take you into his arms and proclaim his love.' Svana's eyes shone. 'I can see it happening. Then there will be a large wedding. I'll cry and blow my nose repeatedly because you look like the Sun Maiden in your gold crown and shimmering new dress.'

A vision of her standing next to Gunnar with their hands entwined, saying their vows like they meant them, rose in Ragn's mind. She frowned at the way her heart beat faster. Obviously, she had slept worse than she considered as she wanted to believe in impossibilities. She made a little shooing motion with her hands. 'You've romance on the brain. Worse than Trana.'

Rather than Svana smiling back at her, her face took

on a stubborn cast. 'I will have to do it tonight, then, saying my wish over the porridge. The *nisser* will see to it that Gunnar Olafson behaves as he was supposed to. I've faith…even if someone else has given up.'

Ragn silently cursed as she fastened the brooches which held Svana's apron up. Her campaign to get Svana to stop believing in the impossible thus far was a dismal failure. 'Gunnar and I are not getting married. Ever. We will be leaving once he has obtained the bride he wants. Do not mention the possibility again unless you want to leave on the next boat to Ile. He remains determined to choose his bride without any help from Eylir or you or even me.'

Svana's face crumpled. 'Did I do it wrong again?' She lifted her chin. 'I will be brave. Today. You will see. I won't flinch at all if the dogs come into the kitchen.'

'You already have been very brave.' Ragn drew the girl into the circle of her embrace and pressed her lips against her hair. It bothered her that Svana blamed herself. She wished she could have her confident little sister back, rather than the girl who seemed to blame herself for all the bad things which had happened. 'You've nothing to do with his decision about not making good on his friend's promise. But you need to help me keep my promise while he searches for the right bride.'

'Maybe he does want to marry you and just doesn't know it. Men can be funny that way. Trana told me! He brought the furs in for you.'

'He brought the furs in because he thought we might be cold and end up sickening.' Ragn was aware the heat on her cheeks increased and was glad of the murky light. And if Svana knew Gunnar had tried to kiss her to seal the bargain, there would be no stopping her vivid imagination.

'Once I ask the *nisser*, it will happen. Like that.' Svana snapped her fingers. 'I want to stay here. I feel safe here.'

'What did I tell you about pretend games? In any case, *nissers* are trickier than Loki, especially at Jul time,' Ragn said a bit more sharply than she intended, but the last thing she required was Svana starting clumsy matchmaking attempts.

'Where will we go when his actual bride arrives?' Svana used her very soft voice.

'Somewhere we can live without fear of Vargr following. Iceland is a long way across the sea. Vargr hates travelling over the water. The witch woman told him to be wary of sea voyages.'

Svana bit her lip. 'Not another sea voyage. I hate the way the boat rocks. I can never get dry. Please, Ragn, for my sake. Closer.'

Ragn shook her head. Svana was incorrigible once a notion took hold. Like herself as a child. Ragn firmed her mouth. Svana was not going to be like her, she was going to be better. 'We will worry about that when it happens. Right now, I can smell porridge. I'll race you to the kitchen.'

'Sometimes stories become real,' Svana whispered. 'I'll not stop believing, just because you tell me to. Not ever.'

'You're up,' Gunnar said, coming into the kitchen just after Ragn took the porridge off the fire.

His rough tunic moulded to his body, revealing the breadth of his shoulders. Her pulse leapt at the memory of how those arms had held her. Ragn inwardly sighed. She had half-hoped her reaction to him had been because of exhaustion. But at least he'd agreed to respect her principles. He would not try to steal a kiss again.

'Good timing.' She turned back to the fire and gave the porridge a vigorous stir. Some of the mixture slopped over and fell with a sizzle on to the fire. 'The porridge with cloudberries is ready.'

'Normally I don't bother with porridge as it is too much trouble to make and then eat when I have a thousand other jobs to be getting on with. But the addition of cloudberries makes all the difference.' His voice flowed over her like warm honey.

Out of the corner of her eye she saw Svana go rigid. Then the dogs came trotting in. One sniffed her skirt before going to sit by Gunnar with a hopeful expression. Svana ran over to Ragn and hid her face in Ragn's skirt.

'Svana, what is this? We cannot have this every meal. Gunnar's dogs mean you no harm,' Ragn said before disaster struck.

'Child, do you know where the woodpile is?' Gunnar asked, cutting across her words.

Svana peeped out from Ragn's skirt. 'I think so.'

'That fire needs some more sticks.'

'I can get them,' Ragn said, putting a restraining hand on Svana's shoulder. 'The dogs frighten Svana. You witnessed it last night. She has to walk past them to get to the door.'

'The dogs will stay here with me. Quick about it now, Svana.' He put his hand to the side of his mouth and said in a loud whisper, 'My mother claimed *nissers* were fond of woodpiles. It may be that he has slept in today.'

A broad smile crossed Svana's face and her eyes shone. 'A woodpile is a good sort of place to hide.'

She ran past the dogs without a second glance. Gunnar resumed eating his porridge, his expression smug.

Ragn put a hand on her hip. 'What are you playing at?'

'Watch and learn. See what happens when your sister returns.' He nodded towards the stone man. 'I take it she hasn't spied that. I plan to use it in the next stage.'

'You should have asked me if your scheme was appropriate. I am the person responsible for my sister.'

He pushed the empty bowl away. 'Last night you asked me to trust you, to leave my hall in your hands.'

'It will be. Svana is a good girl. Very helpful. She is a bit nervous about dogs, that is all. She will settle.'

'I will solve this problem this morning.' He took another bite of the porridge. 'Watch. Learn something new.'

'I know my sister.' Ragn whispered prayers to any god she thought of, but all she thought about was the looming disaster.

Svana rushed in as Gunnar was scraping the last of the porridge from his bowl. Barely giving the dogs a glance, she dropped a pile of sticks in front of the fire. 'No *nisser* in the woodpile. But he could sleep there.'

'Look up,' Gunnar said as a surge of triumph went through him. Svana was indeed like his sisters.

Svana's eyes grew round. 'Where did that come from?'

'My mother used to say that it only appeared when the *nisser* was happy. I think it is a good place for it.' Gunnar struggled to keep his voice steady. 'On the day

I left home, she took it down and gave it to me for protection.'

'Will it protect me and my sister?'

'The answer is, Svana, that even a *nisser* can't stop bad men. You need to put your faith in someone stronger like a warrior and his dogs.' He went down to the girl's level. 'Dogs are very useful, but you have to use a big voice as sometimes they don't listen as closely as they should. Try it now. Try calling their names—Kolka is the tan and black and Kefla is the brindle-coloured one.'

Svana gave another furtive glance at where the two wolfhounds slumbered. She shrank back against her sister. 'Ragn?'

'Try, Svana,' Ragnhild said in a sceptical voice. 'For my sake. Not all dogs are like…like the ones you encountered that day.'

'You've walked past them twice when you were intent on finding the *nisser*,' Gunnar said, trying to make her understand. 'You were so close that you nearly stepped on Kefla's tail when you came back.'

'Gunnar is right,' Ragnhild said. 'You did.'

Svana's eyes widened, but she stood straighter. 'I did, didn't I?'

'Dogs can be great protectors, but first they must know who they are protecting. Hold out your hand and call them to you. Let them know you mean to be their friend.'

Svana whispered their names. As she did it, Gunnar snapped his fingers and pointed to the girl.

The dogs obediently trotted forward and sat in front of the girl.

'Kolka and Kefla will be my friends?' Svana asked in a small voice.

Ragnhild crouched down and put her arms about her sister. 'They want to be, sweetling. I'm sure of it.'

'Trust Ragnhild, child.'

Ragnhild glanced up at him and nodded. Her smile made his breath catch. She finally understood what he was attempting to do. A start.

'Now that you have been properly introduced, they will be fine. Remember to use a great big voice with them,' Gunnar said. 'And they will have any leftovers from your bowl.'

Ragnhild's face softened to stunning and she mouthed thank you.

With a pleased smile, Svana held out her fingers for the dogs to sniff. After they did so, she tentatively touched Kolka's ears.

Svana glanced over her shoulder. 'My sister as well? Should Ragn use a big voice?'

'I believe my voice is loud enough,' Ragnhild said, wrinkling her nose in a delightful manner.

Gunnar bowed towards her. 'Your sister must do as she pleases. The dogs will only attack if they think one of theirs is being attacked or if I give the specific command to kill.'

'I can assure you that you will never have to use that particular command with us,' Ragnhild said.

Her eyes danced with hidden lights. He wondered that he had considered her ill favoured and sallow yesterday.

'Good to know.' Gunnar called the dogs to him. 'I haven't time to waste today, but the dogs are looking forward to a good stew tonight.'

He had barely made it to the hall when Ragnhild

caught his arm. A jolt went through him at her touch. 'Thank you. I appreciate it.'

'I did it for an easier life. I won't have my dogs banished.'

'Even still, it was a kind thing to do. You were right—I should have trusted you. You do have a soft heart.'

Gunnar gritted his teeth. His heart was a tight hard knot. The better part of him had died and lay buried with his mother and his sisters, the family he'd failed. 'Don't get used to it.'

The brewing house smelt of yeast, dried barley and a sort of sweet-sickly smell of ale on the turn. Ragn frowned as she started the job of cleaning out the barrels. A well-run household depended on its weak ale for everyday drinking. The remaining ale was barely drinkable, but she wouldn't risk Svana's health to unknown water. She'd seen too many people become ill through drinking water unwisely.

'Will you make the Jul ale?' Svana asked in a little voice.

'Once I get this batch done. There is barely enough malted barley for it—the grain has not been properly stored.'

'I love your ale.'

'You need to watch and learn. The making of ale is one of the most important tasks a woman can undertake.'

'It is very close in here.'

'It needs to be warm to get the wort to bubble properly.' Ragn peered into the barrel. 'This is part of the trouble—mould. Svana, can you hand me...? Svana!'

Ragn glanced over. All colour had drained from her

sister's face and her eyes had rolled back. Her limbs started to twitch. In less than a heartbeat, Svana collapsed to the ground in a full-blown fit. A scream welled up within her and she rushed to Svana's side.

Ragn whispered prayers to any god who might listening and forced the panic from her brain. After the first few times, she learned that she could only watch and hope. But she turned Svana's head to one side in case she vomited when she woke as she had done twice before.

'What is the problem? I heard a scream.' Gunnar stood in the doorway, his hand on his sword and his face as unyielding as ever.

Ragn moved to block Svana's unconscious form and forced a smile on her face. 'Everything is under control.'

'Kefla came to me, whining. Then you screamed.'

'Svana fainted. She must have locked her knees. She hasn't hit her head and nothing overturned.'

He peered around her to where Svana lay on the ground. Her lashes were dark against her pale face and her legs convulsed. 'She needs to be out of here.'

Without waiting, he pushed past her, scooped Svana up and carried her to the bedchamber. Ragn and the dogs followed in his wake.

As he put her down on the furs, Svana gave a faint moan and her lashes fluttered. 'Ragn?'

'I'm here, sweetling.' Ragn's heart eased. Her sister would recover this time. 'You rest.'

'I… I…'

'Don't worry. The brew house is very hot and you haven't eaten much.' Ragn attempted to keep her voice measured. She'd been overly optimistic this morning. It would take more than a good night's sleep to cure Svana.

'I wanted to make the Jul ale with you, but I'm so tired.' Svana's eyes fluttered close, but her breathing was regular.

'Your sister will sleep for a few hours,' Gunnar said. 'Leave her. The dogs will get us when she stirs. We need to speak.'

His tone allowed for no refusal. Ragn reluctantly left her sister and went into the kitchen. Despite the glowing embers in the hearth, she shivered.

'Does your sister faint often?'

'It was far too close in the ale house and Svana only had a little to eat this morning. I will keep her out of the brew house.'

The planes on his face became harsher. Her stomach became knots on knots. 'How long has she had this affliction?'

Ragn wet her lips. Her heart sank. He knew. He would be like her cousins who had turned them from their door, screaming that the spirit of Angrbord the giantess had taken possession of Svana. 'Fainting is not an affliction.'

'That girl had a fit.'

She crossed her arms. 'How do you know?'

'I know the signs.' Shadows flitted across his face. 'You should have told me.'

'When? When I arrived?' Ragn allowed the anger at the situation, at him for being narrow-minded like all the others and at the world for allowing this to happen to her innocent sister, to spill over. A queer sort of joy ran through her. Shouting at someone was wonderful. 'You might have put us back on that boat and they would have tossed her overboard. Or last night, when you were going to send us away to Ile. Or maybe when

I begged you to let us stay. Svana didn't have a fit on the boat. I watched her all the time. I had hopes she was done with them! What do you know about anything! She isn't Angrbord's mouthpiece!'

He put hard hands on her shoulders. His blue eyes bored into her soul. She was certain he saw all the ugly things she'd caused, knew all the reasons the gods had turned their backs on her. 'I deserved to know. And you are right. She is not Angrbord's mouthpiece.'

'I've lost everything except for her. Can't you see why I tried to keep it from you?'

They stared at each other for a long heartbeat. He let her go and the air rushed between them.

'Because I would have done things differently. I would have treated you with more kindness,' he said in a quieter tone.

'I was afraid,' she admitted, bowing her head.

He watched her from under his eyelids. 'Of your sister?'

'No! For her. I'd hoped the fits were finished. It is my fault. I know the brew house can make people feel weak.' Ragn put a hand over her mouth. 'We will go. It will be easier for everyone concerned. I should not have lost my temper like that at you.'

'How long has she had the fits for?'

Ragn concentrated on the rushes. 'Since the fire. She took a blow to the head, a blow that was meant for me. I turned my back on Vargr and I shouldn't have.'

'Were you the one to hit her? Or to order the attack?' Gunnar asked softly.

'No, I was the one who asked the witch woman to come last Jul which started it all.' The words tumbled out of her explaining how it had happened and how the old crone had gone into a trance the instant she spied Svana.

'But you didn't force the witch woman to make the prediction.'

'I keep thinking if the old crone hadn't spied her, the woman would have said what we agreed in advance. Instead she began moaning and said Svana would cause Vargr's death. Vargr started issuing orders and making demands. Hamthur threw him out of the hall and, as he left, Vargr vowed his revenge. He took it.'

Gunnar tapped his fingers together. 'I've seen warriors suffer from the same affliction after a head wound.'

She stared at him. He knew people who suffered like Svana? 'Do they recover?'

'Some do.' He made a steady shrug. 'It depends on the gods. They remain good warriors for the most part, when they recover.'

'Have you ever known anyone who fully recovered?' she persisted.

The light faded from his eyes. 'One or two. It is no good clinging on to false hope. It is up to the Norns who control all our fates.'

'Did you know what to do because of the other warriors?' she whispered, hating that real hope had sprung in her breast.

'My youngest sister was cursed by a witch when she was small and suffered the fits ever after. My mother refused to put her outside like my relations advised. She nursed her. Svana reminds me of her. I should have guessed there was more.'

'Did she die of a fit?'

'She died of something else.' He turned away from

her for a breath and when he turned back, the mask of a hardened warrior was firmly in place.

Ragn pressed her hands together. 'I'm sorry.'

'Your sister mentioned Jul ale. There is no need for such a thing.'

'Mine was reputed to be one of the best in the Kingdom.'

His frown increased. 'Normally I am away at Jul, renewing my oath, rather than entertaining. Who is going to drink all this ale you plan on brewing? Who will see the flaming wheel?'

'If you are a landholder, you should provide something for your followers.' Ragn's stomach tightened. She'd promised Svana a proper Jul, the one vow she'd considered she could keep. She tried again. 'Your bride will expect to entertain and be entertained. I would hardly like your hospitality to be questioned.'

His eyes blazed. 'No one should question my hospitality.'

'You failed to provide the captain of the boat with ale he could drink. I noticed how much was poured on the ground.'

'Unexpected visitors. My supplies are running low.'

'Some might take it as an insult. I have discovered the trouble—your barrels were not cleaned properly and the wort stank. There is enough malted barley for another small batch.'

'Are you criticising me?' Gunnar's shout resounded off the walls.

'I'm stating a fact.' She crossed her arms. 'When your bride does arrive, you will want her to have a warm welcome.'

'Were you always this stubborn?'

'Only when I believe in something.'

He gave a long sigh. 'Do you have to make it seem like another woman will be arriving on the next tide? Do they come in threes? Or waves?'

'Don't you want more brides?'

'You I can cope with.' A small twinkle appeared in his eye. 'You are a known irritant.'

'I sincerely doubt your friend will have sent another one. Unless you have other men out there searching for your elusive bride?'

He pushed his hands through his hair, making it stand upright. Her palms itched to smooth it down again. 'Eylir is the only one who would dare to do this.'

The muscles on her neck relaxed slightly. 'That is good to know. I doubt you have space for any more housekeepers.'

'I do intend on going north. It is a matter of timing.' His words were far too quick.

'When you have the time and then you can search for your bride in the certain knowledge that your lands are well cared for in your absence.'

'That remains to be seen.'

'Give me permission to do Jul properly and you will see. A little kindness and thoughtfulness pays large dividends.'

His mouth became a thin white line. 'Jul happens elsewhere.'

'Your new bride will expect it. Once it has been done, you will know what needs to be done for the next year.'

'You think I don't know? My mother brought me up well. I choose to ignore it.'

'What I think is unimportant,' she said, choosing her words with care. Svana deserved her Jul celebration.

'You can ignore everything as it happens. You can be in splendid isolation while I do it all.'

'Do you ever listen? We do things my way or not at all.' He rose from the table and clicked his fingers. The dogs trotted behind him. 'Look to your sister. Forget Jul.'

The door reverberated from his slam.

'But I promised,' Ragn whispered. 'And I will find a way to keep that promise.'

Chapter Five

The pile of split logs stood several feet higher than when he first began earlier. Sweat poured down Gunnar's back. There was a certain amount of satisfaction in working off his anger—at Ragnhild, at himself and most importantly the time of year.

He hated thinking about Jul, his mother's favourite time of year. It had been during Jul that his family perished. The house had been raided and his family were left with nothing and starved. Some had tried to blame it on the wild hunt, the spectral hunting party which caused violence and mayhem at Jul, but Gunnar had known who was ultimately to blame—himself. He could have prevented the tragedy, but he'd lingered too long in Kaupang, falling for Dyrfinna who had declared her love and then betrayed him, rather than thinking about his responsibilities.

Ever since then he had tried to forget Jul even existed. He showed up to whichever warlord he pledged his sword to for the swearing of oaths, joined in the wrestling and became blindingly drunk, but then departed.

He gave a loud curse as he split the final log.

Ragnhild was right—his men would expect festivities, complete with feasts and dancing. And the child, she'd expect one. She'd lost everything, but she still believed in the *nisser*.

It was better he endured a proper Jul with someone who would not mind if he was surly. Ragnhild had seen him at his most inhospitable and stood her ground rather than fleeing in terror.

'Gunnar!' Ragnhild ran out with a shawl wrapped about her shoulders. The wind whipped her skirts back against her legs, revealing the graceful curve of her calves. He'd been a fool to reject her when she'd stepped off the boat and now they had their bargain.

'Is there something else that I should be doing?' he said and immediately regretted his tone.

Her brows drew together in confusion until she spied the massive pile of split logs he'd accumulated in a short period of time. 'I wondered what the sound was.'

'Is the sound of chopping wood offensive to your delicate ears?'

She caught her upper lip between her teeth as she examined the pile of split logs and the neatly stacked one just behind him. Her eyes sparkled as if she knew his bad mood wasn't really directed at her. 'You're determined we will not run out of fuel this winter.'

Gunnar followed her gaze. Given the number he'd split, they would be lucky to run out by next summer. 'I seized the opportunity. You said you would have to malt more barley and that takes fuel. My men will need to renew their oaths.'

'Precisely. This hall needs a proper Jul to give it life.'

'Just the oath-taking. And my hall has life.'

'It is a cold and barren place where no one wants to

linger.' She clasped her hands together. 'Jul is about remembering that we need others to survive. Tradition binds people. You want to bind your men to you and keep them faithful. One never knows when one might have need of a faithful ally. Real things, not stories, are what gives Jul its true meaning.'

He picked up the axe. 'I prefer not to discuss Jul.'

'What will I tell Svana? She was in tears at the thought she spoilt the Jul ale.' Ragnhild made a gesture with her hand and her gown fell back, revealing the vivid red scarring on her wrist. 'Never mind. Time she grew up.'

Asa had been like that as well. He'd teased her and pulled her long braid, saying that Jul wouldn't come. It hadn't come for her ever again because of him. He examined the pile of logs. 'Make the Jul ale. My dogs dislike tears.'

She clapped her hands and her face became wreathed in smiles. 'Thank you. Svana will be pleased.'

'I don't want to be inconvenienced. No using Jul ale as an excuse for failing to do things like making porridge in the morning.'

She watched him from under her lashes. 'And the arrangements for the rest of Jul? For my sister? It would show her that life will continue even though we live somewhere else.'

He closed his eyes. Asa's words echoed round and round his brain.

If you don't return on time I will know it is because you are making your way in the world, my dearest brother. When you celebrate Jul, think of me. Always.

He hadn't. He'd tried to forget. Neither Asa nor Brita deserved to be forgotten. 'I want a good Jul ale, one which warms straight to the toes.'

Her eyes sparkled with silver lights, the sort that made him want to believe that things such as curses were made for lifting. And he knew he wanted to keep on seeing that sparkle. 'The rest when the time comes? For Svana? To erase the horrible?'

Erase the horrible.

His selfishness stuck in his throat. For the child who had lost much and deserved a proper Jul, he'd brave the festivities. 'Do what you have to. Make the ale. Get the servants. Make the blasted flaming wheel. Light the Jul log. Just don't bother me with the detail. Or expect me to sing any of the songs.'

The silvery lights deepened in her eyes. 'I will bear that in mind.'

Ragn balanced the overladen basket on her hip as she walked through the yard. Thanks to Svana and her quizzing of Gunnar's men, she had some idea of what the people on the estate needed. There was food for Lars's wife who was suffering from a fever, a new spindle for Coll's woman who had lost hers and some of her grandmother's special herbal remedy for burns amongst the items.

'Where are you going with all of that?' Gunnar asked.

'To visit with the people on the estate. It is part of the lady's job to ensure everyone is well and it gives me an excuse to find women to help in the hall.'

'You want to do this?'

'My grandmother impressed on me that it had to be done by the lady of the estate. She knew of families who starved to death because the lady of the estate failed in her duty. A lady must keep the community together. A good woman trusts her own eyes, rather than employing a steward.'

Gunnar drew his brows together. 'Your grandmother used to do this?'

'Every week when she came to live with us. My father used to say it was the only time the house was quiet when she was away on her visits.'

'If she was anything like you, I can understand how he must have valued the silence.' His eyes crinkled at the corners.

'Do you think I talk too much?'

'You talk more than I do.'

'That is not difficult.'

He gave a half-smile. 'I have grown used to it.'

Ragn shifted the basket to her other hip. 'Then it is all right...what I am doing?'

He nodded. 'If people do not think you care, why should they care about you? Why should they trust you when it matters? I wish I had considered it before.'

Her heart thudded. Hamthur had always told she was an idiot for giving things away to those in need rather than keeping them for the hungry times, but she had still done it. It had saved her life when she was running from Vargr. An elderly couple whom she had given grain to had hidden her and Svana in their barn, giving her time to recover. 'You understand.'

'It is a good idea. I wish I had thought of it.' His eyes grew troubled. 'Years ago.'

'You can only change the future.'

'Ragn, Ragn! You need to come quick! Ever so quick!' Svana banged the door to the ale house open and tugged at Ragn's sleeve just as Ragn tipped the

malted barley into the spring water to begin the pro-
cess of fermentation for the Jul ale. Ragn jumped and
narrowly managed to miss spilling the grain on the
brew-house floor.

'Svana, what did I say about coming in here? We
agreed you wouldn't!'

Svana dipped her head. 'I forgot.'

Ragn put the bucket down and went over to the
downcast child. She gave her a hug. 'I don't want you
to take poorly again, sweetling. The fumes are always
strong when the fermentation starts. What have those
dogs done now?'

'There is a ship coming into the bay. I saw its sails
from the bluff. It is a longboat and…and everything.'

Ragn's heart thudded. Vargr couldn't have discovered them this quickly. Trana would never have betrayed them.

'You went up to the bluffs? On your own?' she asked,
seeking to divert Svana.

'The dogs were with me. Gunnar said I might as
long as I stayed away from the edge.' Her sister gave
a careless shrug. 'I've been searching for the *nisser*'s
hiding hole as it isn't in the woodpile. Only a mouse
lives there.'

Ragn put a hand over her mouth and hid her astonishment. Svana had barely ventured from her side for
weeks but within a few days, she was running about
on her own.

'Who am I to go against Gunnar? Particularly as he
has agreed to sing us one of his Jul songs.'

'That was all your doing, Ragn. He wanted to make
you smile.'

Ragn's cheeks burned and she hoped Svana put it

down to the temperature in the brew house. 'My singing made his ears ache.'

'Is that what you want to believe?'

'His hands were over his ears.' Ragn smiled at the memory of Gunnar's pained expression.

Svana laughed. 'Do you think he will really go north when the light returns? He could stay and…he likes your porridge.'

Ragn winced. Despite everything she'd told her, Svana clung to the forlorn hope that Gunnar was falling in love with Ragn. They had become friends after a fashion. She was not about to jeopardise that.

'And this ship? What does he say about that?'

'Nothing. I came to find you first.'

'We should tell him. Were its shields up or down?'

'The shields are down,' Gunnar said, coming in the brew house. 'Your little helper scurries on quicker feet than I do.'

Svana beamed up at him. 'I try to be Ragn's eyes and ears when she is busy with the ale since neither of you will allow me to properly help.'

'What you are doing is a big help,' Ragn said. 'Now out of here. We have had enough funny turns for one year.'

Gunnar's glance flickered over her and she was aware that her hair was slick with sweat and her dress had damp splotches. She probably had a stain on her right cheek if Svana's pointed look and quick brushing of her own was anything to go by. She inwardly rolled her eyes. She'd give Svana another talking to at bedtime—seeing romance where there was none would lead to disappointment.

'Are you going to get ready for the visitors, Ragn? Gunnar has.'

Little droplets were caught in Gunnar's hair and beard and shone like diamonds. He wore a thick pelt about his shoulders and an intricately engraved gold ring in the middle of his beard. Two arm rings and an ornate-handled sword completed the ensemble.

A warm curl circled about her innards and took her breath away. She forced herself to keep breathing normally. Being attracted to him was not the same as acting on that attraction. She made her gaze focus on a spot above his right shoulder.

'Excellent news.' She managed to sound brisk and no nonsense. 'You never know when raiders might appear.'

'Late in the season for raiders. Njord is unforgiving of travellers on his roads in this season. He dislikes it when the Sun Maiden is in the wolf's belly.'

She wiped her hands on her apron and hoped he wouldn't notice the sweat which flowed down her back. Late in the season for visitors as well. Until the Sun Maiden had emerged from the wolf's belly, few would follow the sea roads. And those that did would stay close to the shore so as to avoid becoming food for the Midgaard serpent. 'How long have you known about the ship?'

'Long enough.' His brows drew together. 'Are you saying that you truly remained in ignorance of it until now? You who proudly proclaim the need for hospitality at this time of year? The standards these days. No true Jul spirit.'

Svana laughed and clapped her hands as she spied the twinkling in Gunnar's eyes.

'The Jul ale required my attention and the other women are busy spinning wool. There remains a pressing need for woollen cloth. I know about the ship now.

My little helper should check and see if the women need any more wool.' She gave a pointed cough and Svana reluctantly left the room. 'Everything is in hand in case of unexpected guests. Although, nothing can be done about the ale. The last lot of barley was badly malted by someone other than me and I had to throw most of it out.'

'I look forward to drinking your fabled ale if it is ever ready.' He gave a soft cough. 'Until then, I make do with my inferior one.'

'Whose ship is it? I presume you know it is friendly as you have not ordered Svana and me to hide.'

He assessed her from under his lashes. Ragn resisted the temptation to scrub her cheek again. 'One of Lord Ketil's, but stationed at Colbhasa so it will be from Kolbeinn, my old commander and now my overlord.'

'Did you part on friendly terms?' The words spilled from her throat before she thought. She silently kicked herself. How to proclaim her fears about friends who become enemies.

The corner of his mouth twitched and he flexed his arms so that the muscles bulged. 'I gave my oath to Ketil and Kolbeinn last Jul and took part in the wrestling. And those who had bet on me had cause to cheer as their purses became heavier. Those who had bet wrongly cheered because I proclaimed I was giving up, having reached the pinnacle of my career. Eylir's winnings were so heavy, he swore he'd send me a Jul present I'd never forget. And then you arrived.'

'You are attempting to change the subject.'

He put a hand on her shoulder. Warmth radiated out through her. 'What do you fear?'

'Every *felag* has factions.' Ragn crossed her arms

about her waist. Gunnar was treating this far too lightly. 'Did Kolbeinn send someone you can trust? Or is it someone who had cause to hate you?'

The semi-indulgent smile vanished. He stroked his beard with a watchful expression. 'The sail belongs to a warrior whom I barely know—Maurr the Forkbeard. He was the favourite to win at last Jul's wrestling.'

'Have you counted the shields? Should it come to a fight, do you have enough men?'

'More shields than I'd like, but that means little. He could be making one last tour of the sea roads before Jul. Kolbeinn normally sends a messenger inviting all his men to attend the swearing ceremony.'

'Kolbeinn has sent someone who would not be swayed by you or any past dealings you may have had. Only you will know if this is a good or bad thing.' She dried her hands on her apron as her brain raced. 'We must proceed with caution and ensure he is fully welcomed. He could blacken your name to your commander.'

The arrogance vanished from his face. He tilted his head and examined her from under his lashes. 'Kolbeinn always chooses his messengers with care. He wants to ensure that ultimately he wins whatever happens.' He blew out a breath. 'You are making me see shadows where there are none, a bad habit of yours, Ragnhild.'

'Has he sent allies in the past?' Ragn filled her lungs with air and held it.

'Before he sent close friends to inspect the hall as he wanted to ensure it was not the same size as his.' He tugged at his beard. 'You are right. There will be a hidden purpose to the visit.'

Ragn allowed the air to leave her body. Gunnar understood the need for caution—something Hamthur never had. And she trusted he was speaking the truth. There was nothing about his demeanour which screamed worry or concern. 'An opportunity for you to prove your loyalty.'

'How?'

Ragn pressed her hands against her apron dress. Gunnar was listening to her, instead of rejecting her ideas out of hand like Hamthur had often done. 'Greet him as if he was Kolbeinn himself. He comes from Kolbeinn and therefore deserves respect.'

'What do you intend to do?' he asked. 'I distrust that gleam in your eye. I want these warriors gone as quickly as possible.'

Ragn gave a half-smile. That sounded more like the old Gunnar who preferred his solitude rather than the new and dangerous-to-her-heart Gunnar, the one who gently teased her and found reasons to make her smile.

'Provide hospitality and demonstrate that all is running smoothly at this farm.' Ragn raised her chin. 'Lack of hospitality is a convenient excuse to behave badly in my experience.'

Gunnar's blue gaze seemed to pierce all the way to the hidden recesses of her soul. 'And you believe a few horns of ale will be enough to avoid bloodshed?'

'My grandmother used to say how a man presents himself at the waterfront makes a difference if he lives or dies, if his hall prospers or not.'

A lesson her husband had never quite mastered.

'Your grandmother had a lot of sayings.'

'One for every occasion. Once I wondered out loud if she made them up and my father boxed my ears for being forward. My ears rang for a week.'

'I see. You were always determined to have your way rather than listening to the voice of reason.'

'I've seen the consequences…when a warrior decided the offered hospitality was a deliberate snub. How do you think this one will react if you growl at him like a grumpy bear?'

'When you look that fierce, Ragnhild, I know to give way.' He put a hand on her shoulder and whispered, 'Put on your best dress. Make these lands proud. Show me that hospitality works. And if it fails, I will growl at them.'

His low voice in her ear made warmth curl about her insides again. She dampened it down and stepped away from him, trying to concentrate, rather speculating on what his touches might mean. Kolbeinn had sent this ship, but for what purpose? 'Where have you hidden the mead? It will be needed.'

'Hidden mead?' He clasped a hand to his chest. 'Why would I do such a thing?'

'To prevent me from using it in such a situation. How many hogsheads, Gunnar? How many have you saved for Kolbeinn? My father always said Kolbeinn preferred mead to any other drink.'

His eyes crinkled at the corners and her heart flipped over. 'Would you take a man's mead?'

'How many?'

'Four hogsheads, in case Kolbeinn ever arrives.'

'Excellent. When this man returns to Colbhasa, Kolbeinn will learn you treat his messengers as if they were himself.'

He came to stand behind her and her body prickled with awareness of him. His breath tickled the back of her neck. 'These warriors will not care as long as it wets their throats and fills their belly. I was one like them not so long ago.'

'Mead it must be.'

'I give in.' He held up his hands. 'I will fetch them from their hiding place. But only two hogsheads.'

'It will do for a start. This Maurr may require a feast. It is lucky you had those sheep slaughtered two days ago.'

'He won't be staying. I intend to be short with him.'

'The length of his visit depends on the reason for his journey, but there are things we can do to ensure he has a favourable impression of this hall.' She quickly rattled off a list of things that would need to be done in the time they had remaining. As the respect in Gunnar's face grew, she smiled inwardly. She looked forward to demonstrating that she could run a hall properly. She had made Hamthur's hall the envy of the surrounding area.

'Impressive. I had no idea so much went into the preparation.'

'I want to be on the shore with you, standing shoulder to shoulder,' she declared. 'In case he has come to enforce the King's decree.'

'And you think by being on the shore, you will accomplish what?' Gunnar crossed his arms, the implacable warrior. 'Your brother-in-law might learn of your whereabouts.'

She drew a deep breath. 'Vargr is in Kaupang. No one will go there until long after Jul. No one will remember me or Svana by then. All anyone used to say about me was how long and lovely my hair was, like a raven's wing. It is short and spiky now.'

'Prickly like you.'

'I take that as a compliment as it means I get things done. He may come about the King's new decree.'

'If he has come about this fabled marriage decree, I will tell the truth, Ragnhild. I'll make it known that I intend to seek my bride when the time is right in the north.'

Ragn hit her hand against her forehead. 'Not even to save your lands? The ones you sweated blood for?'

He frowned. 'It won't come to it. He will give me time. Lying never solves anything.'

Ragn swallowed hard. She refused to lose two homes in a few months. 'Allow them to reach their own conclusions, rather than ramming your version of the truth down their throats. Sometimes one creates a certain impression and people take what they will from it.'

His eyes became ice cold. 'Allow me to do the talking. Remember these lands belong to me, not you. Awkward woman.'

'Awkward is another good description. I take it as a compliment.' Ragn gave a half-curtsy. 'I look forward to hearing your apology later.'

A muscle jumped in his jaw. 'If you disobey me and tell him we are married to save this farm, I will personally put you on that boat and send you off to who knows where.'

She stepped backwards. 'You wouldn't dare. We have an agreement.'

His face became carved from stone. 'Do you truly wish to try me on this? I allowed you to have your way with the people on the estate. Now allow me to do my job.'

'But...'

'But nothing. Trust, Ragnhild, goes both ways.'

Chapter Six

Gunnar silently counted the warriors disembarking from the longboat. Far more than necessary. Only a few short years ago, he would have been one of that number—cold, wet and buffeted by the wind, pleased to be on the shore, but ready to take any opportunity. Now he stood in front of a substantial hall with a beautiful woman by his side. Looking at Ragnhild, it was hard to see the half-drowned woman who had stumbled off the boat a little more than two weeks ago. She might not be conventionally pretty, but she was handsome in her deep blue gown with its heavy brocade trim which proclaimed she was a lady of some standing and then there was her mind. She understood things instinctively rather than prattling on about nonentities as many of the women he'd been with did. Ragnhild was many things, but she was never dull.

He shook his head. To those men on the shore, he was a person to be admired, envied. Only he knew what a hollow sham it was.

'Is it who you said it would be?' Ragnhild asked in an undertone. 'Is he a friend?'

'Maurr the Forkbeard is neither a friend nor foe. I told you I'd defeated him in the wrestling competition last year. Many predicted he'd win it. He could harbour a grudge for that. It was a fair match.'

Ragnhild's smile bordered on the smug. 'The mead will be well received.'

'You are enjoying being right. Allow me to do the talking.'

She made a slight curtsy that bordered on the insolent. 'Your hall. We are here on sufferance.'

'Finally, she agrees with me.'

The warriors approached and he mouthed the ritual greeting. Rather than replying, Maurr glanced at Ragnhild as if he wanted to make sure she was there, as if he wasn't expecting Gunnar to have a wife. He silently cursed Ragn for mentioning the marriage decree, a decree he'd been doing his best to forget, even if it existed beyond Eylir's fertile imagination.

'Are you going to introduce me?' Maurr asked with a false purr in his voice.

Gunnar remembered all the reasons why he disliked the man when he looked at Ragnhild's cleavage as she made a curtsy. With her head uplifted and the sharp autumn breeze whipping the hair from her face, she was a north woman personified.

'Do you come in peace, Maurr?'

Maurr stuck his sword in the ground and proclaimed he had come in peace. Gunnar silently counted the number of blooded warriors again. His instinct screamed to sound his horn and call his men to him and fight, get the first blows in, but it would put Ragnhild and her sister in danger. A watchful waiting game was called for until he ensured their safety.

Maurr's eyes gleamed as he continued his slow perusal of Ragnhild's curves. No one had the right to do that. It was only through years of hard-won discipline that Gunnar managed to force the challenge back down his throat.

He cleared his throat and Maurr's pale blue gaze flickered to him. 'We welcome you to Jura, Maurr the Forkbeard. You must take some refreshment. We hope your stay with us is a pleasant one. Svana, bring your horn forward.'

Ragnhild raised her brow, but she kept silent. He frowned and gestured towards the horns of mead. The sooner Ragnhild completed her task, the sooner she left. Once she had departed, he could think straight.

Her sister came forward with a horn full to the brim. Her white-blonde hair gleamed in the pale sun. Gunnar smiled inwardly. Svana was the picture of solemn seriousness as she carefully made her way over to the captain of the boat. She raised her horn with both her hands, reminding Gunnar how his sister Asa used to practise performing the same task in case she ever graced a large enough hall.

Maurr the Forkbeard took one look at the child, shuddered and pulled back just as she went to hand him the horn. The horn spilled mead all over the warrior and Maurr gave a loud roar. 'Stupid girl! Do you deliberately dishonour me by sending such a creature?'

Svana's face crumpled and a single tear trickled down her face.

'It might be easier if you remember to grasp the horn before you attempt to drink from it,' Gunnar murmured.

'Is this how you greet your guests, Gunnar Olafson?' Maurr asked with a fierce frown. His men crowded around him, as if waiting for his order to strike. 'Dowsing them with inferior ale? Do you mean to insult me?'

Gunnar placed his hand on his sword. His muscles tensed, readying for the fight. 'Ragnhild,' he muttered, moved his head towards the hall.

'Do us the honour of tasting the drink, before proclaiming it inferior,' Ragnhild said in ringing tones before he could order her back. 'You insult Lord Kolbeinn who gave the mead to Gunnar. Was that your intention? Do you intend to move against your overlord? Your lord whom you have sworn an oath to serve? Tell me, what does Kolbeinn do to people who are disloyal?'

Maurr's eyes widened. His men lowered their shields and glanced at each other. They took several steps away from Maurr, demonstrating that they understood precisely what Kolbeinn did to those he considered disloyal. Gunnar struggled to keep his face impassive, but he knew Ragnhild had just tipped the odds in his favour.

'Mead?' Maurr squeaked. 'You honoured me with your best mead?'

'I have treated you like I would treat Lord Kolbeinn,' Gunnar retorted, relaxing his hand. He studiously ignored the superior expression in Ragnhild's eyes. 'Dishonour the messenger, dishonour the *jaarl*, as Ragnhild's grandmother would have it. Ragnhild, will you offer Maurr another chance to taste it before he insults us further and requires me to take measures?'

She made a small curtsy. 'With all speed.'

Gunnar reached out a hand and drew Svana back. She was quivering like a leaf, but she gave him a brave smile. He motioned to the dogs and they immediately sat on either side of her. Her pinched face relaxed. He nodded towards Ragnhild, who appeared to understand the unspoken message that Svana was fine and unharmed.

'Who is the girl? Yours? She is all thumbs and has a cast eye. A witch undoubtedly cursed her. She brings bad luck.'

Gunnar counted very slowly. Slaughtering one of Kolbeinn's messengers would cause more trouble than it was worth. But he would ensure Kolbeinn learned of the insults when he next encountered him. He gave an ostentatious cough. 'Svana is a valued member of my household, Maurr the Forkbeard. You are a guest. I trust you to remember the difference in future unless you care to challenge me for these lands.'

Maurr glanced over his shoulder, noted where his men were and made a low bow. 'I've overstepped. I apologise. Blame it on the rough journey.'

'I accept your apology. Accept the hospitality. Drink.'

Ragnhild hurried forward and wiped the damp from the man's jersey. 'I regret my sister's horn spilled. Svana was over-eager—her first time at greeting such an important personage. Nothing harmed. Shall we move off this cold beach? Perhaps up to the hall and the warmth of the hearth?'

Maurr raised a brow and his gaze ranged over her, lingering a bit too long on the sweep of Ragnhild's neck for Gunnar's liking. 'What relation are you to Gunnar Olafson?'

Ragn dropped a quick curtsy. 'Ragnhild Thorendottar, lately arrived from the north.'

Maurr gave a speculative snort like someone who was judging horseflesh. The urge to tear him apart limb from limb shook Gunnar.

'Your sister, Gunnar?'

'We are unrelated through blood,' Ragnhild replied with a tight smile and glower at Gunnar as if to say that it was his responsibility to explain the precise relationship.

Gunnar made a non-committal grunt and refused to elaborate. Maurr didn't deserve the full truth, after the way he'd stared at Ragnhild's figure. Until he found a wife, Ragn was his responsibility and he refused to have her treated like a piece of meat, available to any warrior who happened past.

He put a hand on her shoulder. Her flesh trembled under his fingertips. He rapidly moved away. 'As Ragnhild said, she has lately arrived from the north. Do I have to give you complete details of her antecedents?'

Maurr gave Gunnar a speculative glance. 'The vision of loveliness has a protector. Pity. I've no wish to create enemies when I come to make friends.'

Maurr's laugh grated. Gunnar frowned as he fought to control the desire to smash the other warrior's head in. Gunnar knew strictly speaking he should correct Maurr's assumption, but instead, he gave Ragnhild a warning look.

'Why would you want to make enemies?' Innocent wonder dripped from Ragnhild's lips. 'We are all friends here.'

Maurr twirled the forks of his beard about his fingers. He'd dismissed her as brainless. Big mistake. Gunnar rubbed his hands in anticipation of seeing Maurr's face when he realised that he'd been outwitted.

'I have come in friendship to all, particularly Gunnar Olafson and his lovely bride.'

His men beat their swords against their shields and shouted their agreement.

Ragnhild shrugged and smiled at Gunnar as if to

say—make the choice, your lands or a small falsehood. 'You give us too much honour.'

'Not all, my lady.' Maurr raised her hand to his fleshy lips, held them there for a breath too long. The man truly did not deserve the truth. 'Not nearly enough.'

She withdrew her hand and signalled for more mead. The servants rushed forward and served Maurr's men while Gunnar choked down the urge to throttle Maurr over his liberties with Ragnhild.

'This estate depends on Ragnhild,' he said rather than enlightening Maurr. 'She has accomplished much in the short time she has been here.'

He noticed with pleasure that her cheeks coloured from the faint praise. He had said no more than the truth. He would give her more praise in the future, he decided, as it made her radiant.

'Why is it that Lord Ketil and Lord Kolbeinn know nothing of your recent acquisition?' Maurr tapped a finger against his beard. 'That Gunnar Olafson has a bride from the north is something you have kept a secret.'

Gunnar tightened his hold on his sword and wondered what Maurr's head would look like severed from his shoulders. He had always considered the man insupportable, but right now he bordered on obnoxious. He made it seem as if Ragnhild was an object rather than a person.

Ragnhild made a curtsy, but kept her eyes low. 'Even the wisest of leaders knows it is impossible to know everything when his holdings are as vast as Lord Ketil's. I've not been here overly long. We considered the oath-taking at Jul would be ample time for an announcement.'

'Is there some reason why you need to know about my intimate sleeping arrangements, Maurr?' Gunnar asked, impressed at the way Ragnhild had avoided any direct lie. She had simply allowed Maurr to assume the announcement would be about introducing her as his bride rather than his intention to seek a bride in the spring.

'Lord Ketil had become concerned that you were unmarried and in charge of such a large estate. The King has decreed...'

'That priority for land be given to married men,' Gunnar finished his sentence for him. His heart sank. 'I have heard about this decree. There was once a time that Harald refused to marry and grew his hair long. Now that he has cut his hair and married the woman of his dreams, he thinks all men should obtain that sort of bliss.'

'He is becoming more dictatorial by the month,' Maurr said. 'It concerns Kolbeinn. Many of us came to the Western Isles to get away from strict laws. And the last thing Kolbeinn wants is any warrior rebelling and swearing allegiance to the Northmen from the Black Pool.'

The Northmen who had settled in Ireland around the Black Pool or Dubh Linn had become Kolbeinn's sworn enemies after they tried to murder Kolbeinn's daughter, Gunnar's former commander, a few years before during the Battle of Dollar.

'I served with Harald in Constantinople. I was at his side when we rocked the boats to get over the Emperor's chain and made good our escape. Afterwards, he clasped me to his chest and called me brother.' Gunnar fixed Ragnhild with his eye so she, too, would finally understand why the King's decree about marriage did not overly concern him. 'He will lose no sleep on my account.'

He inwardly smiled as Maurr's jaw dropped. Maurr obviously was unaware of his friendship with King Harald. He was not some barely blooded warrior who had never mingled with royalty.

'Putting your faith in kings can be risky,' Ragnhild said quietly.

'It is why I have you,' Gunnar retorted.

Maurr dropped the rune stick he carried. 'You can see that the pair of you are well matched. Seldom have I seen newlyweds in such tune with each other.'

Ragnhild made a quick curtsy and retrieved the stick. She quickly looked at it before passing it to Gunnar. 'The King's decree on marriage. Funny how a little thing like that can concentrate minds.'

He mouthed *thank you*. She had understood without his asking that he wanted to know what the rune stick contained.

Ragnhild clapped her hands. 'Drink to peace and prosperity of all ventures. And be glad that Gunnar holds all the King's decrees in such high esteem.'

'Lord Kolbeinn will expect you and your lady to join him for the Jul celebrations. He is currently in Ireland in discussions about what to do with the Northmen from the Black Pool's request for safe passage from their new lands in Alba, but I am sure he will be most interested to meet your bride, Gunnar.'

Gunnar sent his mead spluttering across the sands.

'Tell Lord Kolbeinn we would be delighted,' Ragnhild said before he had a chance to formulate an excuse.

'Was there any particular reason in sending you and not Hring the Stout-Hearted, or twenty other captains in his fleet?' Gunnar asked before Ragnhild did any more damage.

Maurr made a bow. 'Kolbeinn had been concerned that you might actively seek to avoid the decree. He sent someone who would not allow friendship to get in the way of his duty.'

The breath hissed through Gunnar's teeth. 'Lord Ketil need not have worried. Ragnhild arrived.'

Maurr cleared his throat. 'A word to the wise, leave the child here when you journey. Her eyes…'

'Svana goes wherever I journey.' Ragnhild lifted her chin in the air as if daring him to say differently.

Gunnar clenched his fists. His mother would not have spared her words—rather than bemoaning his fate for the past few weeks, he should be the one giving thanks to the gods that his friend had sent him this woman. Instead of being stubborn, he should give in to his fate.

'Ragnhild and her sister will journey with me to the Isle of Man for the end of the Jul celebrations as well as to Colbhasa.' Gunnar glared at Maurr.

The other warrior hastily put up his hands. 'I will inform Lord Kolbeinn to expect all three of you. It has been a hard crossing.'

'You and your company must pass the night here before you travel further,' Ragnhild said, dropping into a curtsy. 'I must insist. Come and taste the hospitality this hall has to offer.'

Gunnar gave Ragnhild a sharp look. If she had remained silent, Maurr would have departed, grumbling about the weather, but he would have been gone and would be nothing but a bad memory.

Maurr's eyes directed their gaze at Ragnhild's

bosom, rather than at her face. 'If you are sure I am not inconveniencing you, we need a hot meal and… witty companionship.'

'Gunnar would not have it any other way.' Ragnhild gave him a significant look. The words of refusing died in his throat. 'Does your wife travel with you or remain at court?'

Maurr's ears went unexpectedly red. 'Ljot remains in Colbhasa, ma'am. She is expecting our first child in the next few weeks. Given the size of her, Kolbeinn's wife Sif believes it to be twins.'

'I look forward to meeting her at Jul.'

'Ljot would rather me travel when the tide was right and will bless you for your offer. She worries unnecessarily.' Maurr's eyes gleamed at Gunnar. 'It will give me a chance to get to know your bride better. Ljot is sure to quiz me incessantly about her. You know how women are—wanting know about babies, weddings and the latest gossip instead of war tactics.'

His loud guffaws echoed over the bay.

Gunnar clung on to his temper. Ragnhild needed to be warned. The man had the morals of a snake. Maurr was the sort of man he would not trust in a narrow corridor where he lacked space to draw his sword. 'The tide turns before dawn.'

'Maurr will be on it.' Ragnhild put a warm hand on Gunnar's arm. 'Until then he enjoys the hospitality of this hall. If you will forgive us, gentlemen, my sister and I must go to ensure we feast well tonight. The meat is roasting on the spit.'

She marched off with her backside swaying. Maurr, despite his pregnant wife, noticed the enticing curve as well.

Gunnar gritted his teeth. Marriage or murder, he was not sure which option he preferred.

'You're a very lucky man to have a bride like that.'

'I could not have said it better.'

'Ragn? Did I ruin everything by spilling my horn? I had one thing to do and I did it wrong.' Svana's timid voice resounded in the kitchen where Ragn had retreated. Ideally, she would have liked to have seen the back of Maurr, but she knew Gunnar stood to gain much if he provided decent hospitality to these men. They were sure to gossip when they returned to Colbhasa. Men always did.

Ragn banged a cooking pot down and began to fill it with barley. 'Svana, I have a feast to prepare. You remember what Mor-Mor used to say—hungry men cause difficulty, but those with a full belly are most apt to sing praises. We want these men to sing our praises. Go to the hall and see what needs to be done. If any of the men start wrestling and get too near the fire, call me.'

Svana twisted her hands. 'Are you sure you want me in the hall? That man Maurr is frightened of me. He dropped that horn of mead just as I was handing it to him. He said I bring bad luck.'

'I do have eyes and ears, sweetling.' Ragn ruffled Svana's hair. 'That man has little say about what happens here. You heard Gunnar. You are welcome here, but more importantly you belong here. You bring me lots of luck. You saved my life when you took that blow to your head.'

Svana rubbed the back of her head where Vargr's cudgel had hit her. 'I remember nothing about that and it no longer aches. You need to stop going on about it like it matters.'

A lump came into Ragn's throat. Svana might say it was nothing, but Ragn knew she'd never forget it. 'That is something. You are healing.'

'I only remember the nasty dogs and the way they snarled. If we had had some dogs like Kolka and Kefla, Vargr would not have dared to come near us.'

'You may be right about that.' Ragn crouched down. She had to hope the ruse had worked and Vargr believed they were dead. He had the lands he'd coveted and he was welcome to them. In the short time she'd been here, she'd lost any appetite for returning to the north and reclaiming her lands. 'We live here and we both have jobs to do. Forget the past.'

'Do you think we will be able to stay for ever? Maurr called you Gunnar's bride.' Svana gave a long drawn-out sigh. 'It is such a lovely word—bride.'

Ragn glanced over her shoulder. The servants were busy preparing the food. 'Maurr the Forkbeard said a great many things, including untrue things about you. Why should I pay attention to what he says?'

Her stomach knotted. She should have corrected Maurr, but her instinct screamed that he'd intended to use Gunnar's non-compliance with the King's decree as a pretext to seize these lands. The one thing in her favour was that Gunnar had failed to correct Maurr. He'd allowed the mistake to continue.

Svana's eyes shone. 'I like Gunnar. He's kind. Do you think…?'

'You are a bit young for him.'

Svana stamped her foot. 'That is not what I meant! And you know it. He said we were his family and we would be accompanying him to Colbhasa. It must be true if he said it.'

'I've learned that holding my breath waiting for things to happen fails to look attractive—I turn blue and fall down. Therefore, I stopped doing it and you should, too.' She gave a decisive nod. 'He will find a reason why he must go on his own to swear his oath and leave us here where we want to be.'

Svana hung her head. 'Because of me, you mean.'

'Sweetling, you heard Gunnar defend you. It will be because he has no wish to live a lie.' The words tasted like ash in her mouth. And it would be a lie. He had no intention of marrying her ever. To parade her in front of his commander as his bride would be wrong.

'He is softening towards you.' Svana held her hand up to her mouth. 'I saw the way he glowered at Maurr when his gaze lingered on your figure. I thought he might challenge him then and there.'

Ragn pretended to be busy with the sweetened barley she had put to soak earlier. Neither warrior had paid any attention to her body, but it was gratifying of Svana to be so loyal.

'I don't care if we go as long as you and I are together.' Ragn swung the cooking pot on to a tripod and put it close to the fire. The sweetened barley would simmer until it was needed. 'What do I think of men and their notions anyway? They have caused me nothing but trouble in recent years.'

'I have caused you more trouble than anyone.'

Instant remorse stabbed Ragn. She put an arm about her. 'You are my only sister and I have loved you since the day you were born, Svana. Run off and see how the servants are getting on in the hall. Be my eyes and ears while I ensure the meal is actually edible.'

'I will go tell the *nisser* not to play any tricks. Today

is far too important.' She called to the dogs to follow her. They trotted along at her heels.

Ragn shook her head. If anyone had told her back in Viken that Svana could recover this quickly from her trauma, she wouldn't have believed them. This place had been good for her sister. Only they would have to leave it. Soon. She couldn't see Gunnar's wife allowing them to stay on. An illogical hatred of the unknown woman filled her. She would indeed be the paragon of grace and beauty Gunnar sought, instead of an awkward woman like her. She contented herself with slamming plates and horns down until she had control of her emotions.

She cast a practised eye over the kitchen. The giant cauldron was bubbling with the hog's meat. Three chickens, salmon and the pork. The remainder of the cloudberries could be added to the porridge for a substantial pudding. A feast worthy of her old reputation as one of the best hostesses in Viken. A bit of stock fish would add to the feast, though.

'Ragnhild, someone else can prepare that.' Gunnar took the pot of soaking stock fish from her fingers. 'We need to speak.'

And Ragn knew her time of reckoning had come.

Chapter Seven

'Before you say anything, that man practically invited himself.' She dumped the remaining cloudberries into the barley porridge. 'Sending him away would have raised his suspicions about why you wanted him gone quickly. This way he can only say good things about the table you keep. Please. I know what I am doing.'

Gunnar's mouth became a thin white line. He beckoned her into a small alcove away from the servant girls who pretended to be busy with the cauldron. There was hardly enough space for the two of them. Her body tingled with awareness of his nearness. Ragn damped it down. Acting on that awareness was not going to happen, not while he simmered with anger.

'I know exactly what happened. I was there.' His breath caressed her ear, making the butterflies swoop in her stomach. He stood two steps closer than he needed to be.

His voice flowed like new honey instead of being ice-cold. She'd expected anger and instead she had this—Gunnar regarding her with an expectant air and speaking in a silky voice. She crossed her arms over her suddenly aching breasts and forced herself to think of the unknown woman, the one who'd have a winning smile and plentiful curves, the one who'd make Gunnar's eyes light up when he claimed her as his true bride.

She pointedly cleared her throat. 'I've saved your hall twice over today. He anticipates breaking inferior bread with you, but we both know my food is superior. He will leave a friend and an ally.'

'Everything was under control until you started speaking.' His brow lowered and the stern Gunnar returned. Ragn heaved a sigh of relief. She could deal with him being grumpy, not the softer Gunnar whose eyes held a distinct twinkle. 'The man assumes you are my bride!'

'And you failed to correct him!' She glanced over her shoulder. 'Keep your voice down unless you wish for him to discover his assumption was wrong.'

A muscle jumped in his cheek. 'There were reasons why I wanted him to leave. There are things we need to discuss and make right.'

'His was a logical enough assumption to make.' Ragn shrugged. The words 'make right' held a distinctly poor ring. He was going to insist Svana and she took refuge in Ile after all. 'I suppose I should be grateful that he considered me your wife rather than your concubine. It could have gone either way.'

His gaze travelled over her from where wisps of hair escaped from her kerchief, down past her meagre curves to where the tips of her boots peeked out. Ragn resisted the urge to hunch her shoulders. He turned away from her. 'You do not have the appearance of a concubine.'

The remark cut her in a way that Hamthur's insults never had. 'Should I be flattered or annoyed by your pronouncement? I suppose it depends on if I ever wanted to play the concubine for you.' She pretended to consider the matter. 'Can't say that I have. I will take it as a compliment. I look like a wife. Excellent.'

His face hardened to icy planes. 'My tongue has always been blunt. I make no secret of it. Why the sudden seeking of compliments? You have always seemed more like a man than a woman in that respect.'

She kept her head upright. More like a man. Proof of his utter disinterest in her. That small faint hope she had of convincing him she was indeed the woman he wanted as his wife disappeared completely. She should be happy. Grumpy Gunnar was a known prospect, but her middle filled with a dull ache from the empty place it left behind. She hadn't even realised that a hope existed until it vanished. She clenched her hand until her nails made half-moon shapes in her palms.

'Men prefer concubines to wives. They lust after them. They dedicate songs to them. Wives are for making sure estates run smoothly and for looking after children. Without looks wives must have large dowries—something to entice a man. I've nothing.'

'I've no time for your trivial concerns. The difference between a wife and concubine! Of all the things you try to distract me with, you chose this! The gods grant me patience!'

Ragn struggled to draw a breath. 'Concerns? Distractions? My future depends on finding a husband!'

'You can stop your search. Thanks to your actions, Maurr considers you my bride.'

'Thanks to my actions, he did not use your status as a single man to wrestle these lands from you. You should be on your knees thanking me. That shingle out there is not red with your blood. I suspect you very much like having your blood inside your body rather than seeping away on the shingle.'

He made a disgusted noise.

'There are more ways to influence people than through your favoured approach—brute force and fear.' The words burst out from deep within her. 'Women are worth more than simple bed companions. We wives excel at making enemies become friends through the breaking of bread.'

'I will hold my hall, Ragnhild, without your help.'

Ragn firmed her mouth. He still didn't trust her ability to help. Getting this feast right would go a long way to demonstrating that she could hold the hall for him when he was gone. 'Is there some reason you dragged me in here beyond a desire to moan and complain about Maurr? The last thing I need when I am preparing a feast is people moaning. Go back out there and smile, instead of grimacing. You are capable of that much hospitality, aren't you?'

His smile was like the sun peeking out from behind a dark cloud and it did strange things to her insides. 'Who is grouchy now? Your food will be perfection as always. You try to distract me because you fear what I am about to say. Two can play at this game, Ragnhild.'

'What precisely do you require, Lord of this hall?' She glanced up at him. 'Better?'

'I require many things from you.' His searing look made her knees go weak. 'But right now, I require a wedding.'

Ragn banged her ear with her hand. Her ability to build dream halls was getting worse. She had started hearing things. 'A wedding? You require a wedding? To whom? When?'

'I might have allowed a minor confusion over your status. Maurr's assumptions are meaningless. But I will not lie to my overlord.'

Ragn's heart beat faster. He was serious. 'I never asked you to.'

'We have been summoned to Colbhasa for Jul. We go married. Properly. All choice has gone. We marry with all speed once Maurr departs. Now do you understand why I wanted him gone instead of lingering like the noxious fumes of five-day-old fish? Instead of preparing for a marriage, I have to be hosting a feast for someone I dislike.'

The air went out of her lungs. He wanted to marry her. More than that, he had just stated they would marry. She put out a hand to steady herself. 'Just like that. You want me for your bride.'

'I warned you before Maurr set foot on the shore. There would be consequences.'

'And the going north in the spring?' she whispered. 'Do you intend for this marriage to last?'

'Why should I go now?' He gave a shrug which emphasised the broadness of his shoulders. 'We are used to each other, even when you chatter incessantly. You will have a home for your sister. And I... I will have porridge with cloudberries for breakfast. I will celebrate Jul in my house, including singing songs.'

Ragn had to smile. 'Is porridge without cloudberries that terrible?'

'I've given in to my fate. Will you give in to yours?'

Given in to his fate. Ragn pursed her lips. 'You make it seem like a death sentence.'

His eyes slid away from her. 'Perhaps it is. Perhaps you should be afraid.'

'Why? You are a good man.'

'I am a cursed man. I may have already brought a curse down on your head.'

The words hung between them. Ragn could see that Gunnar's face held no trace of mockery or good humour, only severe intent. He believed in this curse.

'How can you be cursed? You have your health. You have your hall. Your men look up to you.'

'Nevertheless, it remains. All my family perished after I killed a soothsayer.'

'Did you have good reason for killing him?'

'He had molested young girls and wanted to sacrifice them brutally. I was young. I objected.'

'I am pleased you objected.'

'But with his dying words, he cursed me and my family.'

She shook her head at his obstinacy. Why couldn't he see what had happened to him? 'These soothsayers and witch women cause much mischief with their predictions. I stopped believing in curses somewhere in that dark night when I was running for my life. If you are supposed to be dead, every day is a blessing.'

'All the women in my family died. They will always die. I had no desire to have your death on my conscience, but it cannot be helped—we must marry.'

Ragn stared directly into his blue-flecked eyes. Her heart thumped in her ears. For a man who professed not to believe in superstition, he certainly gave the opposite impression. Svana was not going to cause Vargr's death or stop a storm whipping up out to sea and it would take more than whispered words to kill her. 'It is how you respond to that curse which is important. Curses only have power if you give them that power.'

'I'm serious.'

'Svana and I would be at the bottom of sea if not for you.' She held out her hands, but he did not take them. 'I owe you our lives. Ask me again if I believe in your so-called curse.'

His mouth worked up and down.

'Then it is agreed. We marry, despite the curse.'

'You treat it too lightly.'

'I'll take the consequences.' Ragn dusted her hands on her apron. 'When shall our marriage take place? If Maurr discovers the deception, he'll take it badly.'

'Straight after he leaves. I agree with your assessment of Maurr.'

'Done.' She held out her hand and attempted to control the thudding of her heart. 'We keep this from Svana until the last possible moment. She has trouble with keeping secrets.'

'Does she indeed? I would never have guessed.'

He ignored the hand and watched her mouth. She passed her tongue again over her parched lips, wondered what his lips would feel like. 'Aren't you going to take my hand?'

'A kiss would be more appropriate. We are to be married.'

A kiss? She froze. All Hamthur's jibes about appearance and her disappointing bed-sport flooded back. She wanted it to be different with Gunnar, but feared it wouldn't be. After she'd lost the baby, Hamthur had blamed her for everything.

Ragn retreated two steps. Her feet became entangled in her skirts and she tumbled on to her bottom.

'You are head over heels about this?' He gave a slight laugh. His strong fingers curled about hers. The shock of awareness flooded through her. She snatched her hand away. She hurriedly scrambled to her feet, smoothing her skirt and apron as she did so.

'I wasn't watching where I was going. I've lingered here for far too long.' Her voice sounded husky to her ears. 'I hadn't expected a kiss. I... I thought things would continue as they were. They work as they are now. I keep watch over Svana at night in case her fits return.'

The tension in her neck eased. She had given the perfect excuse for why she needed to keep her distance. She'd experienced enough humiliation at Hamthur's hands to risk a repeat. Her heart kept whispering that Gunnar was a much better man than Hamthur.

'Svana is much improved. Is there a reason you do not seek my bed?'

Reason? She named several in her mind, starting with his lack of desire for her and ending with how she always killed passion, according to Hamthur. 'Are you threatening to use force?'

He lifted a brow. 'Are you saying you are not attracted to me?'

She wrapped her arms about her pulsing middle and slowly shook her head. 'My husband—' she began to say and swallowed the words at his fierce expression.

'Whatever your late husband did, I believe we can safely say that it was in the past. I will give you time if you need it to mourn him.'

She gave a strangled laugh. He thought she still mourned Hamthur. Perhaps she could use that as an excuse? She gave her mind a shake. She was not hiding behind his ghost. 'I have never asked you to.'

He ran a finger along her lips, making them tingle.

'You should know that I have never forced a woman and I have no plans to start. Should something happen between us, then it will happen because it is your choice. My promise to you.'

Never forced a woman. The accusations that Hamthur had thrown at her—how she had unmanned him, how she was awful in bed—resounded in her mind. After the first month, he'd only ever come to her bed when he was drunk. She had to hope that Gunnar would be better. At least he made no pretence about loving her. 'Then we are fine. We know the boundaries.'

'Can you risk a kiss?' The dimple shone in the corner of his mouth. 'Or are you too busy with your feast preparations?'

'Is it the only way to seal our agreement to marry?'

'The most pleasurable way.'

He dipped his head and brushed his lips against hers, no more than the touch of butterfly, but also all fire and heat. None of Hamthur's kisses had prepared her for this dark, all-consuming intensity which infused her being. Her legs became weak and she clutched his tunic.

A little moan escaped her throat and his arms came around her, moulding her against him.

Someone dropped a pan and Ragn realised what she was doing. She jumped backwards. He allowed her to go.

Her mouth panged with disappointment at the kiss's briefness. She kept her eyes on the rushes, but his ragged breathing echoed in her ears.

'I believe the experiment was a success, Ragnhild.'

She glanced up and met his dancing eyes. Her heart did a little flip. She dampened it down. Giving him the satisfaction of knowing how much she had enjoyed what he must consider a brief meaningless meeting of lips would remain her secret. 'I prefer Ragn.'

He smiled. 'Ragn, it shall be. My wife.'

'You take pleasure in teasing me,' she said.

'In the right circumstances.' He gestured towards the kitchen. 'Shall we entertain our unwelcome guest before he starts wondering where we have disappeared to? There again, we are newlyweds. I am sure he will understand if we simply had to retire to the nearest bed.'

'Maurr appears to be a man who is quick to take an insult. Besides, he would not believe it.'

He reached out and rubbed a thumb against her all-too-tender lips. 'Why do you say that?'

'He considers me a wife, not a concubine.'

'Where does it say a man cannot lust after his wife?'

She deliberately turned away. He was definitely teasing her now. It was the main reason why this marriage had to be practical, rather than for any other purpose. She knew the limitations of her charms, but an insidious voice at the back of her brain whispered—what if… what if Gunnar truly desired her? He was a very different proposition from Hamthur.

She silenced it. If she listened to the murmurings of her heart, she might as well start believing in elves and fairies again. 'I've much to do to ensure the smooth running of your household.'

'Our household. It is a joint enterprise now.' His hands grasped her shoulders and firmly turned her back towards him. 'I do believe I have found a way of silencing you.'

She lifted her chin. 'You promised no force.'

Their breath interlaced, and his gaze appeared to trace the outline of her mouth. Her lips throbbed anew.

He gave a slow smile as if he knew and enjoyed the havoc he was creating in her body. 'This discussion is far from over, Ragn. I do find it difficult to resist a challenge.'

'Hardly a challenge.' She gave a decisive nod. 'Wives run households. Concubines warm beds.'

'I have no intention of mistaking what you are!' He gave a low laugh as he walked away.

She fingered her mouth and almost felt the imprint of his lips. It was worrying that a small piece of her wanted to believe that he was interested in her, that he, too, had felt that pull of attraction which made her blood fizz.

She quickly shook her head to clear it. She was worse than Svana with her belief in *nissers*. She refused to give any man the power to make her miserable about her looks and question her competence again. She'd learned from her mistakes. Her destiny was practicality, not romance. The best she hoped for was to gain his respect.

The pot of barley started to bubble over, bringing her back to reality. She ran towards it and swung it away from the fire. Unless she started working properly, she would lose all chance of that as well.

The hall had been completely transformed from the barren and empty cavern that Gunnar had seen only this morning. Now, all the benches were full. Ragn had found tapestries from somewhere to line the walls. The fire blazed and there appeared to be a limitless supply of good food to eat and a watered-down ale for those on the lower tables while the high table had mead to drink. She'd even discovered one of his men had talent as a decent saga teller. How she'd discovered it, he could not guess. Much as he hated to admit it, Ragn had been right to proclaim—good company and food altered tempers. Maurr's men appeared far less desperate than earlier.

Ragn flitted everywhere, making sure they were all made comfortable. All the men seemed to want to flirt with her, but she appeared utterly unperturbed by it, answering comments with a smile, and a deft twist of her hips kept her away from groping hands. Her talent for anticipating potential quarrels and stopping them before they happened was astonishing to watch.

However, it did not bode well for his new quest to get her into his bed, any time soon. The brief kiss they had shared had sent his senses soaring earlier, but she'd pulled back with confused eyes, ending it. Then she'd run from the alcove as if she was the Sun Maiden with Fenrir the wolf on her heels. He had to wonder why. Her husband was not long dead. Did she mourn him? Or was there something else.

'Are you mooning over your wife?' Maurr asked, bringing him back to the reality of entertaining an unwelcome guest. 'Is that why you failed to answer my question about your trees and their suitability for my hall?'

'Trees? You asked about trees?' Gunnar forced his thoughts away from the problem which was Ragn and back to his uninvited guest's request for timber to build his hall. 'I have a stand which are tall enough for your purposes.'

Maurr dug an elbow into his side and sloshed his drink on to the table. 'If she were my wife, I wouldn't be able to think of anything else either. How was the wedding?'

'Excuse me?'

'The wedding—was it here or in the north?'

'A contracted marriage in the north and a small affirmation here. Nothing fancy, but meaningful.' The sweat pooled on the back of his neck. Maurr suspected all was not as it appeared. 'We have had scarce time to think as we have been putting the hall to rights. Ragn is determined to do Jul properly for all my followers.'

'Ah, it makes perfect sense.' Maurr nodded sagely, taking another long drink of Gunnar's finest mead. 'Your wife is someone who thinks of others and their comfort first. I had wondered. None of your men seemed to recall the wedding feast. Or what sort of bridal crown Ragnhild wore.'

'You quizzed my men about my wedding?'

'For Ljot.' He tapped the side of his nose. 'She is sure to ask. I didn't want to get it wrong. My life would not be worth living. How things look is important to her, more than how things taste or how much mead there is. She gets worse, the larger she gets with this baby.'

'Question Ragn about it.' He kissed the tips of his fingers. 'I have more memories of the wedding night.'

Maurr laughed and clapped him on the back. 'Spoken like a true warrior in the throes of early love. I'm envious.'

Gunnar took a gulp of his mead. He signalled to Ragn for more mead.

'You set a good table,' Maurr proclaimed with a loud belch and a further leer down Ragn's front. 'Contrary to the rumours.'

Gunnar tightened his grip on his wooden cup. The man had no right to treat his wife to that sort of scrutiny. Surely the blood money he'd have to pay Maurr's kin would be worth the satisfaction of seeing Maurr dismembered for his inappropriate behaviour towards Ragn. He forced his mind away. He'd deal with Maurr in his own time. Tonight was about ensuring Maurr remained in ignorance over his true status. And in the morning, he'd make things right.

He stood and banged his spoon against the cup. The hall fell silent. 'I shall bid you a goodnight. You will want to get the early morning tide, so you can return to your wife. I hardly wish to be blamed for sending you towards the whirlpool.'

Maurr belched again. 'The night is young. Rest a while yet. We should get to know each other better. I predict we will be neighbours soon enough.'

'Kolbeinn has given you lands?' Ragn asked, leaning forward, stretching the cloth over her breasts. Gunnar glowered at Maurr. 'Do not keep us in suspense! I look forward to welcoming your wife. I'm sure we will become fast friends.'

The way she said it, Gunnar knew that it was more than simple words to her. Ragn was like that—generous and courteous. He hadn't appreciated it enough before and it bothered him. He'd underestimated the strength of her heart. He'd been too busy being annoyed at the disruption to his life to see her value.

The man's ears turned pink under Ragn's blatant flattery. 'The next bay over. It is far more windswept than this one.'

'A pity that this one is taken then,' Gunnar murmured.

'Svana is very tired,' Ragn declared, standing up. 'I shall get her to bed. You know what she is like, always hoping to see the *nisser* in the early morning. She is determined to get her wishes.'

Gunnar frowned. She would put Svana to bed and then claim that she fell asleep, neatly sidestepping his plan to get her into his room. Maurr was bound to find an excuse to check.

Gunnar drained his drink. 'If you will excuse me, I will take Ragn to bed. I would hardly like for her to get lost or delayed.'

Ragn's mouth took on a stubborn cast, causing him to smile inwardly. She wasn't very complicated. She had intended to use Svana as a shield. Her earlier kiss demonstrated her passion. He simply had to figure out what made her fearful and how best to break down her barriers. He wanted a willing wife, not a frightened one.

'Unnecessary. I am perfectly capable of putting my sister to bed. You stay and drink, catch up on the gossip. I swear warriors enjoy a good chinwag more than old women.'

'Your capability is not the question.' Gunnar caught her hand and brought it to his lips. She glared at him, but did not draw away. 'After tonight, I am willing to swear you are the most capable woman I have ever met. The experience is new to me and I remain the eager bridegroom.'

'Enjoy. It will soon wear off,' Maurr called out from where he sat, cradling the jug of mead Ragn had put on the table. 'A word of friendly advice. Soon you will be looking for any excuse to get away from your wife.'

Gunnar struggled to keep from thumping the man.

Chapter Eight

'Is this strictly necessary?' Ragn turned to face her adversary. Ignoring him or running away was not going to work. She needed to get this settled before everything started to spiral out of control, before Gunnar started behaving like Hamthur.

After they had settled Svana with the dogs as guards, Gunnar had insisted on escorting her to his chamber, rather than allowing her to settle down with Svana as she normally did. She was certain the honey scent of mead lingered on his breath.

'What point is there to this besides you drinking far too much mead? I knew something was up when you appeared with the remaining hogsheads of mead halfway through the meal.'

'You mentioned the lack of ale. It has gone to a worthy cause.' He lowered his voice. 'I'd hardly like you to get bothered by any drunken warriors or indeed get lost and discover you sleeping some place altogether different.'

'You're spouting nonsense and you know it. You delight in it tonight. What has got into you? You're positively brimming with good fellowship.' She held up her hand. 'Don't tell me. My late husband used to suffer from something similar when he had too much to drink at the feasts.'

His brow lowered. 'I'm nothing like your late husband. I am about to be your husband.'

'Now I know you have had too much.'

'Here I thought you'd be delighted your sister was safe with all these new warriors about. Kolka and Kefla will guard her well.'

Annoyance at his high-handed behaviour warred with her pleasure that Svana had taken to the dogs. Svana's face had positively beamed when Gunnar informed her of her bedtime companions. 'How do you know that she needs to be guarded?'

He gave a half-shrug. 'It is what I would have done if Asa or Brita had been here.'

'Perhaps I should stay with her, just in case.' Ragn rubbed her temple. Gunnar had to give way and see that it was the most sensible course of action.

'Leave the future to decide for itself.' He put his fingers under her elbow. Her body tingled with awareness of him. 'Our chamber is this way. A day early, but I trust you will remember the way from now on.'

She pulled away from him. 'You are determined to have your way.'

'In this matter, I am entirely determined. Maurr clearly desires my hall, so he does not have to go to the trouble of building his own. He asked questions about your bridal crown, too, because apparently his wife is interested in such matters.'

'Women often are interested in weddings, babies and how children grow. Such things hold society together.'

Ragn fought against the rising tide of panic. The last thing she desired was to be a bed partner for a warrior who had consumed more mead than was good for him. 'I see nothing sinister in that.'

'Should I give him the excuse he longs for?' he asked softly. 'Shall all your efforts tonight have been for nothing?'

Drawing a deep breath, she marched to the room she had always avoided before now, leaving the task of tidying to one of the servants.

Gunnar's bedchamber was a reasonable size and well appointed with an iron-bound trunk at the base of the bed and a pile of thick pelts covering the mattress. A series of tapestries hung on the walls and, in one corner, a small silver cup perched on top of a stand. A warm curl developed in the centre of her being. In a room like this, she could imagine being desired. She ran her tongue over her lips, remembering how his mouth had moved against hers.

'You are being ridiculous,' she said, banishing all thought of that kiss. All he wanted was a warm body after the feast, but she required more. 'None would be the wiser. You should have stayed and spoken with him, found out what his plans were instead of insisting on this...this farce.'

'You were the one who began it by allowing Maurr to make certain assumptions.'

Ragn lifted her brow. 'There is no blood on the shingle or men lying, screaming in agony. I did what was necessary.'

'I'm continuing your good work. Tonight, in this room, is very necessary.' Gunnar placed the fat lamp down on a low trunk where it provided a flickering light. He moved about the room, taking off his fur cloak and sword. When he lifted his tunic, revealing his muscular back criss-crossed with scars, Ragn's mouth went dry and her knees refused to hold her. He turned his head slightly. 'Enjoying the spectacle?'

Her cheeks heated. 'Not really.'

'Your face gives you away every time you stretch the truth.' His voice had dropped to a husky rasp. 'An endearing quality and one I find most interesting in this situation.'

'Do you think the reason for Maurr's doubts is that I look like a wife and not a concubine?' She pointedly addressed the wall beyond his right shoulder. 'That I do not appear to be the sort of woman you'd marry?'

He paused in his disrobing and assessed her from under his lashes. 'I would have considered a lady such as yourself would prefer to be considered a wife rather than a concubine, but for some reason it upsets you.' His brows knitted. 'I will never understand women. If he wonders about you being my wife, it is because you are far too high born for someone like me rather than thinking about your figure.'

'How so?'

'My great-grandmother was a thrall. I can barely read runes. Everything about you proclaims breeding and a cultured upbringing. Maurr simply does not know why you would have chosen me.'

Ragn found it impossible to prevent the laughter from bubbling up. He thought he was beneath her? 'My ancestors did not build this hall. You did. You earned everything from the sweat of your brow. My late husband earned nothing and left even less. And as to our marriage, my choices were limited. Yours were limit-less. I can easily teach you runes if you want to learn.'

He cocked his head to one side. 'What should I have said? That your hair reminds me of a raven's wing? Or your skin is translucent? Would that have made Maurr respect you? Would it have kept him from examining your bosom every time you poured the mead? He should respect you because you are my bride.'

That warm curl whispered its way around her belly and she tried to ignore it. He was baiting her in the same cynical way he'd done with the earlier kiss.

The memory of what Hamthur had been like after he had imbibed too much at a feast assaulted her. He had always wanted to couple whether she wanted to or not. The first feast she had done on her own, she'd been exhausted and he'd been less than complimentary, criticising everything from the spoons to the loudness of her laughter at other men's jokes. Then Hamthur had called her a series of other women's names before settling on Sweetie, pulled her roughly into bed and forced her to have sex with him, stuffing a hand over her mouth so she wouldn't scream. It had been such a change from the gentle way he'd done it in the early days of their marriage. She'd lain there, stunned.

Afterwards, when she had questioned him, he said drunk was the only way he stood coupling with her. And he refused to share her amongst his friends as he'd planned to do because he did not want anyone discovering how truly inept she was. She hadn't known which shocked her more—that Hamthur had planned to offer her to his friends or that he did not want to share her bed or that he'd married her because his father proclaimed it was the only way he'd inherit and he had debts to pay.

'Ragn? Ragnhild? Do you agree? You are worthy of respect.'

Ragn put her fingertips against her temples and tried to banish the painful memories. The woman who had cried, cowered and meekly agreed for the sake of having an heir had vanished for ever.

She marched over to the bed. 'Are you sleeping on the floor, or am I? I am not your bride until tomorrow.'

A gleam came into his eyes. 'You dislike compliments? How refreshing. Most women dote on them. Why is that, I wonder?'

'I've no need for such things and can easily list my faults. When a man uses such words with me, I know he is stretching the truth and desires something from me, something I would otherwise be disinclined to give.'

A dimple flickered in and out of his cheek. 'Is it a fault to have glossy black hair? Or a generous mouth? That is the first I have heard of such a notion. Things have altered mightily since I last lived in the north, but I refuse to believe they have altered that much.'

Ragn schooled her features and attempted to ignore the obviously over-blown compliments caused by the consumption of far too much mead. Someone had to take charge of this before it spiralled out of control. Sleeping in his bed would mean having his faint scent all about her. A reminder if she needed it of how she had reacted to his impersonal kiss earlier. She refused to start believing in her dreams, the ones she had been having lately where he took her in his arms and made slow love to her, where he was considerate and wanted her to have pleasure. Impossible dreams.

This time she kept her feet on the ground, practically assessed her non-existent charms and did nothing to jeopardise the refuge she had found for Svana.

'You know what I mean,' she said, jabbing her finger towards his chest and giving in to her anger at being trapped in this room and having her dreams exposed as the lies they had to be. 'We have an agreement, Gunnar. That agreement does not include compliments. I won't be forced or cajoled into doing things I don't want to, particularly before we are married.'

All the merriment fled from his face. 'Have I done anything to undermine that agreement?'

'No,' Ragn admitted and immediately concentrated on the rushes, rather than the annoyance in his eyes. 'I have experience of men after feasts.'

'But they were not me.' He gave a crooked smile which did strange things to her insides. 'Where will you be most comfortable?'

'I shall take the floor,' she declared with a determined nod. 'Hand me some of the pelts.'

He failed to move. She started to drag one off the bed, but his hand shot out and stilled her. She shook it off. He sat down on the bed with a loud creak. There was no way to remove any pelts without first removing him.

'You are being ridiculous, Gunnar. Move.'

'You will not sleep on the floor. My mother would be appalled that I allowed a lady to sleep on the floor. It is where Kolka and Kefla normally sleep. Her shade would have cause to haunt me if I followed your suggestion.'

'Suggestion?'

'We were discussing the sleeping arrangements. I

merely asked where you would be most comfortable and you replied.'

'The dogs are guarding Svana. Your mother's shade has enough other reasons to haunt you.'

'She never has before.'

'Then she is busily occupied somewhere else and will stay that way.' She tugged at the top fur. 'Let me get this pelt. Remember I don't believe in shades, or curses.'

'You're being grumpy. Are you always like this after a feast?'

'And you are being?' she asked, arching her right brow. 'Pray tell me the difference.'

He remained seated on the bed with an impervious expression on his face. Ragn contemplated simply curling up on the rushes and trying to sleep, trusting that he would throw a pelt or two over her in due course. But he was right—the floor was hard and the rushes needed to be changed. 'What did you think would happen?'

'I expected you to choose the bed and negotiate afterwards on how many pelts you'd allow me.' He shrugged. 'You are the most unlike a woman I have ever met!'

'Are you claiming all the pelts? Expecting me to sleep on the floor without a covering?' She nudged the dirty rushes with her foot.

A muscle jumped in his cheek. 'I made it very clear that you were not sleeping on the floor.'

She shook her head. 'Then you do it. Have as many furs as you need.'

'You already offered me the bed.' He pointed out in a tone she distrusted. 'I accepted your offer with gratitude. I am willing to negotiate on the amount of space you require.'

Her jaw dropped. Negotiate indeed! She knew where

this led. And it all had to do with the after-effects of the feast, rather than a desire for her.

A little voice inside her proclaimed—what if she was wrong, what if the kiss they had shared was something more? She pushed it away. She'd given in to her imaginings before when she accepted Hamthur's overly romantic proposal of marriage and the only path they led to was disillusionment and heartache.

'Allow me to sleep with Svana as I normally do and this nonsensical conversation caused by drinking too much mead can stop.' How she kept her voice even she wasn't sure, but she was proud of the calm tone. 'I am sure we will both get a better sleep and tomorrow will be a day for keeping our wits about us.'

He lowered his brows. 'Leave this room and I will bring you back here, over my shoulder.'

'Why?'

'We remain in a perilous situation. You saw how closely Maurr watched us during the feast. If he gets one inkling of the truth, there will be a reckoning.'

'You are bluffing.'

'It was your decision to enact this scheme. I am merely taking it to the logical conclusion. However, you suddenly seem overcome with maidenly scruples. One can only wonder what your late husband was like. Possibly he was blind and stupid. You are wrong to mourn him like you do.'

'Leave Hamthur out of this! He has no place in this discussion.'

He collapsed back on the bed. His skin contrasted with the fur. Ragn's mouth went dry. 'At last we agree on something.'

'Perhaps I should find a place by the kitchen fire.'

'You hardly want Maurr or one of his men to hear us arguing over something as fundamental as this,' he murmured, turning his head to one side. 'Or discovering you curled up like a thrall beside the kitchen fire.'

Ragn put a hand over her eyes. 'Do you think he will check where we are sleeping?'

'I've little idea what he will do, but it is something I would do if I considered a hall worth having.'

He put his hands behind his head and stared up at the ceiling. The flickering light from the fat lamp made shadows on the vast expanse of his chest. It was almost as if he knew how delectable he looked with the light playing over his skin. Ragn carefully made sure her gaze was on the headboard.

'In the interests of saving these lands, I will sleep in your bed.'

'I thank you for your trust. It makes a good basis for marriage. And you will be sleeping here after our marriage. I do not believe in separate sleeping spaces for husbands and wives.'

Ragn pressed her hands together to stop them from trembling. Sharing a bed and a real marriage. Mead had loosened his tongue. Everything would be negotiable in the morning, after Maurr departed.

'You are right, of course. Sharing a bed with you is no different than sharing with Svana, except I doubt she snores.'

'How do you know I snore?' He rose from the bed and went over to her. The heat from his body encircled her.

'I know how much mead you drank.'

'You only think you know. Thinking can be dangerous at this time of night, Ragn.' He lifted her chin, so she had to look him in the eyes. His thumb rubbed the delicate area under her eye socket. 'There are great circles under your eyes and your skin has gone the colour of tallow. You are going to have to get more rest once you are my wife.'

Ragn gritted her teeth. So much for the vague hope he might have engineered this because he had enjoyed their kiss. He thought she resembled a crone. Like Hamthur before the marriage, he had just been pretending. 'Turn around. I want to undress. I am not doing it for your amusement tonight.'

'Does that mean you might some day? With such a promise on offer, I have no choice but to obey your request.' He dutifully turned his back, but his shoulders shook with barely suppressed laughter.

'Who knows what the future holds?' Her fingers were clumsier than usual as she silently promised that it would never happen. Her body even before the scarring she'd received from the fire was not the sort to entice a man. After they married, she'd undress in the darkness. It would preserve the mystery.

'You may take up as much room as you require. I am kind that way.'

She curled up in a tight ball with her back towards him and pretended not to hear his trousers hitting the floor.

Gunnar dowsed the fat lamp. The mattress dipped, but she noticed he carefully lay on top of the coverlet. He immediately began breathing softly as if his head only had to hit the pillow for him to fall asleep.

She steeled herself not to sleep, but discovered, between the softness and his proximity, her eyes became heavy.

* * *

Gunnar lay in the dark and listened to the sound of her breathing.

It had taken a while, but Ragn had finally fallen asleep. The men on the beach, the feast with its wrestling, songs and ribald jests had not bothered her, but she'd become terrified once they had gone into this chamber alone together.

'What are you frightened of?' he asked softly. 'What did that miserable worm of a late husband do to you? If he harmed you, I swear, Ragn, his death should have been far more painful than it was.'

She murmured some unintelligible words, but her body moved towards his, seeking his heat and somehow it felt right to have her snuggled into him, next to his heart. One hand touched his chest, brushing against his right nipple, making his entire body harden. Her indifference had to be a pretence. His mood lightened instantly. It was not him, but something else.

Gunnar shifted slightly to ease the pain in his groin. He'd given her his word that he would not force her, but he had said nothing about seducing her.

'Have you ever known pleasure in bed? Or did your husband just take?' he asked, but again she only made a low murmur.

He chewed on the back of his knuckle. He would discover her secrets and then he would show her how good it could be between the two of them. And as he was not in danger of giving her his heart, she would remain untouched by the curse.

She might not believe in such things, but he knew it would seek to destroy her.

'I'll find a way of breaking it. I promise.'

* * *

A faint noise like a mouse scrabbling had Ragn struggling to wake from a wonderful dream where Gunnar had declared his undying devotion to her before slowly but surely making love to her. She winced. She'd snuggled up to Gunnar, facing him. Her arm lay across his middle and his was about her shoulders. Anyone chancing on them would swear they were intimate. She started to move away, but his arm tightened about her as a piercing light shone in the room.

A dark shape stood in the doorway, holding a torch aloft. Ragn started to sit up, but Gunnar's hand held her in place, preventing her from escaping.

'A problem, Maurr?' he called out. 'This room is taken. My wife needs her rest. Hospitality on such short notice requires a great deal of effort.'

'None whatsoever,' Maurr said, lowering the torch. 'I mistook my bedchamber. I pray you and your lady forgive my disturbance.'

The light faded to nothing and the footsteps moved stealthily away. Gunnar released her shoulder.

'You were right to insist that we share a bed.' Ragn slid over so that she was on the edge of the bed. Far better to move before being asked to even if her body protested at the cold and emptiness. Her face burnt with heat and she was pleased for the dark. He might have controlled his impulses, but her body seemed determined to enact her dream and she knew the folly of dreaming. All he had to do was lie next to her for her limbs to entangle with his, her face to press up against his and their breath to intermingle.

She'd never slept that intimately with Hamthur. Not

even in the early days when she thought he'd loved her instead of loving her dowry.

Anyone like Maurr would consider that they had just been intimate. An illusion and a lie, but her body yearned for her dream to become real. She concentrated on breathing steadily and hoping against hope Gunnar did not discover the truth and use it against her.

'I know his reputation.' Gunnar flopped against the pillows. She found her body sliding towards him again. He put a casual arm about her. 'We should endeavour to sleep. Tomorrow may be long if he finds an excuse to linger, but he will go. We will be married by night-fall. I will not take the risk.'

Ragn inched her way to the side of the bed and breathed again, even as her body protested at the sudden chill. Her mind had not been working properly earlier. She should have been aware of the risks.

His fingers brushed her hair from the back of her neck. 'Relax. I have given you my word. Tonight, you merely sleep in my bed. We wait for the marriage.'

'Tomorrow will bring me sleeping back with Svana despite your proclamation about married people,' she replied, wriggling to increase the space between them. 'I won't allow your mead-influenced teasing to get the better of me. I know the reasons for our purely practical marriage.'

'Teasing you? Perish the thought.' His voice was full of amusement. 'You are never dull, Ragn. I have had my fill of nameless women with accommodating thighs over the years who fill the silence with meaningless chatter about people I have no interest in.'

'You delight in seeing me off balance.'

He sighed and removed his arm. 'You refuse to listen.'

'I state the truth. We are sharing this bed out of necessity. That particular problem will cease in the morning when Maurr goes.'

'If you say so, it must be true. You know the etiquette of the thing. I am merely a simple warrior.' The way he said it made her pause. He seemed determined to teach her a lesson.

'You are anything but simple. Your proclaiming it is how you disarm other warriors and, dare I say, women.'

'I wonder who you are trying to convince.'

'Goodnight, Gunnar.' Ragn tightened her grip on the mattress's edge. She vowed her eyes would not close again tonight.

She silently resolved that she wasn't going to give in to her desire or her wild hopes. In that kiss they had shared, he made her feel beautiful as if Hamthur's words had been from spite rather than from substance. She knew she was spinning dreams again. The trouble was that she wanted to keep spinning them; she wanted to believe.

Chapter Nine

'Here I leave you,' Maurr said, making the formal gesture of departure. 'I need to travel on to the next holding. But I will inform Kolbeinn and Ketil of your hospitality, far more bountiful than I had been led to believe.'

Gunnar returned the gesture. Finally. He'd been up since before dawn waiting and Maurr kept offering excuse after excuse. Once the man and his men were gone, he'd get on about the pressing business of wedding Ragn and then wooing her. He wanted an enthusiastic bed partner, not one there by duty.

'Any improvement is down to Ragnhild's influence.'

Maurr gave a half-smile. 'You can tell a lot about a man from the table he keeps and the woman he marries, or so my mother used to claim with a slight smile. Yours is clearly a paragon and mine...well, I married her for her beauty, instead of her skill at keeping a house. Her mother swore she'd learn, but I haven't seen any evidence of it yet and we've been married nearly a year. I know who made the better deal.'

'Indeed,' Gunnar murmured.

'We will meet again soon. Our wives will become friends. Perhaps Ljot will even learn to cook. I swear that woman burns porridge deliberately. We can do great things together with this island. Far better than we could have done back in the north where a man would steal your land and your wife as soon as look at you.'

'The gods were with me when I married Ragnhild.' Gunnar struggled not to yawn. He frowned as the full weight of Maurr's statement sunk in. 'You wish to be allies?'

'Kolbeinn hinted that you might be reluctant to follow the King's decree and I should be prepared to take steps, but I see I mistook his words for something else.'

'Kolbeinn is a master at such deception. He cares nought for the outcome as long as he wins, but today he wins with our alliance.'

Maurr tugged at his neckline. 'Agreed.'

'Have you started on your hall? I might be persuaded to sell you timber for the right price.' Gunnar smiled inwardly, enjoying Maurr's discomfort. The man knew he was bested. Now was the time to make him an ally, rather than creating an enemy as Ragn had suggested. He looked forward to informing Ragn the arts of hospitality were no longer a mystery.

'First I must visit several more farms and ensure all is well. Kolbeinn entrusted me with this task.'

'And see if they might be persuaded to trade locations with you.'

The man laughed. 'No hard feelings between comrades. I want the best for my wife and child-to-be. I've fought hard enough to win my lands.'

Gunnar pursed his lips. He had considered as much. This expedition had been a fishing one. A man to watch, but not a friend. 'Then we shall be neighbours in due course. I look forward to it. Just know that this bay was also windswept and unhospitable when I first arrived.'

Maurr peered over Gunnar's shoulder. 'A pity your wife isn't here this morning. I enjoyed her conversation. She is not the usual sort one finds on the Western Isles. Far too fine, if you take my meaning. Such women normally remain in the north. Is there a tale behind her arrival?'

Gunnar barely refrained from hitting Maurr as primeval jealousy coursed through him. Ragn was his and his alone. 'Things are unsettled in the north.'

'It would be bad if you were dragged northwards.'

'No fear of that. I doubt Kolbeinn would permit it. He wants me here, guarding this passage.'

'Even still, I doubt there are many men who deny a jewel like that much.'

'Ragnhild had a full day yesterday and a busy night. I am allowing her to sleep. We are newly wed, after all!'

The memory of how he'd left Ragn with her dark hair against the pillow rose in his mind. He'd departed silently. He had longed to draw her into his arms and kiss her awake, but he had to take it slow and allow her trust to build. He was greedy. He wanted her full participation when they joined.

Today his project of seduction started. Her actions yesterday had begun this game, but he was going to finish it on his terms. He might not be able to give her his heart, but he'd make the marriage pleasant for the both of them.

'I've concern for my wife.'

'A good husband. I wish you joy.'

Gunnar inclined his head. 'I like to think so.'

After the boat pushed out to sea, Gunnar stood gazing at it, plotting his next move.

'Gunnar? Has that man gone in peace, truly?' Svana ran up to him with a splodge of dirt on her face and her *couvrechief* askew. The girl's face was alight with mischief and had totally changed from the scared urchin who had stumbled on to the beach. Her fits appeared to have decreased, but there were moments when she seemed to be listening to sounds no one else heard just as Asa had once done. And he found he welcomed the long-buried memories of Asa.

'You are awake, little one.'

'The dogs wake early.' Her nose scrunched up in the way she had. 'They ate the *nisser*'s porridge this morning. Gobbled it all up, the naughty things.'

'Then he must have finished with it. Trust me, they would not have dared to have eaten it if he required it. Dogs know these things.'

Her eyes grew rounded. 'But there is one.'

'Why would I doubt my mother's words?' He hunkered down to get on her level. A little harmless joy never hurt anyone. Ragn needed to learn that lesson and he intended to administer it. First, he needed to learn more about her past. 'You should keep them in mind as well.'

Svana gave a solemn nod. 'I will. Promise.'

'Where is your sister? Asleep?'

'In the hall, scrubbing it down.' Svana's eyes became troubled. 'She always used to do this after the feasts Hamthur gave. From top to bottom and then bottom to top. Have you hurt her like Hamthur did?'

Gunnar stilled. 'Why would I harm your sister?'

Shadows darkened the girl's eyes. 'Hamthur did. Ragn thinks I don't know, but I do. Hamthur thought he beat her where no one saw, but I knew.'

'He beat her?' Gunnar struggled to control the anger which coursed through him. It was a great pity the man was dead. He wanted to tear him limb from limb for hurting Ragn. 'Often?'

'If he was drunk. Otherwise he'd ignore her. The last feast he tried to push Ragn in the blazing fire in the centre of the hall because he claimed she'd been over-friendly with another warrior when all she had done was to offer the man more ale. She told Hamthur to get out. I was glad he went then and took that woman with him. It was so peaceful, but then they died...' Svana put her hand over her mouth. 'I wasn't supposed to speak about that. The past behind me, yes?'

Gunnar frowned. Hamthur's jealous abuse explained Ragn's skittishness about passion. The sort of ghost he was competing with was very different than a kind considerate husband. And Ragn was stubborn. It would take time to convince her. His mood lightened considerably. 'I would never hurt your sister.'

'I know that.' Svana lifted her chin. 'I never said you would. Hamthur was unpleasant to me and you never are. May I go to the lake?'

'Wouldn't you rather make a bridal crown?'

Svana's eyes bulged. 'A bridal crown? Whose?'

'Your sister and I marry today.'

'Truly?'

'Brides tend to want such things. I have no wish for an excuse from your sister.'

'She lost her crown in the fire, but she managed to

save our grandmother's brooches. She wore those at the wedding as well.'

'I think every bride needs a crown.'

Svana gave a happy little sigh. 'You are serious. Why didn't Ragn say this morning? Why keep it a secret?'

'You would have to ask her, but I suspect she wanted it as a special surprise.'

Svana clapped her hand over her mouth. 'Oh, my goodness! I must catch the *nisser*'s shirt tail now. I have an important question to ask him.'

'Ask him what?'

'That would be telling. Can I tell people about the marriage?'

'Hardly a secret now that Maurr's gone. And I want people to remember her crown, Svana.'

She ran off, shouting excitedly with the dogs at her heels and her fair hair streaming down her back. It was almost as if Asa's spirit lived again and that was a good thing. Maybe he had been wrong to bury the memories. Maybe, after all this time, the gods had forgiven him. Gunnar clapped his hand to his head. He was becoming worse than the child with her unshakeable belief in *nissers*.

Ragn concentrated on scrubbing the flagstones in the hall. She done three-quarters of them and now they gleamed.

Her wedding today was going to be as different as she could make it from the last time. No magnificent feast, golden crown or crowds of women pretending to make her beautiful.

With each swipe of her scrubbing brush, she added another promise. The wedding was going to be very private. Then she would return to her duties. No lavish honeymoon or pretending he cared for her as had happened with Hamthur. The marriage was why she'd journeyed to Jura. It would keep Svana safe because if Vargr did discover they were alive, he would think twice about attacking a warrior with Gunnar's reputation. Solid reasons for the marriage, not that his teasing at the end of the day lifted her mood, or that his delight in her cooking made her try harder or even that she wanted to feel his mouth moving overs hers. Ragn made an angry swipe with the bristled brush at her deluded folly.

This time she kept her heart safe and her dignity intact.

She knew what Gunnar required from a marriage— practical and without complication. She was practical. She had made Hamthur's hall prosperous, so prosperous that Vargr had been convinced Hamthur had cheated him. It was the other part of the marriage she'd failed at.

'Here I find you hiding.' His warm voice flowed over her, making her remember how she'd felt in his arms and banishing all coherent plans. 'Svana gave me an earful. Apparently, I've upset you and I'm to apologise. When she is roused, Svana is quite fearsome.'

'Svana misread the situation. Hardly hiding. Working hard.' Ragn dipped her brush into the bucket before scrubbing the already clean flagstones again. 'I like putting the house to rights after a feast. Everything to be pristine for when the Sun Maiden emerges from the belly of the wolf and your men renew their oaths.'

'You appear to have forgotten we are to marry today. Your scrubbing must wait.'

She rocked back on her heels. Her breath stopped. The weak winter sun silhouetted Gunnar in the doorway, highlighting the breadth of his chest and how it tapered down to his waist and hips. She hurriedly glanced at the muddy pool of water. 'That's just the thing. I'm not sure it should wait.'

'Are you trying to change the terms of our deal? I have made the necessary arrangements.'

Gunnar's voice rang out in the empty hall, echoing all about. She hated that her mood instantly lightened. Gunnar was not having second thoughts. She drew her brows together and forced a scowl.

'Have Maurr and his men departed?' She stood up and was immediately aware of the sodden patches on her gown.

'On the morning tide. I made your excuses, Sleepyhead.'

'You should have woken me.'

'Today will be long enough.' He shrugged. 'You kept the impending nuptials a secret from Svana when you sent her down to the shore.'

'Her screams of delight would have ensured Maurr delayed his departure.'

'I seized the opportunity and told her.' His eyes twinkled. 'Her scream must have reached to Ile, if not Colbhasa.'

Ragn frowned and peered around Gunnar's bulk. Svana knew where she was. She should have come rushing back in to find out the truth. 'Do I even want to know where she is?'

'She believed me and has gone to collect berries. She intends on making you a crown which everyone will remember.' His hooded look made her knees go weak.

'You are to be the most perfect bride ever. Who am I to object to her demand?'

Ragn backed up. Her foot kicked over the bucket, sending its muddy contents all over the floor. She gave a particularly loud curse.

'Problems?'

She grabbed a rag and mopped up the water. 'Nothing I can't handle. My entire day has been like this and it is only going to get worse.'

His smile, if anything, deepened as if he knew that she was using the muddy water as a reason to swear. Where had grumpy Gunnar gone? 'You are right—a reputation for good hospitality can make a difference. I saw that this morning. Maurr's change in attitude was nothing short of astonishing. And it was all down to your efforts. He came prepared to be an enemy and has left an ally, if not yet a friend.'

Ragn paused in mopping up the filthy water. Butterflies started to dance in her stomach. Gunnar praised her. Hamthur had never done that. Part of her reason for making herself busy with the clean-up had been to avoid the inevitable complaints about how dreadful the feast had been and her many errors. 'Will wonders never cease? You find favour with my methods.'

He rubbed the back of his neck. 'I was overly hasty in dismissing your ideas, Ragn. I apologise for doubting you.'

Her hand froze mid-swipe. The new softer Gunnar was far more dangerous than the cross one. 'An apology? What has brought this on?'

'Yes, one must give credit where credit is due.' He gave a crooked smile that made her heart flip over.

'Particularly on one's wedding day. But I warn you—
don't get used to it.'

'I won't. I know what you are like before you have
your porridge.'

His laughter echoed in the hall. 'Everyone else is
shaking in their boots when they confront me. They
fear my temper and moods. They avoid me, but you
delight in prodding me.'

'You only pretend to be frightening to hide your soft
heart. I've seen how you are with Svana and with the
animals on the farm. How a man treats animals can
show a lot about his character.'

A lesson she'd learned after she married Hamthur.
If she had thought to watch how his dogs cringed from
him and his horses shied, she might not have believed
Hamthur's honeyed words, his expensive gifts and his
overly solicitous attention at feasts signified anything
other than his determination to acquire her father's
lands. Ragn pressed her fingertips against her temple.
Gunnar wasn't Hamthur, not at all.

'Hush, you mustn't allow the others to know.'

'Go away and leave me to do this. Then when I am
done, we can talk about the wedding and what needs
to be done before that can happen.'

'Who is being grumpy this morning?'

She risked a glance and he was leaning against the
doorframe. His eyes danced with wicked mischief as
if he knew what she was attempting to do. 'Cleaning
up is the right thing to do. I would be mortified if the
hall was a shambles.'

'At weddings, people notice the bride, not the sur-
roundings.'

Ragn concentrated on the floor. Her stomach knotted. 'And if I said it was the last thing I wanted—to be noticed?'

'You didn't mind yesterday.'

'Yesterday was different, I was doing my part to keep this hall safe. There is a difference.'

He took the cloth from her fingers. 'Tidy yourself up. Be quick about it and smile. It is why you came here. It is about your sister and keeping this hall safe. Go be beautiful.'

'Beautiful is something I can never be.'

'Once we are married, you will have to listen to your husband instead of dismissing my words.'

Ragn bit her bottom lip. When she'd come here, she would have been willing to accept any sort of marriage, but now she knew she wanted something more. She wanted him to believe that she was desirable. She shook her head. Real things, not imaginings. 'Nothing is going to change.'

'If you are not ready by the time the sun reaches its highest point, I will fetch you. All eyes will be on my bride.'

'The best I could do.' Svana held out a crudely fashioned crown made of holly berries interlaced with ivy. 'It isn't gold like your old one, like the one which burned. If you hate it, you don't have to wear it.'

Ragn took it from her sister. She blinked rapidly. 'Gold crowns are heavy. My head ached for days afterward. This one is as light as a feather. I'd be honoured to wear it.'

Svana's face became wreathed in smiles. 'Let me put it on you.'

Ragn bent down and Svana slipped it on. Svana and

her renewed joy in life were the reasons why she was marrying. 'I've worn my best gown.'

'But you need our grandmother's brooches to complete it. 'Where are they?'

Ragn examined the rushes. The brooches. Svana would think of them. 'They are gone.'

'Gone? Gone where?' Svana's brow furrowed. 'You wore them when we met Trana. I distinctly remember you wearing them to demonstrate that, despite losing the lands, we retained our dignity. They were your favourite thing.'

Ragn knelt and put her hands on her sister's shoulders so her face was level with Svana's. 'I sold them and gave the gold to the captain for your passage.'

Svana bowed her head and spoke in a low voice. 'I didn't know.'

'I'd rather have you than any amount of gold.' Ragn wrapped her arms about her sister and held her close until Svana squirmed.

Svana's bones were not nearly as sharp as they had been and Ragn knew whatever her misgivings about the marriage bed and her ability to please Gunnar, they were nothing compared to her joy that Svana would grow up free and healthy. She was doing the right thing and there had to be a way of making this work...for Svana's sake.

She simply had to be logical about it—Gunnar's heart was buried back in the frozen north with his family and this was a marriage of convenience, not one of mutual regard or affection. Practical without complications from dreams or allowing her heart to be trampled.

'Are you ready? Or do you require more time to be beautiful?' Gunnar thundered.

Ragn caught Svana's hand and squeezed it. 'As ready as I will ever be.'

'Then shall we get on with it?'

Ragn emerged from her room to find the hall in her absence had been completely transformed. It seemed like an entire forest had come inside. Holly and ivy hung from the rafters in great swags of green. The hall teemed with people—Gunnar's men and their families.

'How? What?'

Svana clapped her hands. 'Everyone wanted to help once I told them. Even Owain's mother helped with the decorating. You know Owain, the burly man who moved the barrels of ale two days ago. His mother loved the bread you sent back. She made Owain carry her up the muddy track. Her legs might not work so well, but she knows how to twist ivy to make green garlands.'

'I thought we had agreed to a simple ceremony.'

'The orders for this did not come from me. These people simply showed up and started to change the hall,' Gunnar said, catching her elbow. He had exchanged his usual rough wool cloak for a silver-fox cloak which set off his burnished gold hair to perfection. 'They are determined you will have a proper wedding. Something to do with the food baskets you have been parcelling out recently.'

'I was not expecting anything in return.'

'But they remembered the kindness.' His half-smile sent a pulse of heat through her. 'Another reason why your sort of hospitality works. Little things make a huge difference.'

Ragn gave a soft laugh. 'You can learn.'

'You will be amazed at what I can do.'

Ragn swallowed hard. Hamthur had played these

types of word games with her until her head whirled and then after the marriage he'd stopped making that sort of remark and had started finding fault. This time, she was not going to make the same mistake. She knew why she was marrying—a safe home for both her and Svana, not for undying love. *What if?* whispered that growing voice inside her brain. She silenced it. She had stopped hoping for the impossible. She settled for the probable—a marriage based on practicality with neither having any expectations. 'Daylight is slipping through our fingers.'

Gunnar made an elaborate bow. 'Without a bride, nothing can happen.'

The wedding passed in a blur. Ragn was very aware of how close Gunnar stood, how firm his voice was answering the priest's questions and how thin her own sounded.

Gunnar leant in and brushed her mouth with his. Warmth infused her body and her lips parted. The kiss instantly deepened as his tongue touched hers and then retreated. His hands crushed her against the length of his body.

Then the kiss was over. Her chest heaved as if she had run around the hall three times. The cheers from the crowd became deafening. He put an arm about her shoulders and turned to face the crowd. 'Behold my wife.'

Another huge cheer went up which shook the rafters. Ragn stood stiffly. The wedding had been the easy part. She had to stop wanting more than he offered.

'You look beautiful, Ragn,' Svana whispered. 'Good enough to eat. Your hair is growing out and it is all little curls. It suits you.'

After the drinking of toasts and speeches, the women had all gathered in Gunnar's bedchamber to prepare Ragn for the wedding night. A wide range of delicacies as well as a fresh jug of mead had been placed on the iron-bound trunk, alongside two silver goblets and a *tafl* board. The room was warm, but not overly hot, yet Ragn kept feeling faint.

Ragn had been surprised at the number of ribald jokes and riddles the Gaelic women knew. Thankfully most had gone over Svana's head. She noticed, though, with each new round of jokes Svana grew quieter and more withdrawn. 'The wedding went better than I hoped.'

Svana's eyes became more troubled and she gave a half-shrug.

'Two days of feasting if you count Maurr the Forkbeard's visit,' Ragn continued, making her voice sound bright. 'Although you can hardly call what we've just had a feast, more a meal with friends and retainers. And it is far more pleasant.'

She waited for Svana's smile. Instead the girl gave a nervous nod. Ragn covered Svana's cold hand with hers. 'What is the matter? Are you worried the marriage will change things? After tonight, it will go back to being how it was.'

Svana sighed. 'I've been thinking about the brooches and Mor-Mor. They were her favourite. You used to wear them on feast days because they were lucky. You sold your luck, Ragn.'

'Don't think about them. They are gone.' Ragn snapped her fingers. 'Most likely melted down. One less thing to worry about. And I make my own luck, remember?'

'What if Vargr discovers them? He'll know we are still alive, particularly if Maurr speaks about me and the rumours get back to Kaupang.' Svana bit her lip. 'He will come here and it will all be because of me and what the witch woman said.'

'The witch woman also told him not to travel over large bodies of water. He won't come here even if he discovers where we are, which he won't.'

Svana gave a barely perceptible nod as the other women told a few more jokes about the marriage bed.

'Stop worrying.' Ragn patted Svana's hand. 'We are safe here. The dogs look after you.'

This time Svana's smile was real. 'They are my friends now. And they have the biggest jaws I have seen.'

'Vargr would run from them.'

'Are you sure?'

Ragn leant forward and kissed Svana's cool cheek. 'More than anything.

'The master is coming!' one of the women called out.

Ragn climbed into the bed as the women fussed around her, rearranging her under-gown so a shadowy V showed where her meagre breasts started. Ragn resisted the urge to hunch her shoulders.

The door crashed open. The noise from the drums and shields banging to ward away the bad spirits flooded into the chamber. The heartbeat Gunnar strode in on, the women, including Svana, vanished, leaving her alone with him. He'd shed his cloak and tunic, but had retained his trousers. Ragn curled her fists and looked up at the ceiling, willing her breath to remain even.

'Everything is being properly done,' he remarked as

the clanging and banging increased. 'They are driving the spirits away with gusto.'

'Will Svana be all right? Her cheeks were flushed.'

'Owain's wife promised to make sure she was tucked safely in bed.' His eyes danced. 'Relax. No one expects you to emerge from this chamber tonight, least of all your sister.'

'Svana believes she is some sort of matchmaker. She is over-excited.'

'The dogs know to fetch me if anything happens.'

Unable to stay lying on the bed, waiting, Ragn rose and began straightening the furs, struggling to think up another argument for her leaving this room and failing. After the top fur slithered to the floor for the third time, she stepped away, wiping the sweat from her hands on her under-gown.

'That is good to know.'

Gunnar tilted his head to one side, but remained near the door. 'Has the day exhausted you?'

Ragn quickly shook her head. 'Sleep is the furthest thing from my mind.'

The dimple flashed by Gunnar's mouth. 'Excellent. What I plan on doing does not require *sleep*.'

'You brought a torch,' she said, trying to recover from her accidental innuendo. 'You are obviously not in the mood for sleep either.'

Gunnar lifted a brow and began setting up the *tafl* board. 'Do you play? Eylir and I used to play every evening.'

'Years ago,' Ragn admitted, looking at the board with a deep longing. 'When I was a girl, my father and I would sometimes play. I thought myself quite accomplished. My husband hated the game and I have rarely played since.'

There was little point in detailing the temper tantrum Hamthur had thrown when she'd won six games in a row and how he'd refused to play ever after. He had even gone as far as to throw the board on the fire.

'Let me guess. You took far too much pleasure in beating him.'

'I liked to win in those days,' Ragn admitted in a whisper. She had clapped her hands and demanded the ribbons he'd promised while he stomped about the hall. 'I showed him up in front of his friends. He hated losing.'

She winced at the memory of his fist hitting her back as she attempted to move the board, making her spill the pieces across the floor. He'd been completely contrite afterward and apologetic. And she'd been careful never to play again.

Gunnar tapped his fingers together. 'Come over here and examine the board. It will all come back to you.'

She grabbed a fur from the bed, wrapped it about her shoulders and walked over to where he had placed the board. Her stomach knotted. 'It has been a long time.'

'Shall we try a friendly game?' He placed the King piece in her palm. His thumb deliberately brushed the sensitive inside of her wrist, sending a warm tingle up her arm. 'We have all night.'

'Playing a game is a good idea.'

Her fingers tightened about the piece. She wanted to play again and have the exhilaration of matching her wits against an opponent. She wanted to win or if she lost, she wanted it to be because he played the game better than she did.

'When did you last play?' His eyes became an intense blue.

'I gave up after my marriage.' She eyed the bed and then the piece. Which was more risky? 'Perhaps I am too tired to remember the rules.'

'I blame your childish husband. Your skills will swiftly return.' He pushed the board towards her. 'You be black and go first. I see the longing in your eyes.'

She moved a counter and managed to knock over six other pieces. 'I'm terribly clumsy. Perhaps you should find another opponent.'

She rubbed her wrist where the burn had been the deepest and waited for his reluctant agreement.

Gunnar retrieved the pieces. 'I chose you.'

'Did you? I was foisted on you.'

A tiny smile crossed his lips. 'Pay attention as I will only explain the rules once.'

The new Gunnar seemed far more relaxed, almost playful. He ignored her display of bad temper rather than rising to the bait as he had done before. An unease grew in her—he'd glimpsed her vulnerability. 'I will be a poor opponent.'

He held out the King piece. 'This one goes on first. Take it.'

She gingerly plucked it from his palm. His skin gave off a warmth which she wanted to lean into. The torch flickered and cast strange shadows on the board and on the planes of his face. She wet her suddenly parched lips.

'Now place it on the board. Show me where you want it to go.'

'I know where it goes. I know the rules.'

His fingers curled about hers, gently caressing

them. Heat flared inside her. She withdrew her hand and placed it in her lap, trying not to think about how his touch had felt.

'You need to make sure the piece is straight.'

'I have done that.'

'I think it might be best if I came to your side,' he purred as his gaze fixed on where her under-gown met her chest. She forced her hands to stay still and not hitch the gown upwards. 'Guide you through the first few moves.'

Her mouth tingled as if he had kissed her again. 'You stay right where you are.'

'What are you afraid of?' His voice held a deceptive innocence. 'I gave you my word. You are in control of what happens.'

'Me? I'm not afraid of anything,' she lied and focused on the board.

'Anything?'

'A few things like berserkers in the night or fire raging out of control. Sensible things.' She waved an airy hand. 'Things which make a difference to my survival.'

'When did your husband start beating you? On your wedding night? Or was it later?'

She froze. He knew. She shook her head at her own naivety. 'Svana mentioned that! She had no right to!'

He shrugged. 'Answer the question. Did he hurt you after he lost at *tafl*? Is that why playing terrifies you?'

The *tafl* board swam. She blinked rapidly. 'I... I deserved his anger that day. I took far too much pleasure in winning. I showed him up. I learned to manage him better later.'

'Hush. It is not a question of managing or deserving. No true man lays a finger on his wife in anger. Ever.'

He put his hand over hers. The desire to cling to his hand swamped her. It would be easy to lift her mouth and meet his. She swallowed hard, forced her brain to concentrate on the *tafl* board and withdrew her hand.

'Are we going to play? Or are we going speak about someone who can no longer do anyone any harm?'

He tapped his fingers together. 'We play.'

They played for a little while in silence. Ragn noted with pleasure that her memory of the rules and the moves rapidly returned. She enjoyed quickly capturing some of his pieces. He then countered.

Ragn studied the board. Five moves to win. She put a hand over her mouth, weighing up the risks. The fizzing in her blood leaked out, leaving her empty. There was a studied alertness to the way he watched the board.

She made a deliberate error, leaving her King piece open, rather than making the move she knew would lead to her winning.

He scowled. 'Return that piece to where it was. Take your move again.'

She pretended innocence and batted her lashes. 'Why? It is my move. Allow me to make it.'

'Allow me to win without your assistance. Allow me to prove I am different than that miserable worm.'

She bowed her head. He'd guessed. 'Maybe I want the game over.'

'Only someone who played well would see that opening. I want to play the real you. I want to pit my wits against yours.'

She stared at the board, thinking back over the last few moves. 'Did you test me?'

His crooked smile made her mouth tingle. 'I used my instinct.'

'And when we have finished this game?' She glanced over to the bed which appeared to have grown larger.

'When we finish this game, you go into that bed and sleep.'

'Because I look like an exhausted hag?'

He pushed the hair off her forehead. 'Because joining should be a pleasure and not a chore.'

'It has never been for me,' she whispered.

'Then it will be my duty to ensure it happens, but not tonight, tonight is for playing *tafl*.'

'Shall we start over and play properly this time?'

He gave a soft laugh. 'I thought you'd never ask.'

Chapter Ten

'Ragn! Ragn!' Svana ran up just as Ragn finished dressing after her bath the next morning.

She had deliberately chosen a dark blue gown, the one which made her eyes shine and which swirled softly about her legs. Life always seemed better when she wore it. She hoped Gunnar's eyes would light up when he saw it. A few days of romance before his disappointment in her set in. Trusting him with her body was different from trusting him with her heart.

Ragn stopped combing her hair in the weak sunshine. 'Is there a problem, sweetling?'

Svana gave a happy sigh. 'Gunnar says that Kolka and Kefla can sleep in my chamber tonight. They like sleeping on my bed, so you won't need to sleep there as well, will you?'

'How do you know this about the dogs sleeping on your bed?'

Svana tilted her chin upwards. 'They were on the bed, licking my face this morning. I slept ever so well. No bad dreams. And I thought why not for always?'

Ragn put her hands over her mouth. 'I see.'

'Don't you think it is a wonderful plan?' Svana's eyes turned crafty. 'Gunnar agreed. I asked him first because they are his dogs.'

Ragn frowned. Her little sister was indulging in a spot of matchmaking. 'You asked him first?'

Svana's hand twisted her apron about her hand. 'I peeped in and saw you asleep when I went looking for the *nisser*. You were snuggled up in his bed. It made me happy! Then I saw Gunnar.'

Ragn placed her fingers against her temples and bid the sudden pain in her head to go. The last thing she needed was Svana building dreams of a romance. Gunnar had been true to his word—they had finished the game of *tafl* and then she'd gone to sleep. Her eyes had closed the instant her head hit the pillow. When she woke, she discovered a pile of furs on the floor where he'd obviously slept.

'It is something you should have discussed with me first.'

'I would have done except I saw Gunnar before and you were taking a bath. I didn't want to interrupt you. You are on your honeymoon.' Svana put her hand on her hip. The true Svana, the fearless girl, rather than the one who jumped at shadows had returned.

She should be rejoicing instead of getting cross. Svana's excitement was a joy to behold. She simply wished that it didn't complicate things for her.

'As Gunnar has agreed, how can I say no?'

Svana flung her arms about Ragn's neck and buried her head in Ragn's shoulder. The dogs gave joyous barks and ran around the pair. 'You are the best and prettiest sister ever.'

'Idle flatterer.' Ragn disentangled Svana from her.

Svana was not the true culprit here, Gunnar was. He had manipulated the situation and she knew what game he was playing. Honestly, men just liked a challenge.

'Go on, sweetling, go off and enjoy yourself with your new bed companions before I come up with more chores for you.'

'You wouldn't!'

'Want to tempt me?'

Svana ran off in flurry of barking and laughing. Ragn shook her head. Her sister was returning to the carefree girl she had been before everything had happened. She silently vowed again that she refused to allow anything to change that. But something would have to be done about the sleeping arrangements.

'You think you have ordered everything as you wish.'

Ragn burst into the chamber with her eyes flashing and her gown swirling about her ankles. Gunnar forced his hand to move a *tafl* counter.

'Your bath took longer than I expected. Join me in another match.'

Her mouth worked up and down. Gunnar leant back in chair, putting his hands behind his head. 'I see you encountered Svana. Her excitement about the dogs is contagious.'

She sank down on to the stool opposite him. 'I wanted to speak to you about that.'

He held up one finger. 'First we play another game of *tafl*. I want to see how good you are in the clear light of day.'

'You won last night. That should suffice.'

'You should know once will never be sufficient with me.' He smiled inwardly as her cheeks coloured. 'We have time. My men have informed me that I am supposed to be on my honeymoon and that means spending time with my bride. *Tafl?* Or do you have another suggestion?'

Her longing gaze went to the bed. She wet her lips, turning them the colour of this morning's sunrise. 'No.'

'Then we begin.'

Gunnar waited until their fourth game before he sprang his trap on the *tafl* board. Ragn was a worthy opponent. The violence of his thoughts towards her late husband spurred him on in the match. His dreams last night had been of her and slowly initiating her into the joys of joining, showing her that coupling was pleasurable and not a chore. What it was like to have a real man play her body and bring her to the brink of paradise, rather than a selfish spoilt imbecile like her late husband.

'It seems to me that I have won,' he said after he moved his piece and captured her King piece. 'What shall I claim as my forfeit? Shall I allow you to make suggestions?'

Ragn stared at the board for a long time. Her eyes flashed. He smiled inwardly. Underneath her calm exterior lurked a passionate woman and he wanted to free her.

'You lulled me into believing I'd win several moves ago.' She tapped a finger against the board. 'That was wrong of you. I'd never have played for an unknown forfeit if I had thought...'

'Would you rather I had played badly and allowed you to win?'

She slammed her fist down on the table, causing

the pieces to jump. 'I hate it if people make allowances for me.'

'Then you will concede I won and I have won the right to the forfeit.'

'You won fairly and as long as the forfeit is not too onerous, you may have it,' she said slowly. 'My path to winning appeared clear, but I was wrong.'

'You underestimated me. Always a mistake. I thought you would have learned after last night.'

Her mouth curved upwards. 'A lesson I will remember for the next time.'

He gave a soft laugh. 'That's the sort of fighting talk I like to hear. Perseverance. But it still does not get you out of your forfeit. You are spending the rest of the day with me.'

'It's my forfeit?' Her eyes wandered to the bed. 'Oh.'

'I have no objections to spending it in bed, but you might prefer to go hunting for the Jul log.'

'The Jul log? You want my help?' She wrinkled her nose.

He fought against the urge to draw her into his arms and kiss her until they both tumbled into the bed. Taking it slow was harder than he'd ever considered.

'Today is the perfect day for choosing.'

She ducked her head. 'I want to know the truth. Was it easy to set your trap?'

He rearranged the pieces. 'Eylir was the last person to give me a real match and you are better than he is.'

Her smile made his heart sing. 'Even though my skill is rusty?'

'Why would I lie about something like that?' he asked, frowning. He liked Ragn. He didn't love her.

His heart remained buried with his family. 'We shall have to do it again. I'd hardly want to become rusty.'

Her tongue passed over her lips, turning them a deep rose. 'Shall I get Svana?'

He stood up. His body ached to touch her. If they stayed in the room any longer, he would lose control and take her. 'I am claiming my forfeit. We go into the woods alone.'

The colour went from her face. 'Now?'

'Otherwise you will find an excuse why the forfeit would have to be postponed. A thousand things to do in the hall.'

Ragn regarded his hand suspiciously as if she were a frightened animal. He touched her palm and her fingers curled about his. He let go as his control started to slip. She had no idea how delectable she looked with the faint puzzled expression on her face and the way her damp hair had curled about her temples.

He went over to his trunk and held out one of his fur-lined cloaks. 'Put this on. It will keep out the worst of the chill.'

'I have my own. Let me get it.'

'Light fails to linger at this time of year. Already the shadows are lengthening and I suspect your cloak has been misplaced.'

She struggled to give a severe look, but the corners of her mouth twitched upwards. 'Unfair.'

He laughed. 'I have studied your methods, Ragn.'

'I can give in gracefully.'

'The fastening is tricky. Allow me.' Up close, the network of fading scars about her neck was clearly visible. His heart squeezed. She had suffered enough. She would be safe under his protection.

She ran a hand down the fur before starting to take it off. 'Far too fine for every day. I can get my cloak.'

'You did think I wouldn't own such a thing?' he asked, unable to hide the sudden sting. 'Or that I would be unwilling to share it with my wife?'

'I'm surprised anyone but a *jaarl* of a large holding would own such a thing. My father didn't.' Her cheeks coloured as she belatedly realised the implications of her words. 'I didn't mean to imply that it was beyond you, merely that I didn't know such fine things existed. And I am notoriously hard on clothes. Hamthur... I should stop now. You call yourself blunt. I'm far worse.'

Gunnar tapped his finger against his mouth. 'You are doing it again. Comparing me to your late husband. Give me a chance to prove I am nothing like him. As far as I am aware, we have little in common, except having you as a wife.'

Her lashes fluttered and for the first time she appeared uncertain. 'You are nothing like him.'

'Grant me the luxury of using my own things as I see fit, then. The correct response is—what lovely fur, Gunnar, it will keep me very warm in the woods. Thank you.'

She ducked her head as her cheeks flamed. 'I will try to remember that. Thank you for the advice and the cloak.'

'Shall we go? Without any more excuses? Unless you are afraid to be alone with me because you fear lust for my body overtaking you.'

She rolled her eyes heavenwards. 'You do have a great opinion of your charms.'

'Someone has to.'

'Why does choosing the Jul log require such a fine cloak?' she asked, her stride matching his.

'I've no wish for you to cut short the trip because you start shivering,' he said instead of saying how it made her eyes shine and set off her hair.

She glanced over her shoulder back towards where a chink of light from the hall shone in the weak sunshine. 'Svana does love choosing the Jul log. She has definite opinions and is not easily pleased. Shall I call her? It will save time and a pouting child later.'

'It is always best for children to have limited choices, saves tears at bedtime.'

'And you know this, how?'

'One of my mother's sayings. It strikes me as apt. Svana is over-excited about Jul in exactly the same way Asa was.'

'Your mother was a wise woman. It need not have been a forfeit. I would have gone willingly with you… if you had explained your reasoning.'

He lifted the hood of the cloak, so it covered her hair. 'I'll remember that for the next time.'

'There will be a next time?'

'I have to give you a chance for revenge on the *tafl* board.'

She gave one of her tinkling laughs. 'But we agree the forfeit in advance next time. I've learnt my lesson.'

'I'm always open to *persuasion*.'

She looped a stray strand of hair about her ear. Her hand trembled. 'I can't remember when I last chose the Jul log.'

'Did you and your late husband choose your Jul log together?'

She missed a step. He caught her under the elbow,

steadied her and forced his hand to drop away. 'I can't remember if we ever did. Hamthur found it silly.'

Gunnar picked up a stick and tossed it hard, pretended he was tossing at Hamthur's head. It hit an oak tree with a loud thump. 'Why did you stay married to him?'

'Pride.' She shrugged. 'I thought I loved him. My father and grandmother longed for the match as it was the combining of two estates. Things got better for a while, but then I lost the baby I carried and never became pregnant again.'

'I'm sorry.'

'It was after a feast,' she said in a low voice to the trees. 'He was in a terrible temper and kicked me in the stomach. A little boy was born the next day. Perfect, but born far too soon to survive. He blamed me because I had caused him to lose his temper. I had laughed too loudly at another's jokes. I named him Thoren and buried him next to my father. When, at Hamthur's funeral, Vargr offered me gold for the hall, I refused in part because the thought of leaving Thoren's grave was too great.'

Gunnar's gut twisted. She'd lost a child because of that monster and then had been forced to flee because of another one. Ragn's quiet fortitude astonished him. 'You did nothing wrong.'

'I have such good intentions and they frequently go wrong. I never wanted to lose the baby, despite what Hamthur claimed.' Her voice wobbled on the last word.

'I made a mistake with the fastening.' He kept his voice light and deliberately changed the subject. Making Ragn collapse in tears was not his intention. 'It will be falling off your shoulders before we go five steps. I'd hardly like you to slip and land in a puddle.'

She raised her chin and gave him a watery smile. 'If you must, but I dislike depending on others.'

He forced his touch to be impersonal as he refastened the brooches. He would break through her defences. Maybe not today, but soon. He would unlock the passionate woman he'd seen glimpses of. It wasn't as if he loved her, not in that deep-down, all-consuming way that his father had loved his mother. He admired her courage and determination. She had given too much to other people without asking for anything in return. It was time someone looked after her. 'It wouldn't do for my wife to get cold.'

The woods were silent except for the steady drip of damp from the earlier rain. Ragn shivered slightly and was pleased Gunnar had insisted on her wearing the heavy cloak, despite her protests. She doubted if she had ever worn a cloak this fine.

He also seemed to possess an uncanny ability of forestalling her questions and making her confess things that no one else knew, including how she had lost the baby. And he had still not shied away from her.

She breathed easier and attempted not to notice the curve of his neck or how his waist tapered down to neat hips. She had her attraction under control and she refused to be humiliated again.

Gunnar pointed out yet another possibility for the Jul log and Ragn tried to think about it practically. The log needed to burn for several days. Although some people used the same log the entire time, it was easier to get one gigantic trunk and chop it into pieces, always using a piece of the log to light the next bit. The main thing was that the light never went out during the darkest days, giving a pathway for the Sun Maiden and her rescuer, Thor, to follow out of the belly of the wolf.

'Are these all your choices for the Jul log? Do you think they will last long enough?' Ragn asked, trying to keep her mind on the practical, rather than thinking about how Gunnar kept finding little ways to touch her. A hand to get over a log or an accidental brush of his elbow as they walked along. They meant nothing to him, but the touches made her body tingle with anticipation. The suspicion that he knew precisely what he was doing grew.

His warm hand drew a circle in the middle of her back. 'Do you have a suggestion?'

'Yes,' she said and pointed to a stout fallen tree. 'This one's trunk would serve admirably. Shall we return before darkness truly falls?'

She gave an exaggerated shiver. The woods didn't really bother her at night. It was more the creatures in them.

'All in good time. You have to pay your forfeit first.'

'Which is choosing the Jul log,' she argued back. 'We have done that. My mind is made up.'

'I'm not entirely convinced.'

'We can return here with Svana if you wish, but it will suit our purposes. I should go back. People will be wondering where I am. You will want supper. I know what a grouch you are when you get hungry.'

He stopped in the middle of the darkening woods. 'Getting to know each other without interruptions, Ragn.'

'That hall needs someone to run it.' She kicked a pinecone and sent it skittering away. Get to know each other? Gunnar didn't know what he was asking. She doubted that he'd like her once he'd become used to her company. 'Svana should have someone with her, someone who understands.'

'The dogs will look after her. They will find us if there is a problem. Relax.'

She stared up at the dark pines. 'I am trying, but it is hard.'

'Come over this way,' he said, holding out his hand. 'One last potential Jul log. Mind the rock, it is slippery.'

She stepped towards him and her footing missed. Her arms whirled about in the air and she thought she would fall, but he was there. His arms came out and caught her, dragging her up against his body. She put her hands on his chest. His beard tickled her cheek, sending little pulses of warmth through her. 'Thank you.'

He softly cursed before his mouth descended on hers. His tongue demanded entrance and her mouth parted, allowed him to drink. The heat in her middle roared to glowing fire.

A raven crowed, alerting her to where she was.

She dragged her mouth away and stepped out of the circle of his arms. 'Is this wise?' she asked, a shade too breathlessly. 'We are supposed to be choosing a Jul log.'

'You were in danger of falling.'

She took another step back. 'We have chosen one. There is no need to linger.'

'There is something I require you to see.'

'If we must.' She pulled the fur tighter about her neck. 'The weather appears to be turning worse.'

'Humour me.'

Gunnar led the way to a small clearing. At one end, a pond with reeds stood.

Ragn gestured towards the clearing. 'There are no large trees here. I showed you which one was the best Jul log. You are simply being obstinate.'

A muscle jumped in his jaw. 'Can you look in the pond, please? While the light remains.'

'Is this some sort of soothsaying? After what happened, I don't believe in such things.'

'Tell me what you see.'

She glanced in. Her reflection gazed back at her. Her eyes were too large and her mouth a shade too vulnerable and sunrise-red from the kiss they had shared. The twilight had rendered her skin golden.

'If you'd told me I had a smudge on my cheek, I'd have dealt with it.' She scrubbed her cheek with her hand.

He made a disgusted noise. 'That is all you can see? An invisible speck of dirt?'

'A very ordinary face, one on the plain side with too large a mouth and eyes which are far too big and protrude outwards. A nose which is too long, but good for sniffing burning bread.'

He took her arms and raised her to standing. His face was intent. He touched the side of her face with a gentle finger. The touch sent a pulse rocking through her. 'Who created these walls? Who made you think you were ordinary when you are extraordinary?'

Ragn moistened her lips, trying to soothe their sudden throb. Every fibre of her being desired his mouth moving against hers again and she hated that she wanted it. She made her voice overly bright. 'Which walls? Show me the walls.'

Gunnar lowered his brow. 'Do I repulse you? Is that why you stopped the kiss we shared? Why am I not allowed to say I consider you beautiful? Why can't you see it when the reflection stares back at you?'

She blinked twice. He thought her beautiful. He created this whole ruse to get her out here, thinking if she glimpsed herself, she'd understand. It would be easy to love him, but she'd given her heart far too quickly before. Grabbing hold of her emotions, she forced her lashes to flutter. 'You were the one to say I looked like a wife instead of a concubine.'

'Since when are wives less beautiful than concubines? Since your worm of a late husband decreed it?' he asked in a quieter tone, one which ran like the smoothest silk over her skin.

His hands were like bands against her arms and she knew that all she had to do was to lean forward and her mouth would brush against his. She wanted to sink into his kiss and pretend.

She glanced towards the pond and its flickering image. She wanted to believe that her eyes shone that much, her lips were that red and her skin glowed golden, but she knew it had to be a trick of the light. The light was already beginning to fade and so was her reflection. She sighed as she turned away.

'Ragn, answer me.'

'Let me go, Gunnar. Please.'

He held up his hands. 'We return now.'

She took a step backwards and regained her breath. She concentrated on the darkening trunks of the trees. Twilight was fast falling. Soon it would be too dark to entirely see. She didn't like to think about spending the night out in the open.

'My purpose is to look after the hall. I lost my hair in that fire, my only claim to beauty. My ankles, wrists and back are scarred. What you are enjoying now is the thrill of the chase. False flattery helps no one.'

She was proud of how matter of fact her voice sounded, even though her heart was pounding in her ears. She counted to ten, fully expecting him to storm off.

'Who are you to decree when desire or attraction will fade?' he asked, continuing to stand there, blocking her way. 'My grandfather was entranced by my grandmother from the moment he first set eyes on her until the day he drew his final breath. I won't pretend to love you and I certainly do not ask for something which I am not prepared to give, but I enjoyed kissing you and think you enjoyed it as well. I want you in my bed, but only if you want to be there.'

Ragn's breath stopped. When he spoke like that, her heart wanted to believe him, but she knew where following her heart led. Once she had allowed Hamthur's love words to blind her. But Gunnar had not spoken of love, he had spoken of mutual desire.

She knew she should run back to the hall. He would let her go and that would be the end of it. The end of everything. She lifted her head higher. 'Then we will have no more of this nonsense about my beauty.'

He swore. Loud and long so that it echoed off the trees.

He lowered his mouth to hers and plundered it. The fire which had banked inside her raged out of control and she flung her arms about his neck, holding his mouth to hers. She drank from it. He drank back, calling to something deep and primitive within her, a self she hadn't even known existed.

At length, he lifted his mouth. 'Was that the action of an uninterested man?'

With great effort she loosened her arms, but his had come around her and held her close to him.

'You want me? It isn't just the thrill of the chase?'

He smoothed the hair back from her forehead. 'Why were you willing to trade your body for your sister's safety, if the marriage bed scares you so?'

'Having survived one marriage, I thought I would have no problem surviving another. I learned how to divorce myself from what he was doing to my body.' She kept her chin defiantly tilted upwards. 'I thought whoever was to be my husband wouldn't be too fussy. Darkness hides a multitude of defects. And the probability was that he wouldn't be interested in that side of the marriage.' She lifted one shoulder. 'My calculations were wrong.'

Gunnar put his hands on her shoulders. His face appeared grave. 'You have little idea of what truly passes between a man and a woman. I never ever want you to divorce yourself from what is between us. When we are in bed together, there is only the two of us. No more, no less.'

'I was married for three years. You have never been married.'

'Your words fail to alter my point.'

'I know what my husband did with great frequency during our marriage. I had little pride left.' She forced the words from her throat.

'That was not pleasure. That was pain. The domination of one individual over another.' He placed a kiss at the corner of her mouth which calmed the butterflies in her stomach. 'Pleasure is very different. It is about giving, instead of always taking. Are you willing to try with me?'

Slowly she nodded. 'I lied to save my pride. I desire you.'

Desire. There, she had admitted it. Desire was different from love or caring about him. And she knew in her heart that it went beyond simple desire. She'd seen his gentleness.

The smile which covered his face warmed her like the sun. 'The truth gives me joy.'

It would be easy to care for this man, but he'd admitted that he'd never love her and did not require her love. She'd experienced enough humiliation and rejection at Hamthur's hands to last a lifetime.

She closed her eyes and lifted her face. 'Then what are we going to do about it? Is there any point in fighting it? Shall we get it over and done with?'

'I'm going to demonstrate to you what it can be like between a man and a woman and why you are going to crave this over housekeeping.' He lowered his mouth to hers. This time there was a laziness to his kiss as he nuzzled her neck and his hands roamed over her body, cupping her breasts, teasing the nipples over the cloth until they became hardened points before he slid his hands over her bottom and pulled her close.

'Hmm, I like that,' she admitted, laying her head against his chest.

'Then let me show you something else before we return.' He held out his hand and led the way to small overhanging rock.

He took off his cloak and spread it on the ground. 'I thought we'd watch the sunset.'

'You are joking. Svana will worry.'

'Svana knows you are with me.' He patted a space

beside him. 'Sit unless you are afraid of me, unless you don't believe my word.'

Ragn sat down, drawing her knees up to her chest. Against all reason she did believe him. 'This is not easy for me.'

He leant over. His lips touched her forehead and travelled down the side of her face, making it difficult to think logically. 'Overthinking. We are just going to sit and watch the sun turn the sky flame-coloured. Nothing physical, just two people enjoying...'

'How will we get back in the dark?'

'I know my way.'

They sat in comfortable silence, shoulders touching, but saying nothing. The sun peeked out from the clouds, bathing the woods in a red-gold hue. Ragn drew in her breath. 'Lovely and unexpected.'

'I regret that this hillock is too far from the shore and fresh water or I'd have built the hall here.'

Ragn closed her eyes and made a memory. 'When I am old and grey, I shall think on this.'

Gunnar stood. 'Time to go back.'

A vague sense of disappointment gnawed at Ragn. 'Is that all?'

He reached out and rubbed his thumb across her lips. The thrum reverberated against her core. She moaned softly. 'Did you think I'd take you here? In the cold and damp when there is a perfectly good bed piled high with soft furs?'

Ragn ducked her head. 'I've little experience with this sort of thing.'

'Waiting builds anticipation. We proceed at your pace.' His breath caressed her ear. 'When you are ready, I am willing to join you in our bed. All I lack is an invitation.'

She moistened her lips. It would be easy to fall in love with him except he'd admitted he didn't love her or expect her to love him. She tried one-sided love once and it didn't work. 'And if it takes me a long time?'

His teeth nibbled at her earlobe. 'You will be worth waiting for.'

Chapter Eleven

Ragn kept her gaze carefully away from Gunnar's throughout supper. After returning from the woods without the Jul log, she had gone about her chores and tried to forget the kisses. But her heart kept whispering Hamthur had fundamentally lied, she was attractive. She might not have pleased Hamthur, but that didn't mean she failed to please all men. Gunnar had enjoyed her kisses.

Ragn put her hand on her stomach. Those kisses and his declaration changed everything and nothing. And she was starting to spin dreams yet again and there was no place in her life for dreams. She sighed and pushed her trencher away.

'I will bid you goodnight. The dogs and I have things to see to.' Svana made a curtsy and hurried out of the room.

'Svana has become quite the matchmaker,' Ragn said with a feeble attempt at a laugh in the silence which followed Svana's departure. Gunnar had to have seen through Svana's threadbare excuse. 'Pay no attention to her. She will have something else to occupy her interest soon enough. Perhaps I ought to have her do more weaving.'

Gunnar lifted his tankard of ale to his lips. His eyes twinkled. 'On the contrary, I'm gratified that she considers me worthy of such a stratagem.'

Ragn was aware that her cheeks flamed and hastily lowered her gaze to the remains of the food. 'That is one way of looking at it.' She stood. 'There is much to be done in tidying up. It will take me an age.'

He nodded. 'I can't tempt you with another game of *tafl*? You need your chance for revenge. You have trained the servants well.'

Ragn sank back down. He wanted to play with her properly.

'I thank you for the compliment and accept the challenge of a game, but no forfeits. We play for the joy of playing.'

He gave a hearty laugh. 'For now, I will agree to your request, but you will find I am persistent. We will play for forfeits again when the time is right.'

'When that long-off time comes, I will make sure I know what they are before agreeing to them.' She smiled back at him. 'I learn from my mistakes.'

'Always wise. Shall we begin?' They played several games, with them being evenly tied in games won.

'One more to break the tie?' she asked, hiding a yawn.

'Tomorrow. I'd hardly like you to say I won because you were exhausted.'

'We are going to play tomorrow?'

'Having found a worthy opponent, did you think I'd allow you get away easily? I am afraid you are stuck. We will be playing *tafl*. And it is no good saying you don't enjoy it, I have spent the last two games watching your eyes sparkle as you outmanoeuvred me.'

'I believe that can be arranged.'

She rubbed the back of her neck. This was what she thought her evenings were going to be like before she'd married the first time. Playing *tafl* in amicable competition, discussing the day's events and having friendly arguments. It would be easy to fall for him. Ragn gulped. She already had started down that slippery slope of loving him without even realising it. When was she ever going to learn from her mistakes? He wanted her companionship, not her love.

'I must bid you goodnight,' she said.

His gaze targeted her mouth. She hastily wet her lips.

'I trust you know where you are sleeping.'

'I have the general idea.'

'Good.'

She hurriedly left the room before he offered to accompany her. As he'd promised, her trunk had been moved into his room. Ragn rapidly undressed and climbed in bed. She lay still for what seemed to be an age, tensing her muscles, but he never came.

When she woke the next morning, the only sign he had been in the room was a pile of furs, stacked neatly on the ground.

When she arrived in the kitchen, the porridge was already bubbling and Svana sat with the dogs on either side of her. Ragn skittered to a stop.

'Where is Gunnar?'

'Gone out. He said not to wake you.' Svana's smile widened. 'I assume you had another late night.'

Ragn clenched her fists. There was no mistaking

Svana's matchmaking intent. She knew her sister loved her and wanted the best for her, but it did not stop Ragn wanting to scream that her interference would make the situation worse. Ragn held on to her temper with the slimmest of threads. 'Where has he gone?'

'To bring back the Jul log you chose.' Svana gave an overly dramatic sigh. 'I can't believe you forgot it. Sister. You obviously had something far more important on your mind.'

Ragn inwardly sighed. Making a fuss would only encourage her in this wrong-headed approach.

'I thought it would be pleasant for you to have the final choice. You always liked choosing it,' she said pointedly changing the subject towards one Svana was sure to enjoy.

Svana studied the table rather than meeting her eyes. 'I told Gunnar that I trusted him to choose the right one. Trust is important.'

Ragn tapped a finger against the table. Svana's guilty flush deepened. 'What else did you tell him?'

'Nothing very much.' Svana twisted the tie of her apron about her fingers.

'Enlighten me as I know that look, Svana. Your "nothing very much" is something significant indeed.'

'Just that you are interested in him and that he shouldn't give up hope because you were being stubborn as only you can be. I knew you liked him a lot. I told him you had told me that.' At Ragn's sharp intake of breath, she batted her lashes. 'He thanked me. I gave him hope.'

Ragn wanted to collapse in a heap and have the earth swallow her. Svana had no idea the trouble she had caused. 'Stay here. You have made matters far worse.'

Svana's face instantly fell. 'I was only trying to help. He likes how you look, Ragn. You two should have babies. I want to be an aunt.'

Not allowing herself time to think about the possible implications, Ragn grabbed her cloak and headed out into the morning mist. Everywhere sparkled. The spiders' webs appeared as if they were laced with jewels and her breath made soft plumes of steam.

It was easy to retrace her steps from last evening and discover Gunnar standing in front of a stand of trees. The morning mist made it seem like his hair sparkled with diamonds.

He'd just finished ordering several of his men to move the log she'd favoured when she went into the clearing.

He cocked his head to one side. 'Are you coming to check I chose the right one?'

'I wanted to speak to you.' Ragn hoped he could not see she was trembling. Suddenly coming out here was the worst idea she'd had for a long time.

'You are here. I am here. Speak.'

Ragn gestured towards the men who had stopped moving the log and were regarding her with ill-disguised interest. 'Alone.'

Gunnar nodded at his men, who began to move the log again. They had soon disappeared, but the knowing winks and barely concealed crude gestures unnerved her. They had considered she had come out here to have sex with him.

'I must apologise for my men. They keep telling me I'm on my honeymoon,' he said, breaking the uncomfortable silence which had sprung after the last remark faded on the breeze.

She forced her eyes to widen. 'I know what men can be like.'

'What is wrong, Ragnhild? Who has frightened you?'

Ragn's heart sunk lower. She was back to being Ragnhild. Proof if she required that her gut instinct had been correct.

'Svana told me what she had done. I knew I had to come out at once and make things right.'

Gunnar turned away from her and seemed to examine a pile of dead leaves. 'What has she done? What mischief have she and the dogs been involved in?'

Ragn tightened the cloak about her, aware that her cheeks flamed. This was far harder than she'd first considered, particularly after the remarks his men had made. 'She has tried very inexpertly to play at matchmaking. I want to apologise for her inappropriate remarks and suggestions. She has romantic notions in her head. The idea didn't come from me.'

Gunnar shrugged. 'Your sister is young with stars in her eyes. I made it a point to forget her words.'

Ragn bent her head and concentrated on the forest floor. She should have known Gunnar would react like that. She should have ignored it and gone about her business, but she had grasped at any frayed excuse to see him.

'Because I didn't want you to think…' she said to the ground. 'I overreacted. Forgive my impetuousness.'

'To think what? That you had put her up to it? That I would use it as an excuse to take liberties?' His words were barely a whisper. 'Does it bother you that much?'

'Yes,' she answered softly.

He went over to her and gathered her hands in his, drew her towards him. 'That's disappointing.'

'What is?' She risked a glance upwards and her breath caught in her throat. It would be easy to tumble into his eyes and drown. She tried to think of reasons why she shouldn't, but she only thought that she wanted to.

His fingers tightened about hers and a dimple flashed in his cheek. 'I'd had hopes that you had. I had planned on telling you not to use a go-between in future. Unnecessary waste of time.'

Ragn's mouth went dry and she pulled away. He allowed her hands to slide from his. 'You left before I woke.'

'I assumed you would want to be on your own. I apologise and will remember for the future. You want to see me in your bed in the morning.'

Ragn pressed her lips together, trying to work out the perfect retort. Gunnar in this sort of mood was impossible to deal with. None of her usual remarks were working. He was quite deliberately twisting her words. 'That isn't what I meant.'

'What did you mean?' He crossed his arms, but his eyes flared with hidden lights as if he knew her secret attraction to him. 'You complained that I wasn't there and now you intend to complain if I am.'

She put her hand over her eyes. 'I felt bad about sleeping in for two days in a row.'

'The bed agrees with you. Good.'

'I will have to let you sleep in it tonight.'

'Unless you are there with me, willingly and wholeheartedly, the floor is more than comfortable.'

She heard the laughter in his voice. 'Shall I go back?'

'My men are pleased that I am here with you. They were teasing me, not you.'

Ragn's jaw dropped. The men were teasing Gunnar, not her? 'Why?'

'Because apparently I am like a bear with a sore head and should be with my wife. Owain hopes the gods have listened to his prayers and my temper will be much improved when we next meet. They want to spend more time with their wives this Jul.'

'I'm not sure what to say to that.'

'We're beset by people giving unwarranted advice. However, I'm tempted to put it to good use.'

Ragn stilled. 'You are?'

'Up to you. We can return now and make everyone's life a misery or we can remain out here for a little while and warm the cockles of the hearts of those who believe in romance. We don't have to do anything. Just be out here and enjoying the sunshine on our faces.'

'I dislike doing anything because other people say I should.'

'We're more alike than you might imagine.' His infectious laughter rang out. 'We go back to the hall and watch Svana's little face fall. I doubt Svana will end her quest. That girl's determination is only second to her sister's.'

'A back-handed compliment.' She pleated her apron between her fingers. 'Chores need to be done.'

'Before you go, ask yourself—why did you come out to tell me something I already knew? Why are you scared to take a leap of faith when you travelled across an ocean to be here?'

He was giving her an out, she realised with a pang. And Svana's antics had amused him, rather than repulsing him. He wasn't the least bit like Hamthur. She ought to trust him.

Before she gave way to her nerves, she raised herself up on her toes and brushed his lips with hers. His lips were soft and warm. But he didn't draw her into his arms the way he had done before, he stood there watching her with burning eyes. 'I have made up my mind. Perhaps we should give them what they desire.'

He clutched her hand like a drowning man might clutch a spar. She curled her fingers about his and welcomed the warm pulse of desire which fizzed through her.

'It will put an end to their machinations,' she said into the sudden stillness. And once it was done, her gathering dreams of undying love would cease and she'd be able to concentrate on the practical tasks of brewing ale, weaving cloth and making porridge. The longer she delayed, the more her heart dared to dream.

'Other people have no business in your decision.' He lifted her hand to his mouth. His tongue drew a tiny circle on her palm, making it difficult for her to think beyond the sensation. 'Either you are here because you want to be, or you should go.'

'I will stay. I want to be here with you.'

He stood there, looking at her as if she was made of precious glass and might shatter before his eyes. 'Yesterday, you were ready to run like you were the Sun Maiden about to be swallowed by the great wolf.'

'Yesterday in your arms, you made me feel beautiful.'

He started to speak. She laid two fingers across his mouth. 'Hear me out.'

He lifted a brow, but remained silent.

She undid the cloak, laid it on the ground. When she turned back he was watching her with intense eyes. 'I want this. Waiting will make me more nervous, not less. I don't need a bed piled high with furs and expectations. I need you. You asked for an invitation and you have one for here.'

His mouth fell open for several breaths. 'My men should be back at the hall by now, but I will remain here with you.'

'Then I think it is about time we said good morning properly.'

He took her hand and pushed up the sleeve of her gown, drawing small circles with his tongue on her skin and sending little licks of fire coursing through her. His hands worked on fastenings, loosening the gown so he could lift it over her head.

The cool breeze nipped at her bare flesh, causing her to shiver, but he eased her down on to the cloak and the soft fur embraced her. He placed small kisses against her neck and moved until his mouth reached the small mounds of her breast. He took each nipple in turn into his mouth, teased them until they became hardened points. Her body writhed under him, bucking and twisting, seeking to get close to the source of the fire which now consumed her. She reached up with her arms and tugged at his shoulders. He lay down on top of her and their lips locked while their tongues played a game. The tell-tale evidence of his desire pressed against her thigh. A deep dark heat unlike anything she'd experienced before pulsed through her.

She slipped her hands under his tunic. His flesh was warm and sinewy. Indentation from long-ago injuries criss-crossed his body, proof if she needed it of the life he'd endured. She moved her fingers upwards and played with his nipples as he had played with hers. They hardened immediately against her palms.

'Am I doing it right?' she whispered. 'Does this feel good?'

He groaned in the back of his throat and then buried his head in the nape of her neck as his fingers moved lower, exploring towards the apex of her thighs. His palm skimmed her nest of curls, hovered above and his fingers quested deeper into her folds.

Her body surged upwards when they touched her sensitive core, lingering and playing. Round and round his fingers moved until one slipped inside her, making her back arch.

Wave after wave of hot pleasure washed over her. Nothing had prepared her for this. The world slowly righted itself and she was dimly aware of him watching her with an intent expression.

'Was that good?'

She smiled up at him, cupping his face with her palm. 'Beyond imagining. Is there more?'

He captured her hand and moved it to the bulge in the front of his trousers. 'You see how much I want you,' he breathed in her ear. 'Here. Now. In the daylight, not the dark.'

She undid the fastenings of his trousers and his erection sprang free. Hard, hot and silken to the touch. Ready for her. She ran her hand down the length of him.

He groaned. 'Please. Please, Ragn.'

She nodded, knowing that he needed her as much as she wanted him.

She opened her legs, teased his tip with her groin, circling her hips. He rose upwards and she met him, driving him deep within her. Her body was wet and eager for him, expanding to fit his length inside her. She shuddered and collapsed on to his chest and his arm held her. They lay together and then he slowly began to move until the wave she'd been riding crested higher and the clearing rang out with intermingled cries.

Gunnar slowly came down to earth. Ragn had surpassed his very erotic dreams. His joking quip vanished from his lips when he saw her face. He reached out and wiped the single tear from her cheek.

He'd been wrong to take her in the forest. It had been too soon. He offered up prayers to Freyr and all the other gods that he would get a second chance to give this woman pleasure and make her smile. 'What is wrong, Ragn?'

'I never knew it could be so good. You have made me happy.' She wiped away a few more tears as her smile broadened, like the sun peeking out from behind the clouds. 'Will it always be this good?'

'I intend to try.' He kissed away the last tear. 'Do you understand the difference now?'

Her soft laugh ran down his spine. She raised herself on an elbow. 'You might have to show me again tonight, in our bed.'

'My thoughts exactly.'

He pulled her to standing. Her beauty made his breath catch, but he swallowed the words. 'We should get back. In case Svana decides to send out a search party.'

She gave one of her crooked smiles. 'That would never do. She will be smug enough.'

He reached over and kissed her on the nose. His growing feelings for her scared him half to death. He had not been able to protect his family before. How could he hope to protect Ragn?

He screwed up his eyes. Ragn was right—it was what you did after you knew you were cursed which mattered. In his case, he had kept his heart buried. The curse had no power over her as he didn't love her and would never love her. He had learned from his mistakes. This time he would be worthy of those who depended on him.

'We need to return,' he said, instead of explaining. 'I can't abandon my men for the rest of the day.'

Her teeth worried her bottom lip. 'I see.'

Unable to resist, he dropped a kiss on her forehead. 'I doubt you do. My plans are in disarray. I shall be longing for the evening. Do you think we might be able to skip the *tafl* match and go straight to the forfeit?'

Her smile lit up his world. 'Pardon me for altering them, but the forfeit will be far more pleasant after I have won.'

Chapter Twelve

'Ragn! Ragn!' Svana called out, running up to where Ragn was putting the finishing touches on the wheel which they would light on the solstice tomorrow night and send down into the lake. Afterwards they would have mugs of Jul ale. Ragn had already had several tastes and thought it one of her best efforts.

She had made sure the hall had been cleaned top to bottom. Constructing the wheel was her final chore before they would have a few days of rest as the days were far too short to do anything practical. She wanted things to be perfect for the first Jul she would spend with Gunnar. It would set the tone for Juls to come. Ragn hated that her heart was unable to stop spinning dreams, but she also wanted desperately for those dreams to come true.

In the days and nights since they had come back from the woods, Gunnar had found excuses to be with her and Ragn had discovered that the memory of Hamthur's words and violence had subsided under Gunnar's patient tutelage.

On one memorable occasion, Gunnar had shared

the bathing hut with her. However, Ragn still did not feel comfortable with initiating anything, even casual touches. She knew Gunnar was not in love with her, but she kept finding reasons to care about him.

She should be content with what she had, instead of longing for something he couldn't give. And yet, she sometimes wondered—what if she told him how she felt?

Svana had continued to get better and Ragn found despite everything that she wanted to believe. Every time she thought it, she redoubled her efforts to make the hall a better place, to prove herself worthy.

'Ragn, pay attention!' Svana shouted.

'Is there a problem? Have the dogs eaten the *nisser*'s porridge again? I have kept a few berries back for the Jul porridge so your wish can be granted,' she said with a laugh. 'But it would be helpful if you confided what it was.'

Despite her explanations, Svana seemed more convinced than ever that the *nisser* existed and would grant her wish. However, she refused to say why she persisted in that particular belief and Ragn found it easier to go along with it rather than criticise. Her belief in this creature made Svana work harder and not grumble about the chores.

'Two men are here, seeking food.' Svana paused. Her teeth worried her bottom lip. 'I think.'

Ragn wiped her hands on a cloth and tried to ignore the sudden tightening of her stomach. Travellers here? At this time of year? It sounded wrong. Most people would be home with their families. 'Did they come from the sea?'

'No, from the land.' Svana put a hand on the nearest

wolfhound. 'Kolka and Kefla didn't like them, so we came back here before they spotted us.'

'Where were you?'

'Up on the ridge. Don't be angry with me. I know I shouldn't go far from the house, but I wanted to watch the deer.'

Ragn put a hand on her stomach. It was good that Svana had decided to test her boundaries, rather than hugging the house like a shadow. 'You had the dogs with you, didn't you?'

'They are my best friends. We go everywhere together as Gunnar is too busy with his lands and you to look after them properly. He told me this. Ask him.'

'Then it was fine. And they are coming this way and want food?' Ragn drew a steadying breath and tried not to panic. She had to wait for real danger, instead of jumping at shadows.

Svana gave a slow nod. Her shoulders twitched. 'Northmen. Two warriors, but dressed like travellers. Shall I fetch Gunnar?'

'Gunnar has taken the boat out fishing with his men. Last trip before Jul properly starts. He wants to make sure we have enough salmon.'

Ragn focused on the nearly finished wheel and how the kitchen needed tidying, little things so she avoided thinking about the much larger problem—how had Vargr found them so quickly? She had considered that they were safe until the spring. She pushed away the thought and concentrated on the fire. She had no idea if they had come from Vargr. Why would they? She'd been careful.

'I'd feel better if Gunnar were here,' Svana said in a small voice.

Ragn reached over and squeezed her sister's hand. 'Me, too, but we shall have to greet them on our own. It would hardly do to be inhospitable at this time of the year. How would the *nisser* react if we were less than hospitable? We want him to stay.'

She waited for Svana's answering smile, but the girl's face grew graver. 'Will it be like before? Like when the men came? Vargr pretended he wanted to protect us. That ship would have returned to Kaupang by now.'

Ragn cursed under her breath. Even if someone from the crew which brought them here had reported back to Vargr, she doubted that he would have sent anyone this quickly. 'We are on Jura now. Gunnar has a strong sword arm and a good reputation.'

Svana lifted her chin. 'Besides, we have the *nisser*. He won't allow bad things to happen to this land, or where would he get his properly made porridge?'

'If you wish…but there are other reasons like the wolfhounds. Remember how they scared you at first with their teeth.'

Svana laughed and threw her arms about Kolka's neck. Kolka gave Svana's face a lick. 'They are my friends now even if they do eat the porridge!'

Ragn heaved a sigh of relief. Only a few short weeks ago, Svana would have been cringing in a ball rather than even looking at the dogs. Now she ran with them, vaulted over them and slept with them on her bed.

Some day maybe she, too, could stop worrying about strangers. It was that little thing called security, something she hadn't appreciated until it was lost for ever.

Ragn carefully put a poker in the embers of the

kitchen fire before filling two horns with ale. One lesson she had learned was it was better to think ahead than wish she had. Ultimately all she had to do was to play for time and wait for Gunnar and his men to return. They were Gunnar's problem, not hers.

'Are you going to give me one to carry?' Svana asked.

Ragn shook her head. 'You keep with the dogs. Out of sight, but close at hand unless I call you.'

'Is it because I spilt the ale the last time? I want to be with you, Ragn.'

'Keep close, but stay in the shadows, Svana, you and the dogs. If anything should happen, anything at all which makes you uncomfortable, you go outside and wait for Gunnar to return. Promise.'

Svana smoothed the pleats in her apron. 'I wish Gunnar were here.'

Ragn forced a smile. 'He will get here in time. In the meantime, keep to the shadows and you will be safe.'

Her words seem to mollify Svana and Ragn hoped that they would be true.

Ragn went out, carrying the horns. Two ill-favoured men loitered near the entrance way, obviously working up the courage to knock on the door or perhaps checking out where people were and what the defences were.

Ragn tried to think where she had seen the one with a half-shaved head and ponytail disappearing down his back before, but she couldn't be sure. Until she was sure, she waited, watched and was pleased to have the two wolfhounds lurking in the shadows.

She was pleased to see that Svana had turned up her hood and stood beside the dogs in the shadows, rather than being anxious to greet the men.

And so it begins.

Ragn held out the horns and made a ritual gesture.

'A Good Jul to you both,' she called out. 'Are you lost or travelling somewhere in particular? We seldom have visitors here, but you are all the more welcome for it, provided you come in peace.'

The pair exchanged shifty glances. Ragn's heart hammered. She tried to tell herself that she was over-reacting and seeing shadows where there were none.

'We are passing through on our way to another place,' Ponytail said. His eyes seemed to alight everywhere but on her face.

'We are a long way for anywhere. It is unusual to see strangers, particularly strangers arriving by land and at this time of year.' She waited for him to deny it.

'Have you been here long?' Ponytail asked, taking the horn from her without the usual pleasantries.

Ragn held on to her temper. Bad manners indicated nothing. 'Long enough.'

'And is this your daughter? A pretty little thing she is.' Ponytail hunkered down and reached out a paw. 'Are you going to come out into the daylight, Sweetheart? Let me have a good look at you. It has been a while since I've seen silver hair like yours.'

Ragn gestured to Svana to stay still. There was no way Ponytail glimpsed Svana's hair. He must have seen it before. Or worse, he was looking for a girl with silver hair, inward-turning eyes and a slight limp.

Her mind raced. She had to hope that these men were stupid in their arrogance and assumed that she was an idiotic woman. She had to work with what she had, rather than waiting to be rescued.

'She is shy.' Ragn forced her voice to sound eager.

'My husband will return soon. He will want to hear the latest news. He misses such things living all the way out here. You must stay and raise a tankard of Jul ale.'

'Gone fishing?' the other man asked as Ponytail scowled at him. 'I hear the salmon are running well.'

The hair on the back of her neck prickled. The pair had obviously been watching the house. They knew Gunnar was not here, that he and his men had gone out in a boat. Silently she prayed he'd unexpectedly return. If they had watched the hall, they also probably realised there were no other warriors in the hall and that she had sent the servants home early to start their Jul preparations in earnest.

'He will be back sooner rather than later. The days grow short as we get close to Jul.' She gave a light laugh. 'I'm sure he will be interested to hear all the gossip from Viken.'

A muscle jumped in Ponytail's cheek. 'There isn't much to say. Life remains much as it was.'

'That is good to know.' Ragn took a step backwards. Running wasn't an option, not in this skirt. She would have to use her wits and trust Gunnar would arrive before these men acted. Whatever they were up to, it did not bode well for anyone else. 'You must rest a while before continuing onwards.'

The pair exchanged evil looks and she knew that they considered her a naïve fool. 'It is very hospitable of you. We don't want to trouble you.'

'The gods take it amiss if one is inhospitable at Jul. I would hardly wish to anger the gods.' Ragn made sure she batted her eyelashes as if she was a woman with no brain.

All she had to do was to contain the men until Gunnar arrived. It would be far easier to keep them in the kitchen, rather than in the hall.

If they intended harm, she hoped that Gunnar's words about his wolfhounds that first night proved accurate.

She whispered one more prayer and turned towards the men. 'The hot food is in here and the rain has begun again. Of course, it is up to you if you come in or not, but the stew is bubbling away on the hearth.'

The men took the bait and went in, swaggering as they did so. Svana gave a small gasp and pointed towards Ponytail's cloak.

Ragn narrowed her eyes. The silver brooch fastening Ponytail's cloak looked very similar to the device her brother-in-law's followers had used when they had attacked.

She made a little gesture toward Svana, indicating that she should keep to the shadows. Svana's eyes were big, but she did not seem to be in any danger of a fit as she solemnly nodded.

Ragn silently prayed to any god who might be listening that she would be able to solve this problem without endangering Svana. And that Gunnar would arrive back. She hated that she wanted him here, that she wanted to believe he'd solve this problem for her.

She shut the door behind them and quietly motioned for Kefla to lie across the doorway. Svana stayed next to Kolka in the shadows.

'The winter weather can be changeable on Jura. Best to be inside,' she said, walking purposefully over to the hearth. 'Travellers such as yourself must be hungry.'

The pair glanced at each other and shrugged. The muscles in her neck relaxed slightly. They considered her an idiot.

'All right,' Ponytail said. 'It would be a shame not to taste it and see if it lives up to expectations.'

She made a show of dishing out the stew and passing the bowls over. All the while, sweat dripped down her back.

The pair wolfed the meal down, barely saying a word. Her fingers itched to grab the poker, but she fought against the impulse. Wait and watch. Hope for Gunnar and his men to show.

Wiping his mouth, Ponytail made a whispered comment which made his partner chuckle.

'I'm sorry. I didn't quite catch that.' Ragn reached for the poker and placed another in the fire to heat.

Ponytail smiled. 'I merely said that Vargr Simmison sends his regards to his sister-in-law. He wants to know all is as it should be. He worries about you. Wherever you go, he will find you.'

'Does he send his regards indeed?' Ragan said, forcing her voice to stay even as her knuckles shone white against the black of the poker. Worried about her? Worried that she remained alive, more likely. She'd been wrong. Her past was not behind her yet. 'I shall have to send them back to him with interest. Tell him I am no threat to him, as long as he leaves us in peace. I have no plans to return to the north. Go now and tell him.'

'And how do you think a little woman like yourself will force us to go?' Ponytail placed his hands on the table and started to rise.

'Kefla, Kolka,' she said.

Kefla gave a low growl which Kolka echoed. The entire chamber was filled with an otherworldly sound. The colour drained the men's faces as they froze. Kefla came up behind them and sniffed, dripping spittle from her fangs on to Ponytail's boot. The men flinched.

'I would suggest, gentlemen, you remain seated with your hands on the table until my husband arrives home. He can decide what to do with you as you have abused our hospitality.'

'And if we don't?' Ponytail asked as his friend glanced back at the circling dogs.

Ragn poked the reddened tip of the poker so it skimmed the man's cheek. He flinched from the heat. 'You choose which way to die is preferable—dog ripping out your throat or by red-hot poker through your eye. Do I make myself clear?'

Gunnar knew something was wrong the instant he set foot on shore. Everything was far too quiet. No dogs milling about or Svana throwing rocks into the sea. Or, importantly, Ragn standing on the shoreline with her hand shading her eyes as the breeze pushed her gown against her legs.

He had half-anticipated that Ragn would have come down to the shore as she done in the past few days, unobtrusively taking the fish off him and organising the servants as she chatted about her day. He knew he should not look forward to it, but he'd come to do so. He'd started saving up small stories about his day in order to see her smile. He swallowed his disappointment and heaved the final basket of fish ashore. To-night, he'd tell her the truth. It had come to him when they were at sea, he was starting to care for her, more than he had for any person.

He spotted Svana curled up in a ball just above the high-tide line. He crossed the sand in three steps. At his approach, she stood up. Her lips were blue as if she had been outside in the rain for a long while. He looked in vain for his dogs and then he started to worry. Ragn was far too over-protective to allow Svana out like that. Something was wrong and he should have been there, instead of out on the sea, telling tales and catching fish. His curse had returned with a vengeance.

'Where is Ragn?'

Svan opened one eye. 'Inside. There are two men with her. I need to stay out here and wait for you.'

Gunnar frowned. Ragn had sent Svana outside, on a day like this? Ragn assumed that it was safer in the cold air than inside with…? His breath stopped.

'And the dogs?' At his shout, Svan flinched. He swallowed hard and began again. 'Shouldn't they be with you? I thought we had made a bargain about you looking after them when I am away.'

'Ragn needed them. After she had the bad men seated with their hands on the table, she shouted for me to bind their wrists as I am very good with knots. Then she sent me outside again. I was to keep a watch out for you. Have I done well?' Svana ran her hands down her arms. 'It is awfully cold. I forgot to take a thick cloak and didn't dare go back. Ragn wouldn't have liked that.'

Svana's words washed over him. Bad men. Ragn was inside and in danger. He shuddered to think what he might find inside. His heart hammered. They were supposed to be safe here. He had not thought anyone would come at this time of year. He wanted to shake Ragn for not immediately hiding, for not taking greater care. Her easy assurance that she was immune from the curse mocked him. Rather than being vanquished as Ragn

claimed, it remained. He loved her and he had called
the curse down. He hated that he had put her in danger.

He regarded the closed door to the kitchen. He
dreaded to think what was behind that. He only prayed
that Ragn was safe. That the curse had not had time
to work.

'Are you angry, Gunnar?' Svana asked when he
didn't respond. 'Did I do it wrong?'

'You've been very brave, sweetling. I want you to
go to your chamber and change out of those wet things.
Quickly now.'

She gave him a cheery smile. 'When everything is
well, will you send the dogs for me? They are bound to
be wondering where I am.'

'Of course. They like being with you.'

Svana ran off towards the hall and safety. Gunnar
sent two of his men after her.

Gunnar reached for his sword and motioned to his
other men to follow him.

When he opened the door, his heart leaped. Ragn
was indeed there with both dogs flanking her and a
poker in her hand while another rested in the embers.
Two men sat at the table with their wrists bound. Gunnar struggled not to let his jaw drop. Ragn was the most
capable of women.

'Ah, Gunnar,' she said with deceptive sweetness as
she made a small curtsy. 'Do shut the door. We have an
interesting situation here. I need your advice on how
to resolve it.'

Gunnar glanced between Ragn and the terrified-
looking men. It was the complete opposite to what he
had expected. 'My advice?'

'These men happened to visit while you were out.'

Ragn banged the poker on the table for emphasis, making the men flinch away. 'They bring greetings from my brother-in-law. I thought you would be interested to hear the greetings before deciding how best to respond to them. As you can well imagine, I am in a quandary about the entire situation. It goes beyond my experience.'

Gunnar quietly assessed the scene while his heart pounded. Ragn appeared calm enough, but her hand gripped the poker with white knuckles. Most importantly she appeared uninjured from the ordeal. He wanted to tear the men limb from limb for frightening her. But instead he contented himself with flexing his hands. From her pointed look, Ragn obviously had some scheme in mind.

'Vargr, your brother-in-law, sent greetings to you?' he asked, keeping his voice light. 'How did he discover your whereabouts so quickly?'

'Someone must have divulged them. Or he discovered my grandmother's brooches which I sold for Svana's passage and made enquiries.' Ragn's mouth twisted. 'It matters little. They intend to follow me anywhere in the world I happen to go, bringing my brother-in-law's particular form of greeting.'

Ragn tapped the poker in the fire and gave a shrug. Her voice was steady, but the whiteness about her mouth showed her terror at the prospect.

'Do they indeed?' A deep-seated primitive anger washed over him.

'I believe that sentiment goes beyond the realms of acceptable behaviour by a guest.' The steadiness of her voice amazed him. Ragn was truly calm when most women would have been huddled in a corner, weeping their eyes out. 'Kolka and Kefla agreed with me and wanted to rip their throats out. However, it is possible we are being overly hasty. They may still have some sort of use. You decide, seeing how you are the lord here and I am merely the wife.'

Gunnar gave thanks to the gods that Ragn had reacted so decisively. Her quick thinking had saved both her and her sister. 'I'm grateful to you, your quick thinking and your sense of decorum.'

'Your wife is confused. We meant no harm,' the one with the ponytail said with a sickly smile, the sort which made Gunnar wish to punch his face in. 'I look forward to the opportunity to straighten this out. We are strangers here, merely seeking hospitality. Can you call off the dogs?'

'I do dislike blood being spilled in the kitchen. It gives a certain unsavoury aspect to the place.' Ragn's voice remained steady, but he noticed the increasingly pinched look about her mouth. 'These men have been trying to convince me that I am wrong, but I know anyone coming this far and at this time of year in my brother-in-law's name wishes me harm.'

'The lady has no idea what she is on about. There has been a simple misunderstanding.' Ponytail made a face. 'You know what women can be like. They must have their little fancies to give a semblance of truth.'

Gunnar struggled to keep his hands down at his sides rather than fastening his hands about the man's throat.

'You see. That sort of remark always gets me annoyed,' Ragn said, tapping the poker against the table. 'People torturing the truth and considering they will be believed because they are men.'

'Trust me, gentlemen, you do not want to see my wife when she is annoyed. And to put your minds to rest, Ragnhild is one of the cleverest people I know.'

The smile Ragn gave him warmed his heart, but he knew he did not deserve it. He had tempted fate by falling in love with her, even though he knew how his curse worked.

'He is as crazy as she is!'

The violence of his feelings towards the men shocked him. Normally when he was in battle, he retained detached and cool. From Dagmar Kolbeinndottar's experience with her stepmother sending assassins, he knew the assassins would keep coming until the source of the trouble was destroyed. To destroy Vargr, he was going to need Kolbeinn's support.

'Possibly crazier,' he said. 'I have always found Ragnhild to be the model of decorum and hospitality.'

Ragn returned his smile. 'That is very sweet of you, Gunnar. It does my heart good to hear your sentiments.'

'Shall I take over?'

'I would appreciate it.'

He struggled to think of any woman he knew other than perhaps Dagmar who would be as calm as Ragn. And Dagmar had been a shield maiden whereas he doubted that Ragn knew one end of a sword from the other. He swallowed hard. She would have to learn how to defend herself properly. He could not have her that vulnerable again, not now that he knew the curse still retained its power.

'Do you come from her brother-in-law?' he said, putting his sword near Ponytail's neck.

The man stared back sullenly. 'My business is not with you. Keep your long nose out.'

'You invade my home, abuse my wife's intelligence and expect me not to react?'

Ponytailed smirked.

'The one with the ponytail has my brother-in-law's device concealed inside his cloak,' Ragn said in a quiet but firm voice. 'I spied it as he sat down at the table. The design is seared on my memory. Svana independently confirmed it. You may check if you doubt my words. He is trying to provoke. My brother-in-law will claim you attacked first and will demand blood money if this piece of filth is harmed.'

'Would he?'

'I have seen him ruin men before.'

'Excellent you stayed your hand as I have seen that particular played before as well.'

This time her smile was less strained. 'Thank you.'

He stroked his beard. 'There again, they have abused our hospitality and threatened me. The law would be on my side if I removed their heads from their shoulders for attacking my wife.' He glanced at the two men. 'Do you have anything useful to say before I remove your heads from your bodies? Or shall I simply send you back in a barrel?'

'Vargr the Fleet-Footed did send us,' the other one said before he gave a sudden yelp as he was kicked under the table. 'He worries about his sister-in-law and fears men might use her. Since her husband died, she has been prone to strange fantasies.'

'Use her? To do what? Claim her rightful lands, lands which he has already claimed because she is supposed to be dead?'

'She swore vengeance for her husband's death. She might lead some innocent warrior to his doom.'

He nodded towards Ragn and struggled to control his temper. 'My wife considered those lands lost, but I suspect she was mistaken if her brother-in-law feels the need to send men such as you on a journey across the icy seas.'

He motioned to his men who quickly secured the men's hands behind their backs. Gunnar relieved them of their swords, three concealed daggers and a vial of something which appeared to be poison. He threw the poison on the fire where it hissed and let out a noxious fume.

As much as he hated staying his hand, everything had to be done properly. He silently vowed that he would end this threat to Ragn and her sister once and for all time. Ragn had been right. It was how he reacted to the curse which was important.

'You came with peaceful intent?' he asked in a low voice. 'How? Where is your ship?'

'Somewhere safe!' Ponytail dug his elbow into the other's side as if to say that they would soon have the upper hand.

Gunnar nodded to his men who forced the miscreants to standing. The pair obviously considered him some sort of simple-minded idiot. 'I have little time for such games or assassins who carry poison.'

'There is an explanation!' Ponytail shouted. 'You have no idea of the sort of mad creatures you are harbouring! Vargr believes the witch woman's prophecy. That witch can see the future.'

'Ragnhild and her sister have done something to Vargr?'

'Not yet, but they intend to! That woman will stop at nothing to get her lands back!'

Gunnar ground his teeth. One had to admire the man's pure brazen cheek in the face of certain doom. 'Vargr's intentions speak loudly enough without your intervention.'

He gestured to his men who began to drag them from the room.

'You are making a big mistake,' the man shouted 'Do you know what bounty has been placed on their heads? Vargr is not a man to give up lightly. You are only putting yourself in danger. You will lose everything.'

'One of us will.'

Gunnar turned towards the now white-faced Ragn. Admiration for her surged in his breast, but he hated that this had happened to her.

'The pair will have to go to Colbhasa to face justice. Let them become Kolbeinn's problem,' he said when they were alone in the kitchen.

Ragn remained a statue. He went over, pried the poker from her fingers and threw it beside the hearth. It landed with a great clatter.

'Your part has ended.'

'Thank the gods,' she whispered. 'It is over. Svana is safe.'

'You are also safe.' He put his arms about her, stroked her head until her trembling stopped and silently vowed he'd stop the curse. 'You did well. I know very few people who would have had the courage to do what you did.'

She laid her head against his chest. 'I was frightened, but luckily they were stupidly arrogant and didn't notice the dogs until it was too late.'

'You took a grave risk,' he said against her hair. He wanted to shake her and kiss her senseless for being so brave. The depth of his feeling disturbed him. If any-thing had happened to her, he didn't know what he'd do. He hated that his love for her had brought this on. The timing of their arrival was far too close to his de-cision to tell her that he loved her.

'I had the dogs. I knew you were coming back. Time was on my side, particularly after Svana tied their wrists.'

'Was it indeed?'

'Yes, it was. You were always going to return and you have a strong sword arm. Thankfully, those two were far from the brightest and were easily intimidated.' She stepped back from the circle of his arms.

'You were lucky…this time.'

She began to pace the floor. 'I took considerable pains to make Vargr believe we were dead. My sister's life is more important than any handful of dirt.'

He resisted the temptation to pull her back in his arms. 'Kolbeinn will have to hear of this. We go there tomorrow with our prisoners.'

'We—you mean, Svana and I, as well as you?' Ragn asked as if she didn't quite believe it.

He gave a small smile. There was little point in tell-ing her that he didn't dare leave them now. There was every chance her brother-in-law had sent more than one team of assassins. 'Kolbeinn needs to meet you both, particularly as he sent Maurr. We are simply going slightly earlier than planned.'

She glanced over her shoulder. 'Will the hall be safe without you being here?'

As if he'd leave her here after what had just hap-pened! He wanted to keep her in his sight. Trust her to be more concerned about physical things than spend-ing time with him. He knew their relationship was not built on love or mutual admiration, but on the purely practical. 'My men will look after it until we return. We know the danger now and will not be caught unguarded again.'

'And then…after you take these men to Kolbeinn, what happens?'

'I go north once Kolbeinn gives me leave to go.' He willed her to understand. 'Vargr attacked people under my protection. He needs to pay a price.'

'I cannot have other people threatened because of me.' She hugged her arms about her middle. 'When is it going to end?'

He drew her back into his arms, kissed her lips and wondered that he had ever considered her weak. Ragn might be slender, but she was made of steel. Most women would have collapsed in a heap. His feelings for her frightened him half to death. It had only been by the gods' intervention that she remained alive, that he hadn't had to return to another scene of carnage. He was never going to be good enough for her. He was never going to be able to protect her from his all-too-real curse. 'Don't you trust me to look after my own?'

'I want to be there. You need me there if you are going to confront Vargr. I know what he is like and how he behaves. If you want to have a chance of stopping this, I have to be there.' She reached up and stroked his cheek. 'You will let me do that, won't you?'

He half-turned his face into her palm and stopped. Her words and intonation echoed Dyrfinna's right before she betrayed him.

An insidious thought crept about his brain. Ragn was not the sort to give up easily. Had she always anticipated that these men would come? Had she used him as a way of exacting her vengeance on Vargr as Vargr's man had claimed? Why would a woman as accomplished as Ragn be content to be married a warrior like him? She was a woman who always had a plan and she had used him, just as Dyrfinna had tried to use him for her own ends. He truly was a gullible fool. A deep-seated anger filled him, but he struggled to contain it. His heart screamed he should give Ragn a chance to explain.

'I thought you wanted to keep Svana safe,' he said, giving her a look that would have sent most men scurrying for cover.

Ragn's gaze slid away from his. 'She can travel with us, staying with Trana when we go to court. If your journey is to be a success, you will need proof that you speak for me. I am that proof.'

'You have thought a lot about this scheme.'

'My mind turned it over while I waited for your return. It helped to keep me sane. It helped to keep my mind focused.' Ragn smoothed her gown and there was a faint tilt of triumph in her look.

Gunnar clenched his fists. The answer was far too perfect and quick. She had thought long and hard about this scheme. She had planned for this day. The enormity of her betrayal hit him in the gut. 'We will see what Kolbeinn says.'

Her eyes flared. 'That is a sop. You expect him to agree with your assessment. If you want Vargr to stop, you will need my help.'

'It is the best I can offer you. I won't go against my commander.' He struggled to hold on to his temper. 'Why didn't you remain in Viken? Why didn't you find a warrior in Viken to help you?'

She ducked her head and didn't meet his eyes. 'What

warrior would have helped me over the chance to curry favour with Vargr?'

'Or did you think once you had married that you would be able to cajole or coerce your husband into challenging your brother-in-law? Regaining your husband's lands?'

'I love you,' she whispered. 'I didn't intend to and it is the last thing you require, but I do. And on that love, I swear, I did not want this. I did not want revenge.'

The words were like a knife in his stomach. Love? She only spoke of love when he asked her about her schemes to regain her lands. Did she think he was that ignorant that he couldn't see how she was trying to twist him about her little finger? He was not the sort of person women like her loved. He forced his lungs to fill with air. To think he'd been willing to give his love to her freely and all she cared about was regaining her land. His heart protested he was wrong, but he refused to listen.

'You needn't worry. I was going to do my duty even without your added sweetening. Love is the one thing I do not require from you. Ever.'

The words burst from him.

She winced as though he had slapped her. Before he explained, she straightened her back and her face became carved from stone. 'I see. I won't offer my heart again. My sister and I are naturally grateful for your protection.'

The finality in her voice made something in his chest ache, far worse than it had done when he'd discovered his mother and sisters. He pushed it away. She might have used him, but he could give her her heart's desire—her lands. Then they would be done. She'd be out of his life and he could return to his solitude and never have to face the consequences of giving his heart again.

He concentrated on her betrayal. If he could hate her, then the curse he bore would have no power over her. The pain in his chest grew greater. 'As my wife, you will always have my protection.'

Chapter Thirteen

Gunnar's words about her falsely declaring her love to get him to back her quest for revenge rang in Ragn's ears as the boat rocked in the waves, heading inexorably towards Colbhasa. She hadn't said those words for that reason. She'd said she loved him because she meant it and had wanted to say it out loud just once. But he didn't want her love and he most certainly did not return it.

Same old Ragn, same old stupid beliefs in love conquering the hardest of hearts. Her heart protested that Gunnar still wanted to protect her, but she knew the truth—he'd never love her in return, not how she wanted to be loved.

She forced her gaze to keep on the dark grey waves, rather than searching his face for any softening. This mess was not her fault. No one in their right mind could have guessed that Vargr would send assassins over the sea in winter. She had been convinced he considered her dead.

Svana had been right about the brooches. She should never have sold them, but then how would they have escaped? She'd made the mistake long before Gunnar had encountered them. Their marriage was over before it had really begun—how could she stay when he despised her for wrecking the peace of Jura?

With each slap of a wave against the boat's hull, a small piece of her heart whispered she was wrong.

The journey to Colbhasa had taken the better part of the next morning as the winter sea was filled with white-capped waves and a harsh rain had started to fall.

Ragn leant over and pulled the shawl tighter about Svana. Droplets shone on her lashes and the end of her nose, but Svana managed a wan smile. 'You are getting to be a good sailor.'

'The sea isn't as rough with Gunnar being the pilot.'

Ragn's heart squeezed. Svana was always brave and it was clear she hero-worshipped Gunnar. And because of her thoughtless words, she was going to ruin her sister's life again. 'Yes, I trust Gunnar to get us there.'

The two prisoners lay in the bottom of the boat, shackled, while Ragn and Svana sat near the steering board with Gunnar. Gunnar had left most of his men guarding the hall in case of a repeat attack.

The boat was serviceable for travelling on the sea roads in the Westerns Isles, but there was no way it would be equipped to make the long journey northwards.

When Gunnar manoeuvred the boat into the mouth of the harbour, Ragn rubbed her eyes. The sheer number of longboats had to be equal to the longboats which were stationed in the harbours around Kaupang in the winter. She had not appreciated the amount of resources King Harald expended in the west.

'Where is your longboat?' she asked. 'Is one of these yours?'

'I sold my ship when I acquired my land and retired from active campaigning.' He pointed towards a ship with an intricate red dragon on the prow. 'That one used to be mine. You can see where I rammed Thorsten, the leader of the Northmen, from the Black Bay's lead ship the summer before last if you look at the bow just above the water line.' His eyes gleamed. 'That was a battle and a half. I swore five times I thought I'd be in Valhalla before the night fell.'

'Were you victorious?'

He gave a barking laugh. 'I'm here next to you and the other boat lies at the bottom of the sea. The battle helped to convince Kolbeinn that I deserved land.'

Several men ran up to help pull the boat to shore, calling out to Gunnar and preventing him from continuing the story. Ragn noticed with a frown that they did not offer any refreshment. However, Kolbeinn's compound resembled a small city rather than a simple homestead and the rules of hospitality were different.

'Who is this woman?' one of Kolbeinn's guards asked as she was helped ashore.

'This woman is my wife, Ragnhild,' Gunnar called. 'I expect you to honour her as such. And don't tell me that Maurr the Forkbeard kept that morsel of gossip to himself!'

'Your wife?' The man rubbed the back of his neck. 'For once Maurr spoke true. I had wondered if he was telling one of his far-fetched tales when he babbled on about the mead, the wondrous hospitality and above all the kindness of your woman. But this woman does not appear to be your sort at all.'

The entire quayside went quiet. Ragn wanted to hide her face in shame, but Gunnar put his arm about her shoulders and drew her close. 'That is because I never had a wife before. Would any deny her suitability to my face? Her beauty?'

Ragn stared straight ahead. She wanted to hate him on the voyage over, then he did something like that and her heart sighed. In her head she knew he was saying this because the men's words had irked him and that it had nothing to do with his feelings towards her, but her heart refused to listen.

The men on the quayside glanced at each other and awkwardly shuffled their feet.

'I only meant to say that she appeared far too fine for the likes of you. Maurr said that she could read runes and her cooking is God-inspired.'

'We thought it a joke when Maurr proclaimed it,' another finally admitted. 'We never expected you would marry and not to a beauty such as this one either. I understand she keeps an excellent table. Should she come to her senses, I will happily vie for her hand.'

The others echoed the remarks while Gunnar glowered. Ragn shook her head. Hamthur's insidious whispering fell silent in her mind. Gunnar had defended her. With Gunnar's arm about her, she felt beautiful and accomplished.

'What is mine, I keep. Be aware of that and treat my wife with respect.'

Ragn's heart twisted. His touch was impersonal. It was about him gaining respect. It had nothing to do with feelings for her. She carefully wrapped the tattered bits of pride about her heart and kept her back straight as they walked to the large meeting hall where Kolbeinn was keeping court.

The hall was splendid, equal to anything she had seen in Viken—rich tapestries lined the walls and Kolbeinn sat like a king on a raised dais. Everything about him screamed power and prestige, a man who owed his allegiance to the King. Would he be willing to go against Vargr, one of the King's closet advisors, and jeopardise all this luxury?

Gunnar led the two prisoners towards where Kolbeinn sat. As he approached, the hum of voices in the hall fell silent. A finely dressed young woman with a Celt by her side stood at Kolbeinn's right and to his left stood an older plump woman. Kolbeinn's blond hair was shot with silver, but he retained an air of command.

Gunnar's step faltered slightly as he noticed the couple, but then his expression of grim resolution returned. Ragn motioned to Svana to stay at the back of the hall with the dogs. Svana gave a tremulous nod and followed Ragn's request.

'Who is the younger couple?' she asked in an undertone to Gunnar once she had reached his side.

'Dagmar Kolbeinndottar and her husband,' Gunnar said in a low voice. 'I had not expected them to be here. They must have arrived early for Jul and then will return to Ile in time for the Christmas celebrations. Dagmar converted to the new religion when she married her husband. She once was my commander and a very able one as well.'

Ragn stared at the woman. While she knew women warriors existed, most never commanded. Dagmar did not appear to be the sort of woman anyone dismissed lightly.

'Will it help our cause she is here?'

'Kolbeinn remains the one in charge. He will make the decision, not his daughter.'

A stab of envy went through her when she saw the woman's husband bend towards his wife to whisper something and how she put a hand on his forearm. The private look in public proclaimed that they were in tune with each other. For a heartbeat she wished just once Gunnar would look at her with half that much love in his eyes.

She shook her head. Gunnar did not require her love. She'd offered it and he'd thrown it back in her face. He thought she'd used him.

'Gunnar Olafson, you have arrived before you were expected and bearing gifts.' Kolbeinn nodded towards the gagged prisoners. 'Is something amiss?'

Gunnar rapidly explained the situation, giving vague details about exactly how Ragn came to be his wife.

'These men made an unprovoked attack on your wife?'

'And my wife's sister. Their brother-in-law lays claim to their inheritance and wishes them ill. What I want to know is did you give permission for these men to attack me and my family in your territory?'

Kolbeinn tapped his fingers together. 'Who do they serve?'

'Vargr Simmison, one of the King's advisors.' Gunnar removed the ponytailed-man's gag. 'You may ask them if you like. They still have tongues in their foul mouths. I value my gold too much to wish to pay any blood money for these pieces of filth.'

'Is what he says true? Did you go to his lands with the intention of harming his family?'

Ponytail bowed and made an ingratiating smile. 'I serve Vargr the Fleet-Footed who is a great friend of the King's and sits at his right hand after his speed saved the King's life in battle. Their wives are close. I must protest about this action which is not worthy of any who calls himself a Viken and owes his allegiance to the King. Perhaps Ragnhild Thorendottar would care to explain her actions.'

He preened a little after saying his words. Ragn curled her hands into fists and wished she'd done away with him when he'd first arrived. It would have made things much simpler.

She cleared her throat to begin her defence.

'I would not even give Jaarl Vargr Simmison the time of day! Snivelling little coward!' Kolbeinn thundered, turning purple before she uttered a sound. 'Let alone give him the right to attack the hall of one of my men. His father helped himself to my lands in Viken. Vargr helped to ensure I was cheated!'

All colour drained from Ponytail's face. 'I had no idea.'

'Once a man behaves like that, he is ever likely to behave that way again, particularly against a widow as Ragnhild was.' Gunnar spoke softly, but his voice carried to all parts of the hall. A murmur of agreement rippled around the hall.

Ragn pulled Svana closer. For the first time since the pair of assassins had appeared, she allowed herself to hope Gunnar would succeed without losing his life or his lands.

She wanted to silence the bubble of hope, but it rose in her breast. Kolbeinn would have to send men to Harald. They would be safe as Vargr would not want to anger the Jaarls of the Western Isles. The dispute would be settled amicably. She bowed her head and prayed to any god who might be listening.

'What say you, Far?' Dagmar asked in the silence.

'I remember the grave insult. I fully believe him capable of attempting to usurp lands.' Kolbeinn stroked his goatee beard. 'You did well, Gunnar, bringing these men here. I have long wished for a day of reckoning.'

Ponytail scuffed a foot on the ground. 'I wasn't there. That's all ancient history. I was only obeying orders.'

'Pity you were so diligent,' Gunnar said. 'Most men would have found a reason to postpone such a mission until after Jul, but you went straight away. You hungered for it.'

'The King will hear of this.' Ponytail stamped his foot. 'I demand compensation for the manhandling of the King's messengers.'

'What message did you bring from the King?'

Ponytail pressed his lips together. 'This man had no respect for my person. That is all I am saying.'

The hall erupted in a cacophony of rude laughter, oaths and mutterings. Ragn hugged her waist. Against all her expectations, they were siding with her and Gunnar. She sobered. But what would happen when Vargr sent the next assassins and the next ones?

'Why did you not kill these men, Gunnar?' Dagmar asked in a firm voice which carried to all parts of the hall. 'The provocation was great. And you would have stopped his tongue.'

'I can find a way to stop your tongue.' Ponytail gave a leer. 'You should allow your betters to speak, girlie.'

The former woman warrior lifted a brow and the hall

became hushed. Somewhere in the back of the hall, a sword fell to the ground with a great clatter.

Dagmar waited for the shocked murmurs to subside before she gave a pointed cough. 'Forgive me, Far, for my forwardness, but Gunnar Olafson used to be pledged to my service. I feel compelled to ask questions before leaping to conclusions. May I question him?'

Kolbeinn inclined his head. 'Answer my daughter, Gunnar. Why have you behaved in this fashion? Why have you brought these men here instead of killing them? You can afford the blood money.'

Gunnar made a bow. 'Because such men are more useful alive than dead. In my lady's service, I learned it is better I confront the heart of the snake rather than one of its fangs.'

'Vargr the Fleet-Footed has grown more powerful in recent months. That much is true. I have heard rumours of this from others,' Dagmar said, drawing her brows together. 'He may feel that will save him from any dispute, particularly from one of Harald's far-flung territories.'

'Are you saying we should ignore the insult, my lady, because the man giving the insult is too powerful?' Gunnar asked. 'I can't and won't do that.'

'He has been no friend to my father over the years. We should tread carefully and make sure the damage can be contained.'

'Vargr sent men into Lord Ketil's and your father's territory without asking permission. That gives us the right to strike back,' Gunnar said, slamming his fists together. 'He should have sought permission from the overlord of these islands. From your reaction, Kolbeinn, I take it that he disrespected you in the past and you overlooked it. Who is to say what else he will do in the future? How else will he disrespect you and Lord Ketil?'

Kolbeinn made a grunt, but Ragn noticed a gleam in his eye. He approved more of Gunnar's words than his daughter's cautious ones. She whispered thanks to the gods.

The woman nodded. 'There are ways to do things. Acting like thieves in the night goes against our law. Gunnar has done the right thing, Far, bringing these men in front of you rather than murdering them. He owes no compensation to them.'

The entire hall murmured its approval of her words.

'What should I do with them?' Kolbeinn thundered.

'Think of them as a Jul present.' Gunnar bowed. 'From a loyal member of your *felag*. I wish to renew my oath to you this evening and then ask leave to travel northwards and right the insult done to you and this *felag*.'

The entire hall gave a cheer as Kolbeinn beamed.

'We will talk after you make your oath, Gunnar Olafson,' Kolbeinn said. 'Meanwhile, leave these men with me. Disrespect of my authority will certainly not be tolerated.'

'That went better than expected,' Gunnar said as he led the way to the small hut he maintained on Colbhasa. His neck and shoulders were lighter. It was easier to concentrate on the things which needed to be accomplished to get Ragn's lands back rather than to keep finding reasons to hate her. He wanted to hate her. He knew he should hate her for what she'd done, but he couldn't, he cared about her too much.

A dank musty smell pervaded the hut as it had not

been used since the early summer. He immediately opened the small window and lit a fire in the hearth. Svana curled up on a straw pallet next to the dogs and went to sleep while Ragn sank down on a bench.

'The smell will improve soon,' he said. 'The walls are solid. It will keep the rain off our heads for tonight.'

'Do you think Kolbeinn will allow you to go?' she asked, rather than commenting on the condition of the hut. 'Or will he simply ignore the request, deciding on reflection Vargr is too powerful a man to risk alienating him?'

Her voice lacked the sparkle that he was used to. He narrowed his gaze—her eyes were red and her skin blotchy as if she'd spent time crying. His heart lurched. He wanted to draw her into his arms and tell her that all would be well, but the lie refused to come.

'You never know with Kolbeinn,' Gunnar replied truthfully. 'If he wishes to settle scores with Vargr, he will send me northwards. However, he might not give me enough men to accomplish the task.'

'And if not?'

'He will send us to Lord Ketil, but I will find a way.'

She wrapped her arms about her waist. 'Why? Why would you do that for me?'

'Because I swore an oath to protect my land, land I have given my blood for. Vargr will continue to send men until he has what he wants. I refuse to let him win. Do I need another reason? Did I ever need another reason to do what is right?'

She flinched like he had struck her. 'I see. I misunderstood the situation. I would like to join you wherever this journey takes you.'

His heart leapt. She wanted to come. He ruthlessly

stamped it down. She and Svana would be better here where he'd arrange for their protection.

'How well do you fight?'

'I left that to others.' She fluttered her lashes. 'But I would have used that poker.'

'If you can't fight with a sword, what use are you?' he ground out.

'Vargr Simmison is my brother-in-law. My fight. I will play my part. I'm asking to come, but I will find a way to stow away if you attempt to leave me behind.' The fierceness of her expression warred with the sweetness of her face. 'Please, Gunnar. I beg you. I may be of some small use.'

He shook his head. 'You have little idea what you are asking.'

'He has taken everything from me. I will not allow him to take everything from you, too.' She held out her hands. 'I've earned that right, Gunnar. Teach me how to defend myself.'

He picked up a wooden stick and handed it to her rather than drawing her into his arms. Keeping her with him would ensure he'd keep her safe. 'If you are coming with me, you need to know how to defend yourself. Luck was on your side on Jura.'

'I don't believe in luck. I believe in hard work. I will show you that I am worthy of a place on your *felag*.'

Her eyes sparkled for the first time since he'd discovered her standing with the poker. The anguish in his chest eased. He'd missed that sparkle so much that it physically hurt. Sensibly he should tell her to stay and trust his sword arm, but she'd become as necessary to him as breathing.

'Your training begins now.' He handed her the stick.

'You will be ready for whatever happens, Ragnhild. But remember, I am the leader of the *felag*. You obey me. You don't try to manipulate or use me again.'

'I understand. Do you think it will come down to violence?'

Rather than answering her, he lifted his stick. 'Every day until we know Vargr is dead, you will train with me. We start with sticks and then we move to proper swords.'

A loud knock drowned out her reply. 'Enter!'

Dagmar stood in the doorway with a determined expression on her face.

'My father's wife counsels him to send you to Ketil and let him deal with it,' Dagmar said without waiting for the usual pleasantries. 'But Lord Ketil will try to sweep everything under the rushes. He has his own reasons for wishing to appease a man like Vargr Simmison.'

'That would be a mistake,' Ragn retorted and then dropped a curtsy. 'Forgive me, Vargr will continue to disrespect these lands if he is not stopped. It will be the start of a feud.'

'A feud is what Sif wishes to avoid,' Dagmar said. 'I have come to tell you this because you were in my *felag*, Gunnar. You were loyal to me once.'

'Vargr is a bully and the only way to deal with bullies is stand up to them,' Ragn retorted before Gunnar had a chance to speak. 'Your father might consider Vargr a minor annoyance or irritant, but ambition consumes my brother-in-law. Soon he will have to act. It is far better if your father acts before the threat becomes too great. Others waited and lost their lives.'

Dagmar's eyes danced. 'I see you married a woman

unafraid to speak her mind, excellent. About time. Eylir chose well. Even if I expect it took you some time to see it.'

Gunnar stared open-mouthed at his former warlord. He should have guessed that Dagmar would have had a hand in this mess. 'You knew!'

'I made it my business to know,' the woman answered with a tiny smile. 'It was far past time you were married and settled down. What is the point of having lands if you do not have heirs to inherit?'

'Did you give Eylir the benefit of your wisdom as well?'

'I may have said something before he left. He asked if I considered it a good idea.' A faint smile played on Dagmar's lips. 'Can I help it, Gunnar, if I do still feel some responsibility for your worthless hide?'

Gunnar shook his head at her presumption. He would have been cross if Dagmar's actions had not helped to bring Ragn into his life. 'What was Maurr's mission about? Had he gone to take my lands?'

Her robust laugh rang out. 'My father didn't expect you to be married. He anticipated a different outcome.'

'Me losing my lands?'

Dagmar sobered. 'After your display of talent last Jul, who would bet against you? He wanted a fight with the King or rather his advisors, but did not want to be the one to start it.' She waved her hand. 'My father is very predictable. He wanted to show the King that the decrees like that one will not cause peace and what better way than to irritate one of the King's former comrades. I told him not to do it, but my father has his own mind.'

'Your father has the fight he longed for. Vargr is one

of the King's chief advisors.' Ragn clapped her hands together. 'Kolbeinn must give us permission to take the petition to the King.'

'A woman after my own heart. Your luck continues to astonish me, Gunnar.'

Gunnar put his arm about Ragn and drew her against his chest. 'My wife wishes to go with me.'

'I have the right,' Ragn said with a quiet firmness, leaning her head against him.

'They were the focus of the plot, that much is clear.' Dagmar tapped her finger against her mouth. 'Maurr has just returned. His wife died in complications of childbirth five days ago and the baby did not last much longer. He and his men might be persuaded to volunteer.'

Gunnar clenched his fists. 'Maurr—is that the best I can hope for?'

'The man has just lost his family, Gunnar,' Ragn said, putting a hand on his arm. 'He has a boat and we can't afford to be picky. If Kolbeinn is presented with a firm plan, he will be more likely to agree.'

Dagmar gave a husky laugh. 'Remind me not to play *tafl* against your wife. Ragnhild thinks far too many moves ahead.'

'But Maurr! Isn't there anyone else?'

'It depends on what is more important to you—achieving security for your family or your pride.'

Dagmar's brows lowered. Gunnar's heart sunk. He'd offended her.

Ragn asked after Dagmar's children before he explained. To Gunnar's surprise, Dagmar seemed genuinely pleased to be asked and launched into a long explanation about the perils of children cutting their teeth. Their conversation continued for a little while before Dagmar left without answering his question.

'Why did you do that?' he said as Ragn closed the door.

Ragn counted slowly before she answered. When she had her temper under control, she turned to face him.

'Do you intend on huffing and making enemies of all those who would assist us? Is your pride really that important? Maurr has reasons to go across the seas. Let him escape his demons and help us.'

'I will keep my lands safe, Ragn, from all who would harm them. Maurr would have taken those lands. I must consider him an enemy.'

From all who would harm them. The words echoed in her brain. If she had never accepted Eylir's offer, Gunnar and his men would be safe. She would never have known him, never have experienced happiness in his arms. And she knew she could not wish that. She held out her hands. 'I endangered your lands.'

He slowly shook his head. 'You are not my enemy, but we live with the consequences.'

'Changing the past is beyond me,' she whispered. 'I want to make it right as soon as possible. If Maurr's boat is the only option, then I say we take it. If we get there before Jul ends, we can petition the King. It is the custom for the King to listen to petitions in the last week of Jul.'

The cold air encircled Gunnar the instant he stepped out of the door and did nothing to improve his mood. Maurr was the last man he wanted to be beholden to, but Ragn appeared determined to undermine his authority.

As if his thoughts were able to conjure him, Maurr

stepped out of the mists. Harsh new lines were etched on his face. 'Gunnar, I heard of your trouble.'

'I'm sorry for your loss. Losing your family in that fashion makes your heart sore.'

The man started. 'You never knew her.'

'Nevertheless.' Gunnar thumped his chest. 'I once lost my family and the only thing which stopped me from going mad was to find the next fight.'

'The whispers are you plan something suicidal.'

'Word travels fast, but then I suspect I know the source of the rumours.'

'Kolbeinn has a very intelligent daughter.'

'She was one of the most able commanders I ever served under.'

'You need to get there before Jul is out, before your adversary can make another move.'

Gunnar stared at the man. 'Why would you of all people help me?'

'When I stayed at your hall, I saw how you adored your wife. It made me wish I had had that.'

Gunnar pressed a hand to his temple. Maurr had been jealous of his relationship with Ragn? Gunnar had spied something that he'd been too afraid to admit. Even then, he had had feelings for Ragn.

'Ragnhild is a special woman,' he said carefully.

'Less than a half-day after I left you I knew I had to return to Ljot, despite Kolbeinn's orders to visit every one of the newly gifted lands and discover if the warriors were married.' He slammed his fists together. 'We had precious time together before she died. And I owe your wife for that.'

'I see.'

'If you say no, because I am cursed, I will understand. Or otherwise, I say we men of Jura stick together and vanquish those who would harm our lands.'

Gunnar started in surprise. Maurr considered himself cursed.

'I welcome cursed men. They have little left to lose.' He leant closer. 'But as one cursed man to another, it is what you do after you are cursed that determines the course of your life. It took me many years to learn that.'

Maurr gave a half-smile. 'Your lady taught you that.'

'How did you guess?'

'She is a good woman, Ragnhild. I will help you for her sake.'

'Maurr will sail northwards?' Ragn stared in disbelief at Gunnar when he returned to the hut. She had fixed the fire and their living quarters were now comfortable if a little cramped. Svana had fallen asleep in front of the fire again, after making her wish on the *nisser*'s porridge. 'What did you offer him?'

'It was your earlier hospitality that did it. Because of it, he had time with his wife before she died.' A small smile touched his mouth. 'That and it's the first fight he can get his teeth into after his future dreams vanished.'

'But what about Kolbeinn and sending the prisoners to Ketil?' Ragn asked, turning it over in her mind. She'd expected Gunnar to return and announce that he'd tried, but Kolbeinn had refused.

'Maurr offering his ship makes all the difference. Kolbeinn could not order men out on the seas at this time of year. But Ketil and Kolbeinn have wanted an excuse to move against the *jaarls* who hover around Harald like bees about a honeypot. Harald may be tightening his control in the north, but Ketil is determined to keep our traditional freedoms.' He put his hands behind his head. 'There will be an ending to it. You are not going to suffer any more.'

Ragn swallowed hard. 'You are going into battle. How will I not worry?'

'I wanted permission and I have it.' Gunnar's eyes gleamed in the firelight. 'This is not me on my own and subject to blood-money claims. This is me standing against injustice.'

Ragn nodded, beginning to appreciate Kolbeinn's political manoeuvrings. 'A risky strategy.'

'For Kolbeinn, no. For me, yes, but I would have gone without permission. No one threatens one of my own.'

One of his. Her heart lightened. There might be hope for them, even if he had refused her love. 'When do you go?'

'We leave tomorrow. Maurr has promised that his boat will be ready in time. He has no wish to stay here for the Jul celebrations.'

'That soon?' Ragn asked, drawing her knees to her chest. 'It will be dark for most of the journey and the seas stormy. Svana nearly died on the last crossing.'

Gunnar expelled a long breath. 'Svana stays here. Kolbeinn's orders. There is no other way. I am sorry, Ragnhild.'

'Because Maurr considers her unlucky?' she asked around the lump in her throat.

Gunnar shook his head. 'Because Kolbeinn wants a hostage, a surety that I will return. We agreed that Svana is the best person in the circumstances as you threatened to stow away.'

Ragn regarded Svana's sleeping form. How could she abandon her sister? She leant forward to retrieve the covering Svana had kicked off. Svana's lips were softly parted. 'My sister has suffered enough.'

'I spoke to Dagmar and to Kolbeinn's wife. Both are willing to host Svana. She will be treated as a member of the family, rather than as a prisoner.'

'They are?' Ragn paused in her straightening of Svana's covering. 'How much did you tell them?'

'You sound surprised. Both Sif and Dagmar are good people.'

Ragn rocked back on her heels. 'I have seen how others turn away from her because of her eyes and you know she has fits. Not as many as she did, but there are times when she has a faraway look in her eyes.'

'They are fools and idiots—something that neither Sif nor Dagmar can be accused of. The dogs will stay with Svana as well. Neither Kolka nor Kefla is a good traveller. Why I ever let you talk me into bringing the dogs, I've no idea.'

Ragn gave a half-smile. He might grumble, but the dogs were the best protection for Svana. 'I'd like to see anyone get past those two and they do seem to be good for her. She'd be distraught if they were separated.'

He put a heavy hand on her shoulder. 'Then it is agreed. You go with me and leave Svana where she is safe.'

She covered his hand with hers. She wanted to ask him to hold her tight and whisper words of desire that she might pretend were affection, but he pulled his hand out of her grasp.

'I understand,' she whispered. 'But you have done far more than expected. You won't regret it.'

He gave a grunt. 'Be ready for the morning tide.'

Chapter Fourteen

A winter solstice hush hung over Kaupang, the principle town of Viken. Here and there Gunnar saw chunks of light in the buildings. He had to admit that Maurr was an excellent sailor and a fine captain. The winds had been kind and they had arrived during the dark days when the sun never rose. The Sun Maiden was truly in the belly of the wolf, waiting for her rescue, so the King would be in his newly built shining hall with his courtiers.

A thick blanket of snow lay on the ground, piled against the various wooden buildings which comprised the market town, but the harbour itself remained remarkably clear of ice.

Gunnar asked at the quayside and quickly discovered Eylir's whereabouts. He had not decamped to one of his family's estates, but had remained in Kaupang, apparently in the employ of another family. Trana's father, Ragn explained in an undertone when she heard the name.

Gunnar frowned. His friend should have little need to be a sell-sword.

Gunnar pounded on the door, calling out for Eylir.

'Gunnar Olafson, as I live and breathe!' Eylir exclaimed, opening the door. 'What brings you here? I thought you safely cocooned in your new hall.'

'After what you sent me, do you think I'd remain on Jura?'

Eylir took a step back into the house. 'Didn't you like your Jul present? Is that why you are here? To complain? May Loki take your hide.'

Gunnar kept his face still. Eylir knew what he had done and why. But this time, it was his turn to tease. 'I brought her with me.'

Eylir's face drained of colour and glanced over his shoulder. He lowered his voice. 'You are returning her to the north? How could you, Gunnar? You of all men. Did you see the scars she bears?'

'Do you presume to know what my taste in women is?'

'You were always far too particular. Do you know the danger she is in by being here? Or have you done your usual and acted before you considered others?'

Gunnar put his hand on the door frame, preventing Eylir from closing it. 'We discuss this inside. You will help me if you value your life.'

'This is not my dwelling.'

'We are coming in.'

'Are we staying here or going somewhere else?' Maurr muscled forward. He made a disgusted noise at the back of his throat. 'Eylir, you owe me money from that bet last Jul. I wondered where you disappeared off to. If Eylir is the great warrior you have been going on about, Gunnar, we need to have a serious discussion. The man starts punch-ups in empty rooms.'

Eylir tugged at his collar. 'You brought Maurr with you as well. How...lovely.'

Gunnar ushered Ragn in. By the fire stood a buxom blonde, the sort he had once favoured, but who now appeared pale and insignificant beside Ragn.

Her eyes lit with genuine pleasure when she spied Ragn. She ran forward and grabbed Ragn's hands. Ragn kissed her on both cheeks. 'Trana, why are you here? Why are you not with your family on your estates?'

'Long story. I'll explain later. You were supposed to stay away.' Trana's pretty face puckered with concern. 'You promised. Vargr is closer than ever to the King, but I don't think he knows you survived. We agreed— if things alter, I'd send word.'

'Things have altered. He sent assassins.' Ragn rapidly explained about what had happened.

Trana swayed and Eylir rushed to support her. She shrugged off his hand. 'How...how did he discover where you had gone? We told no one. I didn't even go down to the quayside to wish you good fortune.'

'I sold my grandmother's brooches to the captain.' Ragn examined her hands. 'I thought I'd been clever, but obviously not. He must have returned and tried to sell them.'

'There are other explanations,' Gunnar said into the silence that followed her words.

'The important thing is that he found us. Now Gunnar and I are here to deal with the threat.'

Trana nodded. 'Vargr came to see me with mock tears in his eyes. He has taken over Hamthur's estate, including that part which belonged to you because there were no survivors of the tragic fire. I clenched my fists, but kept quiet. Eylir knows how difficult that was for me.'

Eylir cleared his throat. 'Vargr has made it known that you and your sister were killed and that he intends to hunt down the evil murderers who did this terrible thing.'

'Words are cheap,' Gunnar said. 'Is there some reason why he needs both women dead?'

Eylir shrugged. 'With both women dead, he inherits one of the most prosperous estates in all of Viken. And he is a very greedy man.'

'That was in the past,' Ragn said. 'His men set fire to the estate and murdered my retainers. We lost. I learned that night what was truly valuable. It isn't land, but my sister. I wanted to start a new life away from my past.'

'You shall, once we have dealt with your old one,' Gunnar declared. He squeezed her shoulder as if he finally believed her words. The hollow feeling in her chest increased.

Ragn put a hand over his and stepped away from him. 'But first, we need something to eat and drink, somewhere to get warm. Vargr will not make a move tonight, even if he has spies watching the harbour. He will be too busy feasting with the King.'

'My wife makes sense. We need a place to rest and plan.'

Everyone murmured their agreement and Trana offered the house as somewhere for them to stay.

'Vargr suspected you helped us to escape?' Ragn asked in an undertone as she helped to prepare the bread, hard cheese and ale. 'Oh, Trana, tell me that he didn't do anything to you.'

Trana hacked off another hunk of bread. 'Eylir was more than capable of defending my honour.'

'Svana thinks he is sweet on you.'

Trana's cheeks coloured prettily before she turned her attention to the ale. 'I have no idea what his true feelings are. He is hiding something, Ragn. I need a man who trusts me with everything. Now, tell me about your warrior. Did you force him to return?'

'I wanted to disappear. I genuinely thought Vargr would believe my ruse, but he quickly discovered my whereabouts. Gunnar was not about to allow the insult to pass.

Trana gave a huge smile. 'Gunnar likes you and is a far better person than Hamthur ever was.'

'How do you know?'

Trana gave a small smile. 'I made Eylir tell me everything about him.'

Ragn rapidly explained what had passed between them and how Gunnar's heart was buried with his family. And how she'd offered him her love only for him to reject it. Trana listened with a grave face.

'Where is Svana?' Trana asked. 'Before I give any advice, I want to know what she thinks. Does she approve of Gunnar?'

'She has stayed in Colbhasa. Kolbeinn wanted to ensure we would return. His daughter guards her.'

Trana lowered her voice. 'Do you trust them? I've heard things about Kolbeinn.'

Ragn gave a nod. 'She has Gunnar's wolfhounds with her. She is well protected and away from Vargr. Gunnar does this because we are part of his family.'

Trana smoothed a tendril from Ragn's forehead. 'Sweetling, there is always another way. Gunnar could've sent word and Eylir could have acted for you. He has proved most useful to my father.'

'Gunnar fights his own battles and I believe he will need me to help him, even if he doesn't see it.'

Trana put her hands to her mouth. 'You can be a very stubborn woman, Ragn, and Gunnar is a lucky man to have you.'

Eylir gave a knowing smile when he had manoeuvred Gunnar out of the house on the pretext of getting more wood. Maurr had departed to see to his ship and his men.

Gunnar grabbed Eylir's tunic by the neck and shook him before he let him go. 'What you did was wrong. Sending Ragn to me without warning. What were you thinking of, man? It was a huge risk you took. Those two women nearly perished on the open sea. Rogues and fools crewed the ship you used.'

Eylir dusted down his tunic before giving a slow smile. 'So you are not thinking about trading your wife? Good to know. You should be on your knees thanking me, instead of threatening to beat me up.'

'I would have beaten you to a pulp except I have other concerns and you will have a use.' Gunnar fixed his friend with a steely gaze. 'I am here to ensure Vargr no longer bothers me or anyone connected with me. Are you with me? Or do family concerns prevent you?'

'Why is Ragnhild here?'

'Same reason. She desires an end to it.'

'You understand why I sent her.'

'You sent her for your own purposes, nothing to do with me. But she is with me now, not with you.'

A mischievous twinkle developed in Eylir's eye.

'You fit well together. Who would have considered it? Certainly not you. You were always definite about what you desired, but those women never stuck. Ragn is a woman without price. Had I met her before Trana, I might have been tempted, but I did the next best thing, I sent her to you.'

Gunnar struggled to keep his temper. He knew Eylir was winding him up, expecting a reaction. 'Ragnhild is not the sort of woman I would normally have in mind. You knew that. You were more interested in protecting her.'

Eylir dipped his head acknowledging the fact. 'I thought they deserved a chance to live. The brother-in-law is an unpleasant piece of work.'

'Why send her?'

'I know you have a heart, Gunnar, even when you like to hide it under a gruff exterior. I knew you'd do the right thing. Did she make you come north?'

Gunnar shook his head. 'She wanted to make me do this by telling me she loved me. I had already decided to do it. I don't want her love, not that way. I won't be used.'

Eylir's face became grave. 'We don't get to decide who loves us. We can only do what we think is best for them.'

Gunnar pinched the bridge of his nose and tried to rid the buzzing in his ears. 'Ragn came close to dying when I was out on the sea fishing. I didn't even consider that the piece of filth would send men after her. I want it stopped. I want to keep her safe. I want to grow old with her and I'm frightened I won't, Eylir.'

'Ragn survived.' He clapped Gunnar on the back. 'It is up to you to keep her alive. Does Vargr even have to know she is here? Your lands and people were attacked. You have the right to defend them. King Harald will grant you a trial by combat if you ask on the life debt he owes you.'

'I had not thought of it in that way.' What Eylir said made sense—keeping Ragn away from court would ensure her safety. And he knew he'd win any contest, even against a man with a reputation like Vargr's. He might not have been able to stop loving Ragn, but he'd keep her safe from his curse.

Ragn struggled to breathe properly and turned away from the door. Just when she considered everything might be well, she'd overheard Gunnar detailing why she wasn't suitable. After the first few words she withdrew, unable to bear any more about how he had no feelings for her.

'Is there a problem?' Trana asked.

Ragn quickly shook her head. Gunnar had never agreed that their marriage was based on anything but practicality. It was wrong of her to wish for more. It simply hurt to hear the truth. Despite her pledges, she had not changed as much as she had hoped. When was she ever going to learn that chasing after rainbows led to heartache as things slipped through her fingers?

'Not all.' Ragn made sure her lips turned upwards. No one need guess that her heart was breaking.

'Have you told him you loved him when it was quiet? Or did you just tell him after those men arrived.'

'He doesn't want or require my love. I am trying to accept that he will never love me. He is good to me, Trana. I should accept that and not keep wishing for more.'

'I've known you most of my life, Ragnhild. I want you to be happy. Hamthur was rotten to you, but you were stubborn and refused to admit it. You wanted the marriage to succeed because your grandmother had wanted to unite the two families.' Trana plucked at her gown. 'Is Gunnar worth fighting for?'

Ragn blinked. 'What do you mean?'

'You never thought Hamthur was worth fighting for.' Trana counted the points out on her fingers. 'You allowed any woman to run rings round you and claim him as their own. You believed people when they proclaimed you ugly. You stayed with Hamthur because it was easier than leaving.'

'You know nothing about it!'

'You are one of the most determined people I know, Ragn, but in matters of your marriage bed, you give up too easily, way too easily. What I want to know is, is this man worth fighting until your dying breath for?'

Ragn stared at her cousin, astonished that she even asked that question. 'Of course he is worth fighting for. But he thinks I used him. He can't forgive me for putting his lands in danger. I destroyed everything.'

'You have a lot to learn about men.' Trana put an arm about Ragn's shoulders. 'Fight your doubts and your pride. Maybe you just told him at the wrong time. True love is always worth fighting for.'

'Have you fought for Eylir?'

'You are trying to change the subject.' Trana sighed. 'It is over between Eylir and me. Once I thought he might be the one, but then he pledged his sword to my father. And I have always vowed not to marry a man who works for my father.'

'You mean you like to give advice, but not take it.'

Trana's peal of laughter rang out. 'That, too.' She leaned forward and touched Ragn's hand. 'No one can solve this except for you. You know in your heart what you must do. Listen to your heart.'

Ragn squared her shoulders. 'Do you? Have you? Eylir may not be all he seems.'

Trana glanced towards the door. 'Maybe I should start making it a habit.'

'Trana has agreed to lend me her court dress for to-morrow,' Ragn said when they went up into the loft for the night. She wiped her hands on her gown which was now stained and rumpled. Despite Trana's earlier words of encouragement, Ragn knew it would be impossible to have Gunnar reject her love again. She simply had to find another way to show him how much she cared for him. 'I shall be ready in the morning to greet the King properly.'

'Eylir and I have agreed another scheme. It is important I go to the King in the morning before he goes out to his estate to hunt.' He gathered her hands between his. 'Before Vargr has a chance to strike. Before he knows you are here.'

She nodded. 'Going before he goes hunting is a good scheme. I can wake up early.'

Gunnar squeezed her hands. 'You stay with Trana. There is no need for you to go. As your husband, I can speak for you.'

Ragn bit her lip. The old Ragn would have meekly accepted his declaration. 'Those lands belonged to me.'

Gunnar released her. 'There is every possibility that your brother-in-law doesn't realise you have returned.'

'I thought we were working together.'

'Once I know the King will hear my petition, I can produce you as a witness. If we alert Vargr too early, he can escape or hide evidence. If something does happen to me, Maurr has agreed to spirit you away to Colbhasa.'

Her stomach knotted and she understood what Gunnar was trying to keep from her. 'You expect the King to refuse permission. You expect there to be trouble. You are going to challenge Vargr to trial by combat. He is an able warrior, Gunnar, unlike his brother. He enjoys duelling.'

'Whatever happens I want you looked after,' he said, inclining his head. 'I want you to stay with Trana and Maurr where you will be safe. This way no one can claim that you shouldn't inherit my estate should the King turn against me. Maurr will guard the house while Eylir and I petition the King.'

She clenched her fists. This was not how their relationship was supposed to be. 'You settled this with Maurr and Eylir before you discussed the scheme with me?'

He put his hand on her shoulder. 'Let me fight this my way.'

'And I am supposed to accept that?' She pushed him away. 'Just like I am supposed to accept you turning away from me. If you are tired of me, tell me, but stop shutting me out. What did Eylir say to you to make you think that I would sit here meekly while you did this?'

His jaw dropped. Genuine shock crossed his face. 'I'm not tired of you. I want to protect you. Putting you into more danger serves no good purpose. Eylir believes this is the best strategy to keep you out of harm's way.'

She looped her hands about his neck and put her face up to his. She started to whisper that she loved him, but the words stuck in her throat. He'd rejected her words of love before. This time, she'd allow her body to show her love. She arched her body towards his, touched his groin with hers. 'We have tonight then.'

He groaned and pulled her closer. His lips met hers for a hard kiss. The heat was dark and dangerous. She revelled in it and pressed her body forward. His body became all hardened muscle.

He tore his mouth away and put her from him. His chest heaved as if he had run a long way. 'Can't you see that I am trying to keep you alive?'

'Hush. Let me show you how much I trust you.' She trailed a hand down his body until she reached his growing erection, stroked him and felt him harden. With quick fingers, she undid his trousers. His manhood stood proud and erect. She dropped to her knees and took him into her mouth, suckled, going round and round him with her tongue.

He groaned and cupped the back of her head, holding her there. A surge of power went through her. She was doing this to him. She was in control as he lost it.

He tugged at her shoulders. 'My turn to give you pleasure.'

She pushed him back on to the bed and ran a hand down his flank. 'You mean our turn to give each other pleasure.'

A very masculine laugh filled her ears. 'I so agree, but we are both overdressed for this.'

Ragn lay next to Gunnar, her limbs intertwined with his. Their coming together had had a new urgency and edge to it. It had been beyond describing. Both climaxed multiple times. She had allowed her body to say everything about her love for him and he'd responded.

'I knew I'd win you over,' he said.

She raised herself up on her elbow. A scheme began to form in her brain, a way to work together rather than fighting against him. It would work. 'You're making me the bait for your trap. You should have told me in the first place instead of spouting nonsense about Eylir and Maurr and what they thought.'

'Bait? What are you talking about?' He stared at her in astonishment.

'Vargr knows the court. He knows that protocol will keep you tied up for a long time. He will also know a ship has arrived and where it is from. He will guess that I may be on it. We need to make him show his hand. He will come for me once he sees you and you can expose him for what he is.' She kissed his temple. 'You should have told me your plan in the first place. It is sheer genius.'

'I refuse to put you in danger. It is why Maurr will be here to defend you. But you are wrong. I will go to court, put my case and the King will listen. There may be a trial by combat, but I expect to win.'

'If there is a trial, send Eylir for me, no other. I will need to be a witness.'

'Are you paranoid? But, yes, I promise I will send Eylir.'

'I know Vargr and I know what he is capable of.'

'I am trying to protect you, Ragn. Keep you out of danger.'

She put her hand on his shoulder. Vargr would find a way to get to her once he knew she was there. And the best time for him to strike would be when Gunnar was at court. She had to believe that Vargr didn't know they had arrived yet and would not know it until Gunnar announced it to the court. 'Working together we can solve this. It is more important that Vargr is exposed. I am through running. If he comes here, I will be ready for him. You need to trust that you have taught me well. Leave me a sword I can use. It is my condition for remaining here.'

'You do have fanciful notions.' He placed a kiss on her forehead. 'But I will leave my sword here and you can bring it if it comes to a trial by combat.'

'I am counting on you returning in time.'

He pressed the stone man into her hand. 'Keep this safe until I return. You will have more need of it than I.'

Her fingers closed around it. She knew without his having to say the words that he cared for her. He was giving her the good-luck charm he'd always carried into battle. 'I will treasure it. But you make your own luck. You will come back to me.'

Chapter Fifteen

'How long do you think it will take?' Ragn asked Maurr who appeared less than happy at being left behind to guard her. She had kept Trana and Maurr in ignorance about her gut instinct.

Maurr shrugged his shoulders. 'Hard to say, but you will be fine here.'

Ragn smiled back. 'It is good that you stayed.'

'What is Jura like?' Trana asked, putting the pot of pottage on the hearth. 'You two are neighbours. And I have never travelled. Some day I want to see the world.'

Ragn and Maurr started talking about the island and its possibilities, which served as a distraction from worrying about what trap Vargr intended to set.

A knock on the door interrupted Maurr's long-winded explanation of how he intended to build a magnificent hall.

'So soon?' Ragn's stomach knotted.

Maurr motioned for Trana to answer the door. Ragn breathed easier when she saw it was one of Maurr's men. The man twisted his cap. 'You need to come to the boat, Maurr. There is some damage to the hull. Ice, I think.'

Maurr pursed his lips. 'It can wait. My duty is here, guarding you.'

'No, it can't,' Ragn said. Her gut tightened. Everything seemed to be going wrong today. 'If we need to leave quickly, we need a seaworthy ship. Go. We will be safe here until Gunnar returns. Who would attack this house during waking hours?'

'I gave Gunnar my word.'

Ragn put her hand on her hip. 'Trana and I will be fine. You don't have to stay long, just to put your mind at rest. And you are looking after us. We may need the ship. Today. Who knows what sort of mood the King might be in? What lies Vargr might have told the King?'

Maurr nodded. 'I bow to the determined woman. I will leave one of my men outside the door until I return.'

He left with his men and the house went quiet. Ragn leant forward and put the poker in the fire to heat up. 'Just in case.'

Trana's brow puckered. 'In case what?'

'In case Vargr decides to make his move while Gunnar is at court. In case Maurr has been lured away by a false rumour to leave the way clear for Vargr. He will have had the harbour watched, Trana.'

Trana's eyes gleamed. 'I thought you gave in too easily to the men's scheme.'

'Vargr is a wily snake. He needs to be caught. Gunnar agreed to my scheme.' Ragn gave a little laugh. 'Possibly because he didn't believe it would happen, but he agreed to it.'

Trana tilted her head to one side. 'You have changed, Ragn, more than I thought when you arrived.'

'In a good way, I hope.'

'I wouldn't want to be the one to cross you.'

'I shall take that as a compliment.'

Gunnar concentrated on the enormous hall looming in front of him. Ragn would be safe with Trana
and Maurr for the short time he'd be at court. Vargr
would not go after her while he was at the King's hall
as Ragn had predicted last night. It would be later when
he returned from court. Vargr would not take the risk
of moving openly against her until he knew how the
King was going to react.

The main hall thronged with courtiers and ambas-
sadors from many countries. Several wore the heavily
embroidered tunics and cloaks of the Byzantine court
and there was even one from the caliphates in North
Africa. It was clear King Harald's prestige had grown
greatly in recent years. Gunnar gave his token of safe
passage to the guard before he pushed his way forward,
hoping that his old friend had not changed too much.

'Look who is standing next to the Queen—Vargr
Simmison,' Eylir said.

'Are you sure it is him?' Gunnar asked. A sharp-
nosed man whose cloak and tunic rivalled the King's
for their magnificence stood just behind the Queen,
whispering in her ear.

'I have only met him a few times but I'd recognise
his distinctive tunic and cloak anywhere,' Eylir replied.
'You can see why your wife has very little chance of
justice. In fact, it might be better if you give up now
and return to Jura. Let him try to attack you there. You
have men, you can fight.'

Gunnar firmed his jaw. Vargr clearly had influence,

but that did not mean the cause was lost. Viken still had laws and any man could get justice.

He walked up to the throne where his old comrade sat with a bored look on his face as various petitions were put to him. 'Your Majesty, I have come to pay my respects.'

'Gunnar Olafson as I live and breathe. You have ventured to the north,' the King said, rising from his throne with a wide smile. 'It has been far too long. Have you come in search of a bride? You swore it would be the only reason you'd return to the land of your forefathers.'

'Far too long.' The tension in Gunnar's shoulders eased. The King remembered him. 'I am grateful you remember me and my vow.'

'Remember? I owe you a life debt. You helped rescue me from Constantinople.' The King related the story and Gunnar listened in respectful silence while the murmurs from the crowd grew. The ambassador from the caliphate gave him a quizzical look.

Vargr remained standing beside the throne. Ragn's prediction would not come true. Vargr had no idea that she had returned to Kaupang.

'What can I do for you?' the King asked, finishing the story. 'You are here for more than to remember past times.'

'My wife…'

'Good, you are married.' The King smiled fondly at his Queen, who was currently whispering behind her hand to Vargr. 'I have come late to the institution of marriage, but I can recommend the state. You always used to swear that you needed to fulfil your vow to your mother. Is your wife here? Perhaps my wife can use her in her retinue if you intend to remain in the north.'

Gunnar kept his face impassive. 'I have come to you because two men attacked my lands on Jura. I seek justice.'

The Queen leaned over and whispered in the King's ear. He gave an indulgent smile and patted her hand.

Gunnar frowned. The interview was not going as he had planned. It was as if he had been expected. He glanced to where Ragn's brother-in-law stood. A knowing smile crossed his features. Gunnar gritted his teeth.

'Is there a problem, Your Majesty?' the Queen enquired. 'I thought it was why you had *jaarls* in the Western Isles.'

'What can I do about your dispute?' The King waved a languid hand. 'It is a matter for Kolbeinn or, failing him, Ketil. Speak to them. What good is having *jaarls* if one cannot depend on them to administer justice?'

The court obediently laughed.

Gunnar exchanged glances with Eylir. Eylir had been right—Harald had greatly altered from the warlord he once knew intimately. Politics had consumed him. 'Because they came from Viken. Someone from your court sent them and I ask you, because of the life debt you owe me, to give me the King's justice. Put Vargr Simmison on trial. Put him on trial today.'

'Sit down, Ragn,' Trana said from where she sat carding wool. 'You are wearing a groove in the floor. It takes time to petition the King. Maurr will return once he has finished inspecting his ship. You are worrying over nothing.'

Ragn wrapped her arms about her waist. She wanted to go and hide. Despite Maurr's easy words, it appeared the problem with the boat was taking longer than anticipated. Was this how Gunnar felt before he went into battle? 'I have a bad feeling about this. I should have gone. Gunnar will lose his temper and...perhaps we should go to court.'

'You would only be in the way. Trust Gunnar to put it in the right way. Your man can speak without riling people.'

'I trust Gunnar, but I don't trust Vargr. He is a master at twisting things. Gunnar dislikes court manners and runes still confuse him even though we are working on it.'

'Your man is in the right. The King cannot risk alienating his *jaarls* in the west over such a matter. All will be well. No one knows you are here.' Trana patted the bench beside her. 'Come, sit. I am glad to have this time alone with you. I want your advice—how can I convince Eylir not to go west in the spring?'

Ragn studied Trana's form. Her belly swelled slightly and there was a glow to her skin. 'You are expecting. You should have told me last night.'

The corners of Trana's mouth twitched. 'I think so. I haven't confessed to Eylir, but I am fairly sure. I told you that it was complicated. My monthly flow is regular and there's been nothing since October...since you left.'

'It is his?'

'After you left, we were together for one night.' Trana dipped her head. 'But he has refused to touch me since my father hired him to guard me. I fear I am losing him, Ragn. He swears once my father or my uncle returns, he will go west and seek his fortune.'

'What was the advice you gave me, only last night? If you love him, fight for him. Go with him. It is what I'd do with Gunnar.'

'Gunnar married you. Eylir will not consider such a thing until his business is complete. I am certain it means he wants to acquire a fortune. My father spoke of betrothal to someone else...'

Ragn squeezed Trana's hand. 'I begin to think everyone is truly blind. Have you given him a chance to ask you? Or have you simply let him think that you are willing to go along with your father's wishes?'

A distinct rattling like something being knocked over made Ragn stiffen.

'Trana...' she lowered her voice and reached for Gunnar's sword '...someone is out there. It is not Maurr or his men. They would give the correct signal.'

Trana's face went white. 'You hear things. It will be one of the cats knocking over the milk pail.'

'Nevertheless, you had better be prepared to run.'

The door crashed open, allowing a swirl of snow to enter.

'You remain standing there, Gunnar Olafson, ignoring the protocol of this court,' the Queen said, rising. Her beautiful face became haughty. 'Is there something else you require? My husband has kindly heard your petition against the Jaarl Vargr, but you must first seek your over-Jaarl. For too long my husband's former companions have sought unjustified favours. It causes disharmony and factions within the court. Why do you dishonour your King?'

Gunnar clenched his fists and tried to hold on to his temper. Harald had to be made to understand the trouble he was causing before he was dismissed for ever. 'With all respect, my lady, it is the King who needs to answer me.'

'Some people will not listen to well-meant advice.' She leant over and whispered to the King again.

'Did you seek Lord Ketil's advice?' Harald asked. 'Or did you come here because you knew Ketil the White would not favour your suit?'

'Kolbeinn sent me to you because of these.' Gunnar held out the brooches which the men who had attacked his farm had been carrying. 'I suspect you know which *jaarl* they belong to. I suspect you also know that he has no authority to make such raids in the Western Isles. Stop delegating and behave like the leader I know you can be. Grant me the trial of Vargr Simmison.'

The King took the brooches with a frown. 'Where are the men?'

'Kolbeinn has dealt with them as is his right when any attack his *felag*.'

'Then the matter has finished. There is nothing more for me to do. It surprises me that you risked a journey across the sea for such a little thing.' Gunnar detected a note of impatience in the King's voice.

'I wish to get your word that any who might encourage such acts are going against your specific order. You and I parted in peace. Or were your words spoken on the wind? Should I fear more men in the night to take what belongs to me?'

The King weighed the badges in his hand. 'And you ask this on the life debt I owe you? Why?'

'Only you can stop Vargr abusing your name,' Gunnar said. 'If this continues, you face a revolt and I don't want that for you, old friend.'

'For something as minor as this?' The Queen arched a brow. 'It is a matter between *jaarls*, surely.'

'It would be, my lady, but I want to ensure those

under my protection live. If needs be, I want to challenge this man to trial by combat.'

'Why would Vargr be interested in a remote farm on the Western Isles? A witch woman has advised him never to travel overseas again.' The Queen gave a little tinkling laugh.

'It is my right as the husband of Ragnhild Thorendottar, the widow of Hamthur who was unlawfully slain. The man in question confessed to the murder when he attacked her and left her for dead. He has unlawfully claimed her lands.'

A shocked hush rippled around the court. The Queen suddenly developed an interest in her gown. Gunnar kept his face still. Things were starting to move his way. Giving his good-luck charm to Ragn had been the correct thing to do. He made his own luck.

'Ragnhild Thorendottar lives?' the King asked sharply. 'I understood she had perished in a tragic fire. Can you produce her?'

'Ah, now I see, someone is claiming to be Ragnhild Thorendottar.' The Queen curled her lip. 'Do you think you can lay claim to those lands?'

'My wife is at her cousin's. I will fetch her and you can hear from her mouth what she and her sister have undergone. I assume you will recognise her.'

The King turned towards where Vargr had stood. 'Vargr...where is Vargr the Fleet-Footed? When did he leave?'

'Late last night, he told me he feared a plot against his life and has not been here,' the Queen said, her pretty face frowning. 'I was to stall the impostor as best as I could. One of his men wore his cloak, but he has gone now.'

The back of Gunnar's neck crept. Vargr knew where Ragn was. Vargr had had the port watched. Vargr had been one step ahead of them the entire time.

He had thought to protect Ragn by keeping her hidden, but Vargr had outplayed him. He should never have left her alone with just Maurr for protection. He should have brought her with him. 'I need to go.'

'The King has not dismissed you, Gunnar Olafson,' the Queen warned.

'I wait for no man's permission to save my wife's life.'

Ragn had little time to react as Vargr and five of his henchmen barged in. She grabbed an eating knife, stuck it in her belt and reached for Gunnar's sword with the other hand.

'Vargr! Get out! You have no right to be here!' Ragn pointed towards the door with the sword. 'Even in this country, you are not allowed simply to enter a private dwelling without invitation.'

'Ragnhild, my sweet sister-in-law, how very pleasant to see you again. And in such good health as well.' Vargr made an elaborate bow. 'The reports of your death appear to have been false. But reports of your return were correct. It is why I had the port watched. Every step you and that so-called warrior of a husband have taken has been noted.'

'Whatever you want, I refuse to comply with it.' Ragn said between gritted teeth. Taking on six men was an impossibility. Her only hope was that Gunnar had noticed Vargr's absence from court and was on his way back. 'Last time I ran. This time I stand my ground.

You are nothing but a swaggering bully, Vargr, whose scheme is about to collapse about his ears. Now get out!'

'Are you the owner of this dwelling?'

'You have no right to be here,' Trana said, bustling forward. Her entire being bristled. Ragn put out a warning hand. 'Leave now! Or I will…'

'Who are you going to alert?' Vargr's sneer increased. 'The King? He and I are like one on this. Ragnhild is a traitor. She attacked one of his emissaries. Her lands and her new husband's lands will be forfeit. The Queen understood my disquiet and agreed that one of my men should stand in for me today.'

Ragn's mouth went dry. Gunnar had blundered into a trap. If she had gone to court, she would have seen the impostor immediately. Instead she had stayed here. Vargr had anticipated what they were going to do, but then Vargr had always been good at *tafl* and thinking ahead. 'You had best have proof of my guilt! There will be a trial, Vargr.'

Her brother-in-law gave Trana a hard stare. 'If you are sensible, Trana Ragnardottar, you remain alive and unhurt. Otherwise you will suffer the same fate as your cousin. I take it that you were responsible for spiriting her away despite your denials. You thought I would not find out. It is good that others are more honest than you.'

'You mean the sea captain,' Ragn said. A cold fury descended.

'It is amazing how sailors talk when they have golden brooches to offload.' Vargr nodded towards Trana. 'I'd forgotten how pretty your cousin is. It would a pity if her looks were spoilt.'

Trana gave a small cry and wilted. Ragn gritted her teeth. Vargr had to have made a mistake.

'Allow me to handle this,' she said in an undertone. 'Stay here. Wait for Gunnar and Eylir. Whatever happened at court, Gunnar will find a way to return. That baby you carry is important. I will survive until they find me. Courage.'

Trana gave a small nod to show that she understood. 'I was willing to stand shoulder to shoulder with you, but I'm no warrior. I'm not brave like you.'

'And me, Vargr?' Ragn asked and her stomach knotted. She waved the heavy sword, drawing his attention away from her cousin. 'What do you want from me? Am I supposed to go meekly to my death?'

He moved swiftly, put hard fingers about her upper arm, forcing her to drop the sword before she had the chance to react.

'I thought you would not have the wits to use it. Did you really think you'd prevail against me and five of my men? The odds were always in my favour, Ragnhild.'

Ragn muttered a curse as he twisted her arm. Every breath he remained here was another chance for Gunnar to arrive. Panicking was not going to solve anything. 'You have little idea about my wits.'

'We have unsettled business.'

'I thought we said everything we had to say to each other when you threw the lighted torch in my hall.' Ragn forced her voice to be steady as her mind raced. They would have to drag her out. She could scream as they did so. People would notice. Anything to delay. Anything to allow Gunnar or Maurr to return. 'Those lands belonged to my family, but I offered them to you in exchange for my sister's life.'

'My father should never have favoured my brother over me.'

'Your father is long dead. Your brother is dead.'

'Hamthur turned our father against me. You with your feasts and being kind to people helped him. I should have inherited the better estate.'

Ragn swallowed hard. He was talking and his men were just standing menacingly in the doorway. Good. Now to keep him talking. 'I will not apologise for making those lands prosper. Hamthur's lands only prospered because of my inheritance and because I managed the lands. I offered to teach you to improve your lands.'

He snapped his fingers. 'We are wasting time. I won't allow you to destroy my world.'

'Leave Trana here and I will go quietly.'

His smile showed no mercy. 'Trana comes with us so she can understand precisely what happens when people cross me. Nothing will happen to her if she obeys, but she does need to learn a lesson.'

'I had no plans to come back until you sent your assassins. That was wrong of you, Vargr, endangering others.'

Vargr put his face close to hers. The madness shone in his eyes. 'I had thought the witch woman was speaking of Svana and then I realised—she was speaking about you. You are the one who is destined to destroy me unless I destroy you first. I see it now.'

He put his hands about her throat and closed. The world started turning black at the edges. Her hands flailed, brushing the eating knife in her belt. With her last conscious thought, she grasped it and pushed the knife upwards into his belly. He gave a grunt and his grip loosened.

She drew a life-giving breath as she spun away from him and grabbed the poker.

'Catch her! She has stabbed me.'

One of his henchmen grabbed her arms, forcing her to drop it. She kicked out ineffectually. 'You will never get away with it. My husband will not stand for it.'

'What, your new husband? I have the measure of the man. A loner. No one to worry about.' He shrugged. 'I fancy he will be at the King's hall some considerable time as the Queen has taken a dislike to him. Maybe you two will meet in death. It would be fitting. You will die for attempting to murder me. I could not have planned things better.'

Ragn thought of all the things she had left unsaid and how she would have clung to Gunnar far tighter when he went to the King's hall if she'd known what was going to happen to her. She should have told him that she loved him last night and made him believe it, instead of allowing her body to whisper the words.

'I pity you, Vargr. You think only of power and gain. I know what love is and what difference a good man can make in the world.'

'Do you indeed?' A stern voice sounded from the door.

Ragn went weak at the knees. Vargr had lied. The King had not detained Gunnar. He had come as he'd promised he would. 'Gunnar.'

'Unhand my wife.'

Vargr's henchman increased his vice-like grip on her arm.

'I am taking her with me as is my right,' Vargr said, putting a hand over the growing stain on his tunic. 'We shall see what the King says—the witch stabbed me in the stomach. She intended to kill me and she must pay for her crimes.'

'Are you terminally stupid? That is barely a scratch,' Ragn shouted.

Vargr went red in the face. 'Who are you calling stupid?'

Gunnar raised his brow. 'I am happy to fight you for her. You and me. We shall see who wins.'

'The Queen will insist on a trial by ordeal rather than a trial by combat,' Vargr said with a sneer.

'You are friendly with the Queen. I hadn't realised.'

Vargr preened. 'She does what I say. My wife is her closest confidante.'

'Truly?'

'The King is so besotted with her. His decree about marriage has meant that I have been able to increase my holdings as I knew it would when I suggested it.' He gave an arrogant laugh. 'I am the ultimate power behind the throne.'

Gunnar's brow furrowed and he appeared to ponder the statement. 'Does he, indeed? It does not sound like the Harald I know from old. There was only one leader in his *felag*—Harald. Shall we ask him? Harald, who leads this country?'

Gunnar stepped to one side. The King strode into the room. 'I run my country as I ran my *felag*,' the King proclaimed and Vargr went white.

'I believe you heard everything, Harald,' Gunnar said. 'I regret my wife inflicted a slight wound on this piece of filth rather than killing him outright, but one cannot have everything.'

'This is a family dispute,' Vargr said, gesturing to his henchman who released her. 'A quarrel which got out of hand. Nothing more.'

'Is it, indeed?' King Harald arched his brow. 'Interesting way you quarrel, Vargr.'

Vargr wiped his hand across his face. 'I demand the right to avenge this wound!'

Gunnar looked at Harald. 'Do I get my trial by combat?'

The King tapped his hand against his mouth. 'My wife has been overly hasty. She spoke without due consideration of the situation. She has been badly advised in recent months. That ends now.'

The colour drained from Vargr's face. 'I can explain. He has twisted my words. I merely came to talk to my sister-in-law and discover why she has spread such lies about me. She attacked me, unprovoked.'

'You make no demands of me. I have heard enough,' the King thundered. 'Your lands are confiscated for plotting against the Crown.'

The King's bodyguards removed Vargr and his henchmen. Ragn ran swiftly to Gunnar and he put a reassuring arm about her shoulders. At his touch, her knees threatened to give way, she leant her head against his chest and heard the steady thump of his heart and his arm tightened further.

'You are arrived in time,' she whispered. 'I knew you would.'

'You are alive and that is the only thing which matters,' he said against her hair.

Harald coughed and gave a low bow. 'Gunnar, I see this time I must thank you for saving my throne. Had Vargr been allowed to continue, he would have alienated many powerful *jaarls*.'

'I thank you for your opportune intervention,' Gunnar said, keeping his arm about Ragn's shoulders.

'He will be properly punished,' the King proclaimed. 'He bore false witness and swore that Ragnhild Thorendottar was dead. Her lands will be restored to her. You can be a *jaarl* in Viken properly now, Gunnar.'

Ragn closed her eyes. Once, seeing Vargr punished and getting the lands back had been her dearest wish, but now she wanted to be where her heart was. 'My husband's lands are where I wish to be. We are carving a new life and I intend to live that life.'

Harald bowed towards them both. 'I'm sure some deserving warrior will be grateful for such a fine estate. I will ensure you are properly compensated for it.'

Gunnar pulled her tighter. 'I would go where you wanted,' he said in her ear.

'Good, then we go back to Jura. Back to our home.'

As the King and his men started to withdraw, the door banged opened and Maurr rushed in with a drawn sword. When he spied Gunnar holding Ragn, he halted. 'Someone sabotaged my ship and the guard I left has gone missing.'

'I believe we know who that someone might be— Vargr Simmison. I suggest you apply to the King for compensation,' Gunnar said. 'And I believe you gave your word, Maurr. You were going to stay here. You were going to ensure Ragn did not get into any trouble.'

Maurr reddened. 'Ragn told me to go. She said she would be safe with just a guard outside. I never thought the man would be so brazen to do something like this in broad daylight.'

Gunnar tightened his grip on her shoulders. 'Did you, Ragn? That was very reckless of you.'

'That's right. I told him to go.' She put a hand to his cheek. 'I trusted you would be back in time and you were. It is in the past. Besides, we might have needed a swift ship.'

Gunnar gave a low growl. 'It is well I am in a good mood, Maurr.'

'I left one of my men guarding the door. I am not completely careless,' Maurr retorted. 'Where is he?'

A quick search found the unconscious man dumped in an alleyway. Maurr and his men took him away to be seen to.

'I am not feeling so well,' Trana said when all was quiet and collapsed on the floor in a faint. Eylir went pale and lifted her up, fanning her face and begging her to speak.

'I think Trana has something to tell you,' Ragn said, grabbing Gunnar's hand. 'We should leave them alone.'

Gunnar nodded and led her to the loft where they had slept the previous night. His arms came about her and held her tight. For a long while, neither said anything.

'There are things we need to say to each other as well,' Gunnar said against her hair. 'You took far too many chances. You should have gone with Maurr to the ship. You knew what was going on. You must not take chances like that. My heart can't take it.'

She reached up and stroked his face. Her heart turned over. 'Does that mean you have feelings for me?'

He gave her a look which took her breath away. 'I love you with every particle of my being. I was wrong not to tell you before. I was going to tell you that day the men arrived, but then they did and I thought my growing love for you nearly caused your death by calling down that curse. I hated that I nearly destroyed the woman I loved. If stopping loving you was the price I had to pay for keeping you alive, I would have gladly paid it.'

She laid her head against his chest and listened to the steady beat of his heart. He loved her. 'Were you able to stop?'

His arms tightened about her. 'I tried. I tried telling myself that you had used me. That all you wanted was vengeance and to return to your old lands, but my heart refused to listen as you are very easy to love. Your bravery and the size of your heart put me to shame. I decided I would defy the curse.'

'I am very glad your heart showed sense. Now do you see that the curse has no power over me and never did?'

He turned her, so she had to look directly into his eyes. 'The image of you in danger will haunt my dreams for months to come. When I was racing over here to save you, I realised that the only power the curse had was in my mind. It stopped me from trying to make a difference. And then I knew, I could save you.'

'I never thought Vargr would use a decoy at court,' she admitted.

'Next time, you go with me. It is the only way I can ensure your safety—keeping you with me at all times.'

She laughed softly. 'You can't decide when someone's life will end, Gunnar. The important thing is to have them part of your life and to let them know that they have made your life better. In the past few weeks, you have shown me what it is truly like to live and I love you for it.'

'My life has meaning because you are in it,' he said, placing his cheek against hers. 'I was busy dying inside and didn't realise it. But then you arrived and demanded I fulfil another's promise.'

'I was wrong to do that.'

'I fell for you when you defiantly stood with that spoon in your hand and the pot of stew bubbling on the hearth. You made me remember what it was like to be cared for. You looked like a goddess.'

'Hardly that.' Ragn smiled. 'I had an ulterior motive— I was determined to have a hot meal for Svana.'

'Then you found my mother's good-luck charm. I knew she'd have approved of you and the way you are kind to people, the way you make other people's lives better.'

Ragn put her hand against Gunnar's cheek. He turned his face into her palm and kissed it. 'I know I would have liked your mother as I know the calibre of her son.'

'You have my heart, Ragn. I thought it dead and buried with my family, but it was here all the time and waiting for you. You made me remember my family and those memories have brought my family back to me. What more can I say?' He pulled her against his body. 'You are the most beautiful woman in the world to me. Some day maybe you will believe me.'

Ragn's heart skipped a beat He thought her beautiful and she knew it did not matter what anyone else thought. His was the only opinion which counted. 'You love me?' she asked softly.

'Utterly and madly. I am not afraid who knows it either.'

'There was a method to my kindness that day—I wanted a home for Svana,' she confessed. 'I wanted her to have a Good Jul.'

'And in doing that you reminded me of all the good I cut myself off from. I regret that Maurr forced my hand. I wanted to woo you properly rather than forcing the wedding.'

'You say that now, but I am glad that he did arrive and made us both see how we felt about each other.'

'Do you think you could find a corner of your heart for me?'

Ragn gave a laugh. 'Only a corner?'

'As much as you can spare. I require your love, Ragn. I always did. I was a fool to say otherwise. Forgive me?'

She pretended to think about it. 'Recently I have discovered that people do not have a small capacity to love, but a large one. I love you, Gunnar, unconditionally. My life is better for having you in it. I don't know how long the fates will allow us to be together, but know that I'd rather have a short time with you than a life of loneliness. Now kiss me like you mean it.'

'With the greatest pleasure.' He bent his head and tasted her lips.

Epilogue

Winter Solstice AD 878—Jura

The faint noise made Ragn turn her head from where she was lying on the bed, looking at the tiny bundle in the cradle.

'Were you asleep?' Gunnar asked in a quiet voice.

Ragn shook her head. 'I was far too busy watching our little girl blow milk bubbles.'

'She is absolutely perfect.' Gunnar reached out his finger to touch their baby's cheek. 'Asa is smiling at me.'

Ragn struggled to sit up. Her body remained tired from the birth a few days before, but the pain had been worth it when she held their baby girl in her arms. This baby was the living symbol of their growing love for each other. Gunnar had named her after his youngest sister, Asa. 'She is indeed. She knows her father.'

Gunnar's face became wreathed in smiles. 'And her father promises to make sure she is well looked after. My family means everything to me.'

Ragn curled her fingers about his, knowing that he still bore the scars from how he'd lost his family. 'Is there some problem? We have your mother's charm protecting the house.'

'Svana came to see me earlier. She said that she knows we have a *nisser* and she wants to make sure that everyone says a wish over the porridge. I am supposed to say a wish for Asa tonight.'

'I thought she'd outgrown believing in *nissers* along with her fits.'

In the past year Svana's fits had faded to nothing. And thanks to the suggestion of Kolbeinn's wife of covering Svana's straight eye for a little time each day, Svana's inward-turning eye had strengthened. Ragn agreed with her prediction that when Svana grew into a woman, she would have any number of warriors vying for her hand.

'Apparently Svana made a wish on the porridge last Jul that you and I would have a girl before the next winter solstice. And the *nisser* has delivered. She is now certain that she will get a sword for Jul.'

Ragn collapsed back against the pillows, laughing. 'You know she would never reveal to me what she asked last Jul. She simply said that we would both know when it happened. I thought she was very nervous about the birth with her constant questions about when the baby was due and if I knew the sex. I never imagined she put the *nisser* to such a test.'

'It is lucky that I purchased a sword for her the last time I visited the blacksmith on Colbhasa.'

'Svana has hardly been subtle about her desire to be a shield maiden. The sword can be from us. She has already had quite enough for one lifetime from the *nisser*! She mustn't get greedy.'

Gunnar's laugh answered her own, before he grew

sober. 'I know you do not necessarily want our children to believe in such things and so I am asking—does Asa get presents from the *nisser*?'

Ragn studied the cradle for a long while. Gunnar was asking, instead of demanding, but she knew how much joy he'd taken in this year's celebrations. 'Once I might have thought that people should only be practical and believe in things they could touch, but I was wrong. Such things allow for hope and anticipation. Life isn't about what you can touch, it is about what and who you believe in and I believe in you.'

He put his arm about her shoulder and settled on the bed. 'And you taught me that a heart grows the more it gives. The only time you are cursed is if you stop trying and close yourself down.'

'I agree. We both learned that.'

'Will you join me in the wishing over the porridge, my beautiful wife?'

Ragn thought back over the year and how they had both grown in love and confidence. She might not be beautiful to everyone, but she was to the people who mattered most to her. 'Of course, although I can't think of anything to wish for, everything I desire is here with me in this room.'

'Then we shall have to wish that it continues for as long as possible and use everything in our power to ensure that wish comes true.'

'That is the sort of wish I agree with wholeheartedly!'

She turned and put her arms about him and there was no need for words as they watched their baby sleep.

* * * * *

*If you enjoyed this story
don't miss these other great reads
by Michelle Styles*

Taming His Viking Woman
Summer of the Viking
Sold to the Viking Warrior
The Warrior's Viking Bride

Author Note

Because the Vikings were the last great European civilisation to become Christian, it remains possible to see echoes of their pagan midwinter festival of light in the Christmas celebrations of the lands they conquered. Jul, or Yule, was the period from about the eighth of November to the twentieth of January, when the Sun Maiden went into the belly of the wolf and was rescued only through the intervention of Thor.

The festival involved much feasting, as when it was dark and cold outside people remained close to the hearth. It was also a time of renewal and the swearing of oaths. This makes sense when you consider how much preparation would have gone into creating a successful war band.

Part of the Yule feast included swearing solemn oaths on boar's bristles. The boar would be sacrificed as an offering to the gods—in particular Freyr. Some speculate that this is why the boar's head—or indeed a ham—is traditional at Christmas. Other things such as specially brewed ale and a flaming wreath were also part of the Jul tradition.

In Norway there remains a tradition of the *nisser*,

or elf, who looks after a farm being given rice pudding on Christmas Eve. The *nisser* served much the same function as a brownie—doing good deeds in secret so long as they were respected. If they were not respected they would play tricks.

There are no primary source documents written by Vikings during the reign of Harald, the man considered to be the first true King of Norway. Because of the movement of Viking war bands during this period, it is thought that he might have insisted on more obedience than previous warlords. However, we do not know what his actual decrees consisted of, or how much control he actually exerted over the Western Isles. Various sagas do record that the Western Isles and the Isle of Manx were under his overlordship.

If you are interested in learning more about the Vikings in Scotland and Ireland, or even the general era—these books might prove useful:

Adams, Max, *Aelfred's Britain: War and Peace in the Viking Age* (2017 Head of Zeus Ltd)

Ferguson, Robert, *The Hammer and the Cross, A New History of the Vikings* (2010 Penguin Books)

Jesch, Judith, *Women in the Viking Age* (1991 The Boydell Press)

Magnusson, Magnus K.B.E., *The Vikings* (2003 The History Press)

Marsden, John, *Somerled and the Emergence of Gaelic Scotland* (2000 Tuckwell Press Ltd)

Oliver, Neil, *Vikings a History* (2012 Orion Books)

Parker, Philip, *The Northmen's Fury: A History of the Viking World* (2014 Jonathan Cape)

Williams, Gareth ed., *Vikings: Life and Legend* (2014 British Museum Press)